Kissed by the Rain

ALSO BY CLAUDIA WINTER

Apricot Kisses

Kissed by the Rain

Claudia Winter

Translated by Maria Poglitsch Bauer

amazon crossing

Text copyright © 2016 Claudia Winter
Translation copyright © 2017 Maria Poglitsch Bauer
All rights reserved.

Previously published as *Glückssterne* by Goldmann in Germany in 2016. Translated from German by Maria Poglitsch Bauer. First published in English by AmazonCrossing in 2017.

Published by AmazonCrossing, Seattle

www.apub.com

ISBN-13: 9781503934962
ISBN-10: 1503934969

Cover design by Shasti O'Leary Soudant

Printed in the United States of America

"Man has control over everything

Except his own heart."

—*Friedrich Hebbel*

Prologue

Frankfurt, September 1952

She wasn't afraid, not the tiniest bit—well, maybe just a little. You see, it was so dark inside the wardrobe that she couldn't see her hands in front of her face. And there was this weird smell of old wood, dust, and mothballs. She pulled her legs up to her chest, rested her chin on her knees, and felt ashamed. Lucy, in her favourite book, *The Lion, the Witch and the Wardrobe*, was much more courageous than she was. Lucy also hadn't stupidly shut the door behind her. But according to Mama, Lucy was just imaginary, and the magical wardrobe she climbed through to reach the enchanted land of Narnia was made up, too, as was the man with goat legs, and the talking lion, Aslan.

But she couldn't completely give up believing. She stretched out one hand, touched the soft fabric there—Mama's dresses, not worn since the baby went to live with the angels—and fumbled deeper among the rattling wire hangers. If she believed hard enough . . .

She exhaled with disappointment as her hand touched the back of the wardrobe. There was no secret exit, only coarse wood that didn't even budge when she cautiously pressed against it.

She gave a start when the door was flung open and a small figure slipped in to join her. This time, the door stayed open, and in the dim light, dust particles danced in her hiding place.

"Li! I've got it," her sister said in an excited voice.

Her stomach tensed up. She had hoped that the idea was only a joke. But she should have known better. Bri never joked around.

"You aren't scared, are you?"

A frown played across her sister's face, with its perfect doll's mouth and huge marble-like eyes. Bri sat across from Li, mirroring her posture—her back against the wall of the wardrobe, arms wrapped around her knees. Even though they didn't look alike at all, everyone always realised right away that they were twins. It was as if the good Lord had decided to have some fun and create two completely different figures out of the same piece of clay. Unfortunately, he had done a better job with Bri, and sometimes Li resented that.

"N-no. Of course I'm not afraid."

She gritted her teeth and squinted. Sweaty fingers grabbed her arm, and she felt something hard and cold pressing against her skin.

"Better open your eyes, then, to see where you're cutting."

The door of the wardrobe was open. Li could still run away. She wouldn't, of course. She never did.

"Why don't you go first?" she whispered.

"I already did, you coward. Go ahead, do it, before I bleed all over Mama's clothes."

Bri laughed her usual laugh, the one that meant Li was a stupid little goose, even though Li was older by twenty minutes. Bri had acted like the older sister and flaunted her unwillingness to do what was expected of her for as long as Li could remember.

Li gripped the knife. Should she count to ten and press down very slowly? Or was it better to go fast? Would she faint? "Ow!"

"Finally. Give me your finger. Press it against mine. Like that. And now"—Bri paused dramatically—"swear."

"Bri, I'm bleeding!"

"That's the idea, stupid. Come on, swear."

"I forgot what I'm supposed to say."

"Good grief, Li," Bri complained. "You've had since yesterday to memorise it."

Now Li was in tears, ashamed that she couldn't even remember a few lines. She sobbed because she was hungry and bleeding and stuck in this stupid wardrobe—and because she could never say no to Bri's nutty ideas.

"Don't cry." Bri's voice was very gentle now.

Li swallowed and sniffed even though Mama had told them not to do that since it could give you a stroke. She'd said that's what happened to Uncle Walter.

"I'll go first. I, Brigitte Markwitz, swear by everything I hold dear"—Li opened her mouth to ask what that meant, but Bri raised a finger and continued—"that I will never abandon my sister Lieselotte."

"I, Lieselotte Markwitz, swear by everything I hold dear that I will never abandon my sister Brigitte," Li responded.

Bri smiled. Her smile was like an angel's. That's why Li wasn't the only one who couldn't say no to her.

"This oath is valid for this and all future lives."

"Future lives?" Li swallowed. She loved her sister, but sometimes she was a little scary. She would ask Mama about that later, at dinner.

"And may I drop dead if I break this oath."

"And may I drop dead if I break this oath," repeated Li, even though it gave her the creeps. "Also, we'll find two princes, two handsome princes, who are also brothers. All four of us will walk down the aisle together . . . or we shall never marry."

Li's eyes grew wide. That part hadn't been on the crumpled paper Bri had given her the day before. What had got into her?

But Bri did not scold her. Instead, she just looked at her, first with an astonished expression and then with the admiration she usually reserved for their big sister, Adele.

"Yes, all four of us will walk down the aisle together," Bri quickly agreed, and took her twin's hand.

Li's heart leapt with joy. She no longer cared that Bri was squeezing her hand too tight, or that her finger hurt pretty badly. At that moment, she was the happiest girl in the world—no, in all possible worlds in all of the books on the shelf over her bed. Starting today, she would never again feel lost in this strange house that belonged to Mama's new husband, and which was supposed to be her new home. She had Bri, after all—forever.

1

Frankfurt, April 2016

"It's gone!"

I closed my eyes. It couldn't be. "What do you mean, gone?" I said calmly, hoping I had imagined the note of panic in my mother's voice.

"I mean, *gone*! I have no clue what could have happened. I took it out of the safety-deposit box a few months ago and put it into our safe. And when I checked this morning . . ."

She gesticulated with her brush as if trying to paint in the air what could not be described. I dodged a rust-coloured splash and it landed on the Victorian lampshade instead. Mama began to pace around the studio that used to be our greenhouse. I took a deep breath, a long gulp in, and then exhaled in three short puffs, the way I often did before a difficult client meeting. But this was not a client meeting. This was my own personal Armageddon.

"Mama, a ring cannot simply vanish from a safe."

My mother came to an abrupt halt, her round face spattered with paint, and pouted. "So you don't believe me."

I opened my mouth for an acerbic reply but thought better of it and walked weak-kneed to the safe in the living room.

"It's one-six-zero-three-eight-six," Mama said behind me.

"You used my birthday?"

"So what? You know I'm not good with numbers."

"Jesus. You might just as well have left it open."

I bit my lip and entered the numbers. The green light that flashed on was accompanied by an elegant buzzing sound. A brief glance inside the safe confirmed the shattering truth—it was empty except for a few papers and a folder. The royal-blue velvet box was gone.

"I'm sorry, Josefine," my mother whispered.

I should have consoled her. Instead, I walked to the French window and looked out into the garden, where my father was planting seedlings. Normally, it would have amused me to see him using a yardstick and Mama's cooking twine to plant the seedlings in a perfectly straight row, but right now, I didn't find the scene funny at all.

"Did you ask Papa?" I mumbled. It was a rhetorical question. My mother replied with a derisive snort.

My father was interested in climbing roses, carrots, and his compost heap. He probably didn't even remember that the ring existed or what it meant to my mother's family—and to me.

"Have you seen any signs of a break-in? Did you call the police?"

"Of course not!" Shocked, Mama dropped the brush. Mirabelle, who had just dared to venture out from under the sofa, yelped and scurried behind the walnut sideboard. I frowned, watching the whippet cower. Our pretty little house in Bad Homburg's Hardtwald had offered asylum to many abused and abandoned greyhounds over the years, to the displeasure of our well-heeled neighbours. But this latest rescue's behaviour was the strangest yet.

"She's not so bad," said my mother. "She's started letting us pet her. She only eats chicken and mashed potatoes, but . . ."

"Mama, why haven't you reported the theft?"

I turned to her with crossed arms. After looking at me for a while, she lowered herself onto the couch. Mirabelle sneaked up and crouched at her feet. The dog's ears, spotted and bat-like, were raised like radar antennae, ready to register everything that could possibly harm her.

"Your grandmother's going to be beside herself over this silly piece of metal," Mama mumbled, petting the trembling bundle of fur.

"That 'silly piece of metal' is worth a fortune! And it might mean the end of my wedding."

"Come on, Josefine, nobody still believes in that inane superstition."

"Grandmother does. When she finds out that I can't wear the ring at my wedding . . ." I swallowed hard, but the lump in my throat did not budge.

"She doesn't have to find out!" Mama declared. "We could use another one, a lookalike." The expression on her face wasn't like her at all. "All right, forget I said that. But let's look everywhere before we start confessing things to your grandmother."

She went to the sideboard next to the fireplace accompanied by a small, crouching shadow that pressed against her calves.

My family's fear of Grandmother's rage never ceased to amaze me. But I was not exempt from such fear. I lifted the top of the desk next to me, determined to locate the ring.

After rummaging through all of the drawers in the house, emptying cupboards, and peeking into two drainage pipes, I had returned to my office in downtown Frankfurt. I glanced at my wedding to-do list and then leaned back and looked out through the panorama window. The skyline was capped by a breathtaking blue sky streaked with candyfloss clouds. I usually felt tremendous satisfaction at the sight of the futuristic, gleaming skyscrapers of Frankfurt's cityscape. Today, my stomach contracted as if I'd eaten something rotten. It felt like a nightmare.

For nine years I had waited for the passionate scene that has inspired writers and filmmakers all over the world—someone bent down on one knee in front of me. But I knew from the start that Justus's proposal would be less romantic than I had imagined as a little girl.

In the end, he never even knelt down.

My fiancé was . . . Well, he was a temperate man, reserved in matters of the heart. But he made up for it with his loyalty, constancy, and reliability—and I appreciated especially this last quality very much.

Anyway, declarations of love plastered on skyscrapers and exploding hearts in the night sky are overrated. I had truly been delighted when, two months earlier, I found a dove-blue Post-it note in my signature folder with an engagement ring taped to it.

"I'm going to make junior partner next quarter. Marry me!"

The note was written in Justus's little boy scrawl, which not even his secretary could decipher. Normally, he dictated even one-line memos. Yet this note he had written himself. Plus, dove-blue is my favourite colour. It was so—

"Humiliating."

I jumped as my door flew open. There was no chance to escape—my uninvited guest had already crossed the room and planted herself squarely in front of my desk.

"Frau Ziegelow, how nice to see you," I lied nonchalantly, sliding the wedding list under a folder.

"I've had it, Frau Sonnenthal."

With a sob that reminded me of a kicked cat, my client slumped her Rubenesque body into a visitor's chair and began fanning herself with an official-looking piece of paper. I pushed over the box of Kleenex that sat ready for its usual Tuesday deployment. I sometimes wondered whether Frau Ziegelow mistook our meetings for therapy sessions.

I waited until she had dabbed her eyes and energetically blown her nose before pointing to the wrinkled document in her hand. "May I?"

She dropped the paper on the desk. My blood pressure rose when I saw the letterhead—Melwin & Co. Even though the divorce was long since finalised, my client's ex-husband spared no expense in making her life difficult. When I read the subject line, I could feel my obliging smile evaporate.

"This is a restraining order."

Frau Ziegelow wrinkled her nose. "I don't care what it's called. It can't be legal. I am entitled to advertise my hair salon."

"On your ex-husband's car?"

She pursed her cherry-red lips.

"It says here that you attached three posters to his Audi, advertising your salon and covering your husband's salon's logo." I examined her sternly over the rim of my glasses. True, it was a serious legal matter, but the image of my client, all 265 pounds of her, scaling fences by moonlight and attacking her ex's Audi TT with a roll of adhesive tape was not without an element of comedy.

"Strictly speaking, it's my car, so I can do with it whatever I want," she answered.

"Frau Ziegelow, our settlement gave him the Audi and you the convertible," I reminded her as gently as I could. "You got the two penthouse apartments downtown and he got the house in Sachsenhausen. You got the Tausendschön beauty salon and he got Cuts and Curls. Worst case, your former husband could sue you not just for injury to the interests of his company, but for property damage, too." I shook my head and pointed to the letter. "This stipulates that you may not come within 110 yards of your husband's salon. Considering all the things you've done these past few months, I would say that's letting you off lightly."

"Come on, it was a few scraps of paper on his prehistoric display window!"

"You mean a wall-sized poster, pasted on with special glue?"

"So what?" My client angrily jingled her bracelets. "He owes me after stealing two of my workers. The second one's probably warming the old perv's bed, too—on *my* mattress, no matter what the settlement stuff says."

I looked at her without saying anything. For some reason, I liked this woman who seemed unable to let go of the love of her life. I had always liked her, ever since I had first started at the firm, fresh out of law school, when my assistant, Lara, had led the distraught woman into my office, declaring that I was the best family lawyer at the firm. That was true then and now, since I was the only lawyer dealing with family law at Maibach, Roeding & Partners to this day.

Catching Lara watching through the glass, I silently cursed the architect who had come up with the fishbowl design of these offices.

I got up with a sigh and signalled to Lara to bring two cups of coffee from the vending machine. Then I lowered the blinds. I was sure that one of my colleagues would tattle on me since, in these hallowed halls, transparency was key. The great Maibach simply could not understand that some clients needed a little privacy.

Feeling uneasy, I turned back to my desk and saw Frau Ziegelow reading my wedding list.

"That's private and personal," I said, annoyed at myself for sounding guilty.

"You're getting married?"

She looked up at me with shining eyes and her frown turned into a warm smile that somehow did not fit into this room, permeated as it was by years of tears and hurt feelings.

"Child, I'm so happy for you! Who's the lucky guy? How long have you known each other? Where will the wedding be, and, most important"—the hairdresser eyed my ponytail—"when will you finally come to Tausendschön and let me take care of that hair of yours?"

I adjusted my ponytail uncomfortably. There was another unwritten law in this office—lawyers were not to have any personal contact with their clients. This was a pity, since the Tausendschön was one of the city's best salons.

Lara's appearance with coffee and cookies saved me from having to invent a polite excuse to avoid Frau Ziegelow's invitation. I watched Lara totter across the deep-pile rug, set down the tray in slow motion, and beam at me for approval. I suppressed a tart comment. She didn't act that way on purpose. She simply lived in the same dreamland as my great-aunt Li, who spent all day buried in her books.

"Thank you, Lara."

I took a chocolate cookie and turned away from her to show that her duty was done. But my assistant stood as if nailed to the floor.

"You can go," my client took over, pointing to the door. Only then did Lara leave.

I gazed at my wedding list while the chocolate melted between my fingers.

"You've got to toughen up, child," Frau Ziegelow said. "Or your employees will walk all over you."

"Is everything all right in here, Frau Sonnenthal?"

The blinds flew up with a snap. Reacting without thinking, I pushed the cookie into my mouth and stared at Justus, who was standing in the doorway, frowning. My client was visibly irritated, but all I managed was an awkward grin while chewing like I had a huge spoonful of peanut butter in my mouth.

"Everything's just fine, thanks." Frau Ziegelow quickly took a cookie. "Frau Sonnenthal is a wonderful lawyer. She always knows exactly what her clients need."

My fiancé's iron-grey eyes lost their look of disapproval, and his posture relaxed. I took off my glasses. Justus always said their frames covered too much of my face.

"It's good to hear that, madam. We at Maibach, Roeding & Partners always strive to make our clients feel well taken care of until the very end," he said in the tone he used for children and dogs. I had often told him to not to talk like that. And his final words made it sound as if my client were headed for the guillotine.

"Until the very end?" echoed my client with a smile. "I hope not, Herr—"

"Grüning. Dr. Justus Grüning. I'm a colleague of Frau Sonnenthal," he answered without missing a beat.

My hands were trembling as I set my cup down, splashing coffee into the saucer.

"I see—a colleague." Frau Ziegelow appraised me.

Justus bowed elegantly and closed the door with a polite "It's been a pleasure" to Frau Ziegelow and a warning "Keep the blinds open, Frau Sonnenthal" to me.

We sat in silence for a few long moments. Then my client spoke.

"Please tell me that wasn't your intended but just a lover."

"A what?" I almost choked on my coffee.

"I was afraid of that."

"I have no idea what you're talking about."

"You're flustered by him, and not in a good way." I was going to protest, but Frau Ziegelow continued. "Besides, he addresses you so formally."

"We like to keep our personal and professional lives separate," I replied, which sounded lame even to me.

"Utter nonsense."

"With all due respect, I don't believe that my relationship is the topic of this consultation—ouch!"

A be-ringed hand had darted across the table and now grasped my wrist.

"Never make the mistake of getting married with half a heart, especially not to a man who obviously doesn't have one at all," my client whispered in the tone of a psychic who has seen terrible things in her crystal ball.

I tried to pull my hand away, but she wasn't finished.

"Frau Sonnenthal, I like you. You're a young lady who knows what she's talking about, most of the time. But now it's my turn to give you some advice."

I glanced at the clock on the wall. My next client was due in ten minutes.

"We choose men for three reasons—because our heart tells us something, or our brain, or our sexual organs. The latter is exciting, but doesn't last long. Our intellect has the most persistent voice and is apt to overpower everything else, especially the tender and mostly timid stirrings of the heart."

"Frau Ziegelow, I've known Herr Dr. Grüning for nine years. Believe me, I've heard all kinds of voices by now."

"But have you listened to them? Nothing happens without a reason, and fate whispers to our heart so quietly that we don't always hear it." Frau Ziegelow's dark-brown eyes were focused so intently on mine that it was difficult to look away. "But you have no idea what I'm talking about, huh?" she asked, finally letting go of my hand.

I shook my head and tried desperately not to think about my grandmother's ring disappearing just before the wedding.

"Well, it's none of my business. I'm meddling, as usual." Frau Ziegelow blinked and then pointed to the Melwin & Co. letterhead with studied casualness. "I want my ex-husband to stop poaching my employees. And to stop bad-mouthing me to my customers—though I know it might be difficult to prove he's doing that. Maybe we could formulate our own restraining order. Could you do that?"

"If you stop taking the law into your own hands, I definitely can. Could *you* do that?" I answered, still a little rattled by her crystal ball lecture.

Frau Ziegelow nodded.

"Good. I'll notify your husband's lawyer. I'm sure my colleague will talk some sense into his client. And you must promise me in return to obey fair-practice rules and regulations from now on." I smoothed out the document and filed it in her folder, which was already bulging and had to be secured with a rubber band. "I guess that's it for today."

She firmly shook my hand, holding on a little longer than necessary. "Was it worth it?"

I immediately regretted my question. Already on her way to the door, Frau Ziegelow paused.

"What I mean . . . you and . . . your husband, er, ex-husband . . . all of that," I stammered, blushing, and gestured towards the overflowing folder.

She gazed at the recorded proof of her broken marriage before turning away. "I wouldn't give up one minute with the bastard."

Frau Ziegelow's sad eyes stayed with me all the way to our home, a sky-blue town house in Frankfurt's West End. They faded away as I fumbled for my vibrating mobile phone in the hallway next to the mailboxes. I opened Mama's text message with trepidation.

Grandmother wants to see us. Tonight, 7:00 p.m. Kisses.

The hallway light cycled off with a low clicking sound. In the dimness, I leaned against the wall and listened to my breathing. The text gave me forty-five minutes to get to my grandmother's house if I didn't want to incur her displeasure, as she considered being late a mortal sin. I opened the mailbox with a sigh. There was the *Wochenblatt*, a flyer with ads for summer tyres, and a few official-looking documents addressed to Justus. I also found a birthday card from my cousin—three weeks late as usual, and opening with an apology. I didn't even try to decipher the rest of Charlie's scrawl, and just stuffed everything in my briefcase before hurrying up to the fourth floor.

I was dumbfounded to find our wheeled suitcase standing by the open door. Clattering noises emerged from inside the apartment and I almost tripped over Justus's duffel bag.

"Sweetie?"

The tension in my stomach grew worse as I set my briefcase down and hung my coat in the closet. I jumped when my fiancé suddenly appeared next to me.

"What in the world are you doing?"

I didn't know whether to be shocked or amused. He was standing in front of me in camouflage fatigues, like a soldier on furlough—well, except for the Panama hat.

Justus looked at me smugly. "Do you know where my Jack Wolfskin jacket is, Finchen?"

"You donated it to charity last year when they collected old clothes," I replied, trying to remember when Justus had decided to enlist.

He frowned and began to rifle through the closet.

"Would you please tell me what you're up to?" I said to his back.

"Combat survival training" was the hollow-voiced reply. My coat fell from its hanger. Justus pulled his winter coat from the farthest depths of the closet with a satisfied look on his face. "I told you about it." He brushed a bit of lint off the tweed and grimaced.

"Did you?" I was confused.

"Maibach wants me to prove I'm a tough guy before signing the partnership agreement."

"Really. So he's sending you off to—where, the Congo?—three weeks before our wedding?"

"Actually to the Westerwald—campfires, tents, the complete macho programme," Justus smirked. "They're picking me up soon. Get this— they'll blindfold us, so we don't know where we're—"

"But you hate camping!" I interrupted. "Besides, we're supposed to choose the wedding cake, and I have to go over the guest list with you before we order place cards."

"It's just for five days, Finchen." I really hated that particular diminutive of my name. "Your crazy aunts will be delighted to taste their way through all the cake shops in town. You girls don't need me."

"But—"

"There's no but. There are things a man simply has to do," he said, emphasising each syllable. "Especially if a pay rise of tens of thousands of euros is involved. I am sure you agree with me there, Josefine."

I said nothing. When Justus used my full first name, any further discussion was futile. It had been like that since we were students, and was one of the things I had learned to accept. He gave me a peck on the forehead and stuffed his coat into the duffel bag.

"There's still time for us to sit and have coffee," I said, trying another approach. "I have something important I need to tell you."

"Is it about that horrid Frau Ziegelow? I'm sure it can wait till next week. I don't understand why she constantly wastes your time—and why you let her! Dump that clown on one of the peons."

I contemplated his chiselled face, shimmering grey eyes, and long lashes. Justus had a slight squint, which sometimes gave the impression that he wasn't looking straight at you, but at something behind you. I had always considered it strangely attractive. Now, however, it underscored my impression that, mentally, he had already left the apartment.

"Okay, fine, it can wait," I forced myself to say, and was relieved to see his disapproving expression disappear.

We had always disagreed on how to interact with clients. He preferred to deal with them in writing only. But poor Frau Ziegelow wasn't even what I'd wanted to discuss. I had wanted to tell him about the missing ring, though, on reflection, it was probably better if I dealt with that on my own. I was quite sure he wouldn't understand my grandmother's superstitions about the heirloom.

"I'll call you. Wait, actually . . ." He reached for his Blackberry and handed it to me with a sigh. "No mobile phones allowed. I'd better leave it here."

"Well, whoop-de-doo!" I cried. I couldn't help it. "How am I supposed to talk with you about the cake?"

"Come on, Finchen." He pulled me abruptly and forcefully against him. "I don't care if it's chocolate cream or that awful buttercream your granny goes gaga over. I'll still say yes when the priest asks. So don't worry about the silly cake."

My body finally relaxed. Justus always had this wonderful, clean scent of shirts fresh from the cleaners and of mouthwash. Since his tight embrace made it hard to breathe, I could only whisper, "Super."

He held me out at arm's length and pulled the elastic band out of my hair. "I like this turquoise blouse on you, but you should wear your hair down." He gave me a wink, shouldered the duffel bag, and left.

I stood motionless in front of the closed door for a while. Then I looked at the clock. I had less than ten minutes to get to my grandmother's house, so the shower I craved was out of the question. I grabbed my trench coat and sighed. Now that I thought about it, I'd prefer running around the Westerwald in fatigues to putting myself in the matriarch's line of fire. But as it turned out, there also were things a woman simply had to do.

2

As a child, the house of my grandmother, Adele von Meeseberg, had always seemed like an enchanted castle in a fairy tale—but I was never sure whether a good or an evil queen lived there.

Even at thirty years of age, a strange feeling of awe and enchantment still overcame me whenever I passed through the wrought-iron gates, from which two stone lions gazed down on me. I parked my car next to Mama's Audi under the old cherry tree in full April bloom. Out of habit, I leaned my head back and looked up at the white façade with its transom windows. There was one dormer window that stood out from the rest—oval shaped and bordered with carved stone flowers, the only aberration in the baroque architecture of Villa Meeseberg.

"Are you planning to grow roots there or will you honour us with your presence sometime today?" said a gruff, raspy voice. My great-aunt was leaning against one of the red stone pillars of the entrance, smoking.

"Aunt Bri! I thought you'd quit."

She looked at her hand and opened her eyes wide. "Oops! Where did this come from?" She hastily took one more puff, stomped out her cigarette, and gingerly picked up the butt.

I knew of no other woman her age who could kneel down so elegantly, and none who wore dresses that revealed their knees.

Bri straightened up and tossed the butt into Grandmother's cherished rose border. "Believe me, the drama inside is way more harmful than a little nicotine. Smart decision, by the way, to come late."

"It wasn't intentional. Traffic—"

"Josefine, I beg you, don't destroy my hope that, for once in your life, you might do something inappropriate."

Bri adjusted her hat, which resembled an upturned, eggshell-coloured mixing bowl. She always wore atrocities on her head, inviting endless teasing. But my great-aunt had always done what she wanted, and my cousin Charlie seemed to take after her.

Aunt Bri linked her arm with mine and led me inside.

"The entire clan is assembled." She motioned with her chin to the drawing room and rolled her eyes. "And, as usual, the indignation of our first-born son is enough to shake the chandeliers."

My heart sped up. Uncle Carl and Aunt Silvia were here, too? Was my grandmother so upset about the missing ring that she'd convened the entire family council?

"How bad is it?" I whispered to Bri on our way to the massive double doors.

"Bad? According to Carl, your cousin has been abducted by human traffickers and sold to Russian drug lords. But if you subtract the lurid details he invented, it's actually just a girl in love who eloped with her beau." She shrugged. "Happens in the best of families. My hysterical nephew, of course, thinks we should call the feds because Charlotte isn't returning his calls."

I spun to look at Bri, nearly bumping into the armour of my ancestor Philipp. "Hold on. We're here because of Charlie?"

Bri had to tilt her head to inspect me from under her hat. "What other reason does my sister have to round us up like cattle in the middle of the week? And at this hour." She made a face. "We don't even get cake!"

I followed Bri into the drawing room, my hands clammy. The first person I spotted was my mother. She was perched on the Biedermeier sofa next to a distraught Aunt Silvia. Charlie's mother always cried easily, and red eyes below her dyed-blonde bangs was not an unusual sight.

"Twenty-five thousand euros in tuition. For nothing! Does the girl think that money grows on trees?" roared Uncle Carl, commanding the room as he paced in front of the fireplace.

I snuck over to join Papa, who was leaning against the window and studying the lilies on the wallpaper. His warm smile made me feel better immediately. Bri steered towards the bar, but paused to nudge her sister Li, who had dozed off despite the noisy discussion.

"Charlotte is twenty-four now. Twenty-four! You'd think my daughter would be old enough to realise that life isn't a damn computer game she can just pause in order to take off for Scotland with some bum."

"Watch your language, son," Grandmother said in a biting tone.

Uncle Carl stopped abruptly and pointed at his wife. "Charlotte should have gone to boarding school, like I always told you."

Silvia convulsed with sobs and Mama tried to soothe her in the same tone she used on dogs in distress. When I tried to catch her eye, Mama looked down guiltily, confirming my suspicion that she had yet to mention our own problem. Charlie had once again managed to send the entire family into a fit. And she had done it without even being present.

"Scotland is enchanting, and so romantic. Rich green meadows with all those sheep and craggy cliffs . . . as long as you have good, warm clothes and don't catch a cold. I read that it rains quite a bit," Aunt Li piped up. Bri almost choked on her Scotch.

I suppressed a grin. Li was so adorably naïve.

Carl took a deep breath that made his smoker's lungs whistle and strained his shirt buttons. He had gained at least ten pounds since I'd last seen him.

"With all due respect, Lieselotte, I can do without your travel advice."

"Sit down, son. And you, Silvia, pull yourself together."

My grandmother was not a tall woman, but after she raised herself from her armchair, I wasn't the only one who forgot to breathe for a moment. Even Papa, who was not easily cowed, seemed ready to salute. Adele von Meeseberg was in her late eighties. Despite her stooped posture, she had lost none of the grace and pride common to women who could look back on an upper-class life and were used to telling others what to do.

"Could we approach the matter objectively?" she said into the silence.

"Cocktail, anyone?" Bri jingled the ice in her glass.

I was tempted to raise my hand, but somehow didn't dare.

"I have to drive," grunted Carl, though everyone knew that this didn't normally stop him.

Aunt Li glumly pointed to her floral teacup on the side table, and everyone else said no, pretending, more or less convincingly, that they weren't used to drinking. I really would have liked to know what Grandmother was thinking—I couldn't help but notice the hint of a smile on her lips.

"Charlie dropped out of college," Bri explained as she refilled her glass. "Or, to be precise, she was taken off the university rolls since she apparently struggled in her exams."

"You mean she failed them because she hasn't seen the inside of a lecture hall in six months," added Carl.

"Business Administration never was a good fit for her. If you had allowed her to study what she wanted—"

"A von Meeseberg who cooks for people? Over my dead body!"

"Don't be such a snob." Bri's eyes flashed. "A talented chef can go far these days."

"Do you seriously believe Charlotte has the discipline to work her way to the top in a temple of gastronomy?"

"If you do what you love to do, you can achieve amazing things," Bri responded, and I silently agreed with her.

As a child, when Charlie wasn't hunting for spiders in some corner of the basement, you could find her helping out in the kitchen, and she had remained an avid baker to this day. Her cheesecake was a revelation. Unfortunately, she'd never found a diplomatic way to make her domineering father understand her gift. So, at a young age, my cousin had rebelled. And she'd carried on rebelling ever since.

Bri took a gulp of her drink. "Anyway, the girl was expelled from that chichi private university and she sublet her apartment to a classmate, who claims that she went—"

"Why the hell to Scotland of all places?" interrupted Uncle Carl.

"Well, I think that Scotland is quite—"

"Shut up, Li," Carl and Bri shouted at the same time.

Aunt Li threw up her hands.

"She could at least have told us," Silvia whined.

"But she did." Li removed her glasses and cleaned them with her jumper.

All eyes turned to the small, plump woman who almost disappeared in the armchair, a book balanced on her knees as always. I marvelled, not for the first time, at how different my great-aunts were, despite being twin sisters. I had never seen Bri with a book in her hands, but Li studied even brochures as diligently as if they were Mann's *Buddenbrooks*.

Aunt Li put on her glasses and looked around. "What is it?"

"Would you kindly explain what you just said, Li?" Bri suddenly seemed nervous.

"They were delightful—a young, great love, so full of hope. The two are made for each other. By the way, Bri, I'd like some apricot liqueur, the Italian one. It's delicious." She sighed. "The little summerhouse was empty anyway."

"You mean to say that Charlotte was staying here in the backyard? With her boyfriend?" The words just slipped out of my mouth.

"We *are* living in the twenty-first century. You no longer have to be married to sleep in the same bed." Li blushed and smoothed down the crocheted book cover. It was just one of her many awful handmade creations that lay around all over the house, or which she frequently gave to people who had no intention of ever using them. "And by the way, he isn't some 'bum,' as Carl claims. He's a musician—a very nice, talented young man."

"Spare me the details! When did all of this happen?" screamed Carl.

Poor Li was visibly confused now.

"Three weeks ago." Pouting, she added, "Charlotte asked me not to tell anyone about her travel plans. She also said she'd leave her phone at home. So it makes no sense to call her."

"Oh, Li," said Bri, shaking her head and emptying her glass.

A muffled sound came from the sofa. Mama had her hand in front of her mouth and looked very pale. "I completely forgot," she whispered, fidgeting. "Charlie spent a night at our place last month."

I looked at her in disbelief.

"Knew how to handle a hedge trimmer quite well, her boyfriend did," mumbled my father.

"Well, isn't that wonderful? A conspiracy—in my own family," grumbled Uncle Carl, his face crimson.

"She said something about water damage in her apartment . . . Was I to turn her away?" Mama blinked. Then, her eyes suddenly widened and she looked at me, trying vigorously to mouth something I couldn't begin to decipher.

"Are you all right, Mathilde?" Li asked.

"Of course I am, Aunt Li. I just suddenly remembered where I . . . last saw my amber necklace!" She gave a little cough and tapped on her ring finger. "I've been looking for it for the last few days."

"Isn't that the worst? I feel like all I do is misplace things. Just the other day, I . . ."

Li's voice seemed to fade away as I finally understood my mother's pantomime—the chronically broke, currently homeless Charlie staying in my parent's house, their daughter's birthdate as the less-than-secure code for the safe . . .

I brushed a strand of hair from my forehead, noticing that my palms were clammier than ever. It wouldn't be the first time Charlie had filched something. But could she really have done that to me? I looked up at my father.

"Papa?" I whispered. I felt numb. "Did you by any chance take the velvet box from the safe?"

"What velvet box?" he asked.

My breath caught in my throat. So the little monster really had absconded with my ring. I exhaled and started to laugh hysterically. Uncle Carl gave a start.

"It seems that several people in this room have lost their goddamn marbles. Care to tell us just what you find so funny?"

"Don't attack Josefine just because she's doing what we all would like to do," Bri interjected. "I honestly don't understand your goal for this meeting, my dear nephew. As you said yourself, Charlotte is twenty-four. An adult. Nobody can keep her from travelling wherever she pleases. You'll have to postpone your sudden paternal yearnings until your daughter gets tired of either her friend or the Scottish rain. Josefine's the only one with reason to be upset—Charlie would've been a lovely maid of honour. Which reminds me—we're having a wedding in three weeks, people, so let's talk about pleasant matters, such as flower arrangements and cakes! Li, why in the world did you order those funeral flowers after we'd already agreed on white calla lilies?"

By that point, I really needed schnapps or chocolate cookies—and plenty of either. Mama responded to my gloomy look with an equally melancholy head shake.

"We're not finished discussing this, Bri," thundered Carl. "I have by no means exhausted all possibilities—if I have to, I'll hire a private detective to bring my daughter back to Germany."

"A bounty hunter," Li corrected. "The correct term is 'bounty hunter.' And before you shush me again, I have no doubt that Charlie is doing splendidly in Scotland." With her chin raised, she turned to her sister. "Regular white lilies are on sale right now. Don't be so old-fashioned, Bri. And you'd better explain to me why you promised Mechthild she could do Josefine's hair even though she cheated when we played cards last week. Why are you validating that horrible woman?"

Uncle Carl cast a condescending look around the room. "Fine. Just go on quibbling about flowers and hairdos while *I* am trying to save my child. I will do everything I can to bring Charlotte back and make sure she graduates. I owe it to her since her mother was such an abject failure."

"Amen," said Bri, filling her glass for the third time, this time to the brim.

With my arms wrapped around me, I stood at the window and watched Mama's Audi pull out so fast it sprayed gravel all over the yard. It was after ten by now, and neither of us had worked up the courage to tell Grandmother about the ring—not when Uncle Carl took Silvia by the arm and grouchily said goodbye, and not during the quarrel between Bri and Li about who had made a bigger mess of the wedding preparations. Now it was my turn to leave without having achieved anything.

I smelled roses even before my grandmother joined me. She looked out of the window into the darkness of the garden, as attentive and alert as if she were expecting a late guest. Her voice, on the other hand, was weary.

"What is it you have to tell me, Josefine?"

Two hours of Uncle Carl's ranting and the spectre of Charlie hovering over us like a demon bent on sowing discord had strained her nerves as well.

"I don't know what you mean," I answered with forced cheerfulness, but I'd much rather have thrown my arms around her the way I used to as a little girl.

As an adult, my relationship with Grandmother had become less overtly affectionate. It was simultaneously deeper and more distant. I admired my grandmother so much that it would have felt disrespectful to take her hand without an invitation. Yearning for her approval, I feared the slightest sign of her displeasure.

"I'm old, not senile," she replied, and walked to her armchair. "Something has been bothering you all evening."

With her hands folded in her lap, she stiffened her back, as if sitting up straight was a carefully rehearsed process. It reminded me of how often she had exhorted Charlie and me to keep our composure in every situation. I didn't think my grandmother even knew how to slouch in a chair.

"Have you changed your mind about the wedding? It can happen, you know. Your great-great-aunt, for instance, just before—"

"Absolutely not," I snapped. The thought alone was absurd. I never changed my mind once I'd made a decision. That was something only indecisive people did—people like Charlie, people who didn't have real goals in life.

"Josefine, if you've realised that your fiancé is not a good match for you—"

"Justus and I are an excellent team. You don't have to worry about that," I assured her.

A strange expression crossed her face, but maybe it was just a shadow from the crackling fireplace.

"What is it, then?"

I hesitated. Maybe Mama was right. Maybe we shouldn't tell her. It couldn't be too hard for a skilled jeweller to create a replica of the simple gold ring. And properly cut glass didn't look so very different from a genuine diamond, and if Grandmother didn't look too closely . . .

"I won't bite your head off, no matter what it is. Besides, I can't imagine you've done anything worse than broken a piece of china. Unless we're talking about your great-grandmother Helene's china—that I would hold against you."

"The bride's ring," I whispered, feeling my heart sink. "It went missing . . . from the safe."

I could have dealt with her crying out in horror. Even a temper tantrum, composure be damned. If she was so attached to Great-Grandmother Helene's ugly plates, how much more unthinkable would the loss of a family heirloom from the Thirty Years' War be?

But she just sat in her chair like a statue, her face strangely waxen from the glow of the fire. She was silent for what felt like an eternity.

Then she turned her face to the window and sighed—a sigh that expressed everything, from disappointment to sadness, all the way to resignation. "That's unfortunate," she said quietly to no one in particular.

"I think Charlie has it. So maybe it's not really gone; it's just . . . somewhere else."

"Such things do not happen without a reason."

"Grandmother," I pleaded, irritated to hear Frau Ziegelow's words echoed. "It's only a ring. A piece of metal that—" I fell silent when I saw her face become impenetrable.

"You cannot walk down the aisle without that ring, Josefine—not if you want my blessing."

I was familiar with the feeling that now threatened to crush my chest like a corset laced too tightly. I only managed defiance for a split second—there was no sense fooling myself. I'd been raised in a house where tradition was revered and where Grandmother's word was law. A wedding without Adele von Meeseberg's blessing was as inconceivable as a church without a priest. I'd sooner cancel the wedding than carry on without Grandmother's blessing.

"Please don't do this to me." I trembled as if I were standing barefoot in a bucket of ice water.

"What does the number twenty-six mean to you?" my grandmother continued.

"It's the number of failed marriages in our family," I replied in a flat voice. I hated myself because I was about to let a stupid superstition ruin my life. But the only rebellion I could muster amounted to two clenched fists behind my back.

"What do they all have in common?"

"They lasted no longer than half a year . . . and . . . none of the brides wore the ring when she said 'I do.'"

Goosebumps rose up on my arms even though I had heard the stories hundreds of times and had long ago stopped believing in the connection between the ring and failed marriages. Our family's tragic history of doomed lovers had been part of my life for as long as I could remember, and the dissolution of some unions hadn't just been messy, but bloody. As a ten-year-old, I had relished making Charlie cry with the terrible details of one or another of those tragedies, but for a while, I'd actually believed that the women in our family were cursed, and that the only way to stave off the curse was to wear that special ring during the wedding ceremony.

As I got older, those stories met the fate of most fairy tales—they were put away and largely forgotten. But my grandmother had never grown out of them. She was still convinced that any marriage in our family undertaken without the ring's protection would end either in divorce or in the cold waters of the river Main.

"Go ahead, call me a foolish old fossil." She raised a hand to stop me from objecting. "I know very well what my lovely clan whispers behind my back. But, whether it's a curse, fate, or coincidence, I will not be responsible for my favourite granddaughter becoming the family's next suicide risk." A hint of a smile played around her lips. "But of course, the choice, dear Josefine, is yours to make."

"I have a choice?" My voice was very low and submissive. If I'd been standing next to myself, I would probably have shaken myself silly and screamed at myself. It was frightening how well I could control my emotions.

Now Grandmother smiled. "Well, you said that the ring wasn't lost, just elsewhere. You have three weeks until the wedding—if I have the dates right."

I was amazed. Was she seriously suggesting that I—

"Let me quote your great-aunt Li—Scotland is an enchanting country."

Driving home, I thought about the relationship between Charlie and myself. As a teenager, I was convinced that the sole reason for my cousin's existence was to make my life difficult.

On my tenth birthday, for instance, the little monster had discovered how to use matches and proceeded to burn down the table with all of my presents on it—all the while with a huge grin on her face. When I was fourteen, I had a huge crush on a boy named Marius Goll—that is, until Charlie, in whom I had stupidly confided, splashed my secret on the wall of the gym in red paint. *Jo loves Marius.* The feeling was not mutual, which became clear when Marius made fun of me in the cafeteria, in front of the entire school. Charlie always insisted that she'd actually done me a favour. Thinking back, she had never had anything good to say about any boy I liked.

I hit the brakes, stopping in the middle of the rain-drenched road. Other cars screeched to a halt and someone honked. I switched on my hazard lights and, grasping the steering wheel, I bent forward and gazed into space.

Charlie didn't like Justus either.

I sucked in air until it felt like my lungs might burst. Then I exhaled in short puffs until I was so empty I felt dizzy.

Charlie had been against my marriage from the start, and now she had found a way to prevent it. Even if I flew to Scotland, where the heck was I going to start looking for her?

I stared at the squeaking windscreen wipers for quite some time. Then I started the car, turned off the emergency blinkers, and stepped on the accelerator.

I was still furious when I arrived home and immediately went to my briefcase. Working on that stupid restraining order was exactly the distraction I needed right now.

When I pulled out Frau Ziegelow's folder, a postcard fell to the floor and landed face up—the belated birthday card from Charlie. My pulse quickened. I knelt down and looked at the image of a Victorian stone building in the middle of unspoiled moorland that immediately reminded me of . . . No way.

Unsettled, I picked up the card and flipped it over.

Fàilte! O'Farrell Guesthouse, Kincraig, Scotland.

The hairs on the back of my neck stood on end. It was getting harder to doubt that some strange power not only meant to derail my wedding, but also wanted to transport me to a foreign land. I closed my eyes until I felt strong enough to decipher the scrawl that confirmed what I already suspected.

> *Dear Jo,*
> *I'm sorry, but I had no choice. You should marry someone who deserves you.*
> *With all my heart, even if you never talk to me again.*
> *Charlie*
> *P.S.: Justus is an idiot.*

3

"Is there anything else I can do for you?"

The Asian flight attendant wore false eyelashes and a name tag that didn't seem to fit her—Candy Dee. She had already come to my seat three times since take-off.

"Would you like some more water?" Candy Dee asked in a tone usually reserved for mentally challenged patients.

I managed to nod, but the rest of my body felt paralysed—bolt upright and engulfed in fear. I was panicking because I was flying to a country I only knew from movies, because I'd left before my vacation time request had been processed, because I could imagine Justus's reaction when he found out, and because I had no idea what I would do if I didn't find Charlie, or even what I would do if I did. Not to mention I was terrified of flying.

"You may undo your seat belt and lean back if you wish."

Candy Dee was still in caregiver mode. My knees trembled and I tried to calm myself by focusing on the tray table in front of me.

"Everything is fine," I replied hoarsely, knowing that Candy Dee didn't believe a word.

She nodded sympathetically and continued down the narrow aisle, repeating her spiel as she went.

I definitely didn't feel fine. Upon boarding, I had made a beeline for seat 14E and immediately fastened the narrow belt around me, clinging to its modicum of security. I'd barely noticed the other passengers, too preoccupied with digging my fingernails into the armrests and surviving take-off.

Only now did I dare glance around. What I saw pushed my pulse rate right back up.

I was trapped, jammed in between a teenager with earphones and a mountain of a man who constantly wiped his sweaty, receding hairline. I would never be able get out fast enough in an emergency—provided I was even alive or capable of getting into one of the life rafts. They had those inflatable rafts on board this plane, right?

I cautiously tapped the shoulder of earphones kid, who swayed to whatever he was listening to with a glazed expression on his face.

"Would you mind swapping seats with me?" I begged. "I'm afraid I might have to—" I pointed at the bathrooms and mimed gagging. My grandmother would have been appalled.

"Sure. No problem, man."

He jumped up and I slid into the aisle seat.

I felt much safer here, especially because now I could see the flight attendants' station through the half-open curtain. Candy Dee was talking with a blonde colleague and their laughter calmed me immediately. It seemed that no plane crash was imminent.

I looked at the businessman on the other side of the aisle, rustling his newspaper and mumbling to himself. He was an attractive man—not in the classical sense, but . . . Now he smiled and a cute dimple appeared.

For some reason, I couldn't tear my eyes away from him, and I soon became painfully aware that I was staring at this stranger for far too long. I took note of his dress shirt, loosened tie, and nice trousers.

Expensive shoes, well polished. His hands were sturdy, but pale, uncalloused. No wedding ring. Not a Scot, but probably an English businessman, I thought, feeling proud of my ability to read people. I was rarely mistaken. Brown eyes.

I jumped. The man had noticed me. He looked me up and down as if trying to decide whether we knew each other. I quickly lowered my eyes. How awkward. At least he had helped dispel the images of aeroplane parts bobbling in the ocean. I now felt confident that I would arrive in Scotland alive.

Remembering my cursory Internet research, I shuddered. Scotland offered everything I detested—forces of nature, driving on the left side, whining bagpipes, sheep stomachs stuffed with innards, men in strange outfits who probably smelled like sheep. However, I was engaged, so I shouldn't be getting that close to any Scotsmen anyway. This was also true, of course, for attractive, unmarried Englishmen.

Reassured, I closed my eyes—only to open them with a start a few moments later. Snippets of conversation in English drifted over to me, sprinkled with quiet laughter.

"Sure, I thought of you, Maisie . . . Yes, I got it, just the one you wanted . . . I look forward to it, too . . . I'd say in two days . . ."

He was on his phone. On an aeroplane!

"Excuse me," I hissed, leaning into the aisle.

"Not at all . . . quite a bit . . ."

"Excuse me!" My voice was tinged with hysteria.

He covered the mouthpiece and leaned towards me with a blank look. A faint scent of . . . I shrank back. This guy, unbelievably, seemed to smell of chocolate cookies.

"Yes, may I help you?"

"You . . . your . . ." My hands were trembling.

The man looked at his mobile phone, a puzzled look on his face.

"Phone," I managed to say, ashamed of sounding like a breathless psycho.

He frowned and seemed to think about what I'd said. Then he nodded with an aloof smile . . . and resumed his phone call! "Sweetie, what did you say? . . . Oh yes, sure . . ."

I was speechless. He leaned back and murmured to the person on the other end of the line as if it was the most normal thing in the world to make a Boeing 737 crash. I imagined the wildly spinning altimeters in the cockpit, the plane listing to one side, spiralling into the depths, until . . .

Oh god, we were all going to die.

"Are you all right, miss?"

In my panic, I hadn't noticed that the jerk had finished his call.

"Didn't you listen to the flight attendant earlier? You're not allowed to use a phone on a plane," I snarled in German, too angry to remember my English.

He peered at me sideways, a look of mild amusement on his face.

"It was important," he answered in surprisingly correct German, and seemed to be about to say more when his phone started to vibrate. He immediately switched to his mother tongue.

"Jennifer? I'm on the plane . . . Well, just the usual trade fair craziness . . . Definitely a few interesting options for the Edinburgh branch. Looks like we're landing on time . . . Dinner at your place sounds wonderful . . . Yes, I like . . ."

I felt sick. This man had to be stopped.

I unlatched my seat belt with some difficulty, gave the Englishman a dirty look, and walked with as much dignity as my wobbly knees allowed towards the flight attendants' station.

Candy Dee was not pleased. I could see it in the look she exchanged with her colleague and from her reluctant march down the aisle to verify my accusation. I ducked nervously into the bathroom, but half wished I'd followed her to watch. Candy Dee represented authority here, even though she was five foot nothing and sounded like a little girl.

I returned to my seat five minutes later, head held high. Unfortunately, the scene I found there did not resemble the one I'd imagined I would see.

Candy Dee sat in my seat, her childlike, knobby knees turned towards the Englishman. Their heads nearly touched across the aisle as they looked at photos . . . on his mobile phone. They didn't even notice me until I cleared my throat. Candy Dee jumped up as if I'd caught her sneaking a cigarette.

"Nevertheless, Mr. Murray, I still have to ask you to turn off your phone," she said sweetly, with a blissful smile.

"Why don't you call me Aidan, Candy? And you know what?" He cast an amused glance at me. "Why don't you take my phone, so I won't accidentally annoy anyone? I'll pick it up later."

I rolled my eyes and dropped down into my seat, almost forgetting to buckle myself in. Candy Dee left, grinning like a teenager with a crush. I shut my eyes defiantly, determined not to open them again until we'd landed.

Someone gave a little cough to my left. "Excuse me, miss?"

I grudgingly looked over.

"You snitched on me! What's the word in German . . . *verpetzt?*"

He looked at me, seemingly fascinated rather than annoyed.

"I had to save all of us, Mr. Murray," I muttered, setting him straight.

"I see," he said, pursing his lips.

"Stop that!" I snapped, forcing myself not to stare at his mouth. It was surprisingly soft, almost feminine.

"What am I supposed to stop?" he continued in German.

"The puppy-like dramatics. Maybe they work on Maisie, Jennifer, and Candy Dee, but I'm not buying what you're selling." To stress my point, I wiggled my hand with the silver engagement ring Justus had given me.

"Whoa! What's bugging you?"

"I have no problem with bugs, just with people who endanger others because they think the rules don't apply to them."

He laughed. "And you obey the rules by eavesdropping on private conversations and denouncing people to the flight crew instead of asking them politely to turn off their phone. You didn't have many friends in school, did you now?"

"But I did ask you!"

"No. You just informed me, not very politely, that I had a phone—I was aware of that—and also that they're not allowed."

"You—" I gasped for air. This guy was simply unbelievable.

"How can such a pretty woman be so uptight?"

He leaned across the aisle and I automatically pulled back. But that did not deter Mr. Murray.

"You look like a girl who never let her classmates copy her homework." He stroked his chin.

"Whereas I'm sure all your friends let *you* cheat," I answered, trying not to let on how right he was.

Grinning, he eased back into his chair. "You seem to know how to think on your feet. What do you do for a living?"

"I'm a lawyer," I replied.

"Perfect. And what brings you to beautiful Scotland? A case?"

"It's none of your business."

"What's wrong with a nice little chat?"

"Maybe I don't want to chat with you."

"Believe me, that's exactly what you want." He gave me a meaningful look.

At that moment, the aeroplane began to tremble like a massive animal in pain. I winced when the seat belt sign switched on with a loud ding.

"Just a little turbulence." Aidan Murray shrugged. "Look at me and answer my question. Why are you flying to Scotland?"

"It's . . . private," I moaned, clawing at the armrest again. His eyes were green, not brown, as I'd thought at first—green with gold flecks. The plane rumbled and rattled. A child began to cry. Candy Dee and her colleague scuttled around, calming passengers, and finally retreated to the jump seats, their backs straight as arrows.

"I'm going to die," I mumbled, gritting my teeth to keep them from chattering.

"Why Scotland?" The awful man exuded calmness.

"I'm visiting someone," I said, gasping for air.

"A man? Maybe the one behind this?" He gestured towards my engagement ring and placed his hand over mine nonchalantly. The soft pressure was strangely reassuring.

"I'm visiting my cousin," I lied, and pushed my glasses up. My pulse rate must have been 180 at least.

"Is she as pretty as you are?"

"Much too young for you." I managed to grin. "Besides, she isn't crazy about Englishmen in suits."

"You think I'm English?"

"Well, you don't look Scottish."

"And what do Scottish men look like, in your opinion?"

"They're taller and more muscular. They wear lambswool jumpers . . ." *And they definitely wouldn't smell of chocolate cookies.*

"Well, now, I'm about six feet tall and have quite a few muscles. My pullovers are in my duffel bag—alpaca, by the way. Lambswool is for women." He winked. "You don't look like a lawyer either, by the way, even though you're talking like one."

"Is that so?" I really needed to stop holding my breath. I already felt quite dizzy.

"Annie Stone," he replied, staring at me so intently that I had to turn away. "My primary school teacher. Her face was as grim as yours."

I chose to ignore his impertinence. "So you're really Scottish?"

"*Gu cinnteach*, madam." Grinning, he stuck his thumb in the air. "That was Gaelic," he added, as if that was necessary. "It means 'for sure.'"

"And what were you doing in Germany? Visiting one of your girlfriends?"

"I sold a flock of sheep."

"You're joking."

"Just a little."

"Very funny."

"But it did make you smile."

"Touché. Your point. And I'll even add half a point because your German isn't bad."

"My mother's from Flensburg." He tilted his head to one side. "Tell me about the guy to whom you're recklessly willing to give away your heart."

Even though he was joking, I felt attacked.

"I'm not giving anything away. Believe it or not, there are still some people who take marriage seriously!"

"What makes you think I don't take it seriously?"

"I don't get the impression that you're much for commitment."

A strange expression flickered over his face. He pulled his hand away and turned to look out of the window past his seatmate. I felt my cheeks burn. Had I been holding hands with this womaniser the entire time? How embarrassing. But I wasn't myself, what with this horrible flight . . .

"It's almost over, ma'am. We're about to land," he said.

I leaned forward and peered out. Indeed, lights appeared through the fog. A city.

Aidan chuckled and I suddenly found him less unpleasant. His nearness was actually calming—and the flight wouldn't last much longer, thank god.

"All that's left is a safe landing in Edinburgh, Miss . . . ?"

"Josefine," I replied quickly. "I'm Josefine."

"Josefine." The way he pronounced my name was unusual—drawn out and soft—as if he had secretly added a few vowels.

My seat was vibrating. The landing flaps went out—I felt an uncomfortable pressure in my ears.

"Aidan . . ."

I squinted and tried to suppress visions of a crash landing. What did it matter? I would never see this man again, whether we arrived safely or not.

"Aidan, until we're on terra firma, would you mind holding my hand as you did before?"

It was thanks to Candy Dee that Aidan Murray disappeared from my life even faster than I had hoped he would. She showed up before the seat belt signs were turned off. Ignoring our clasped hands, which we quickly dropped, she instead gave Aidan a look so seductive that any other woman would have considered it a declaration of war.

"Your mobile phone, Mr. Murray." She blushed. "Aidan." She bent down and whispered loud enough for me to hear, "I saved my number. Just in case you're in Frankfurt one of these days and want a personal tour of the city."

"What a generous offer, Candy," Aidan replied, showing off the dimples that probably secured him offers of sightseeing tours from every woman on the planet.

Candy Dee sauntered off with swaying hips and giggles that reminded me of the squealing piglet sound one of Charlie's old dolls used to make. Charlie had dragged that doll everywhere until I was so sick of the constant oinking that I made the doll disappear. It was probably still languishing in Grandmother's rain barrel behind the shed.

I feigned rummaging in my handbag while Aidan retrieved his bag from the overhead compartment. Absentmindedly, I applied some lip gloss—I had carried the small jar with me for years without ever having opened it. It had been a birthday present from Charlie, who didn't care that I never used the stuff. Why did I mind Candy Dee's behaviour? I tore at the seat belt, which apparently did not want to release me.

"Push first. Then pull." Aidan pushed my hands aside. The clasp opened with a soft click. I was free.

"Thank you," I said, with as much aloofness as I could muster.

He looked at me for a moment, and then his dimples went back into action.

"Whatever it is you're really looking for, Josefine, know that nobody asks you to give your heart to Scotland. But if you do, Scotland will love you back."

And he left. Taken aback, I watched his tall frame head towards the exit and disappear into the multicoloured mosaic of caps and hats.

What Scotland gave me first was a problem smelling of peppermint drops. The woman behind the car rental counter shook her head sympathetically, pushing a strongly scented peppermint sweet around in her mouth.

"Sorry, miss."

"But I even paid in advance!" Flustered, I waved my voucher in front of her and rifled through my handbag for the third time. It was an act of pure desperation since I now remembered where my driver's licence was—in the glove compartment of my Mini Cooper, which was in its parking garage in Frankfurt.

The woman transferred her mint from one cheek to the other. "As I've told you already, without a licence, I'm not allowed to give you a car."

I groaned. "I don't believe this."

The mint clicked against her teeth. "That's the law. No driver's licence, no car."

"What would it cost me for you to bend the rules?" Determined, I pulled my chequebook out.

The clicking ceased. "Did you just say what I think you said, miss?" she asked sternly, and looked at me with much less compassion than before.

I felt sweat break out on my forehead. Had I fallen so low?

"Well, you see . . ." I swallowed and looked over my shoulder.

The bearded man behind me in line stood there with a blank expression on his face. His wife checked her watch and sighed. I leaned forward and waved the car rental woman closer.

"It's a matter of life and death," I whispered nervously. "I have to be in the Highlands as soon as possible. Would twelve years of driving without an accident and five hundred pounds be enough for you to help me out a little"—I glanced at her name tag—"Deborah?"

Deborah peered at me without a word. Then her ample bosom trembled and she uttered a sound that hovered between disbelief and resignation. "Why don't you try a peppermint drop, miss."

Annoyed, I looked at the little metal tin she pushed towards me.

"Take one. They're good."

I took one of the powdered sweets and put it in my mouth.

"Delicious, no?"

"Terrific," I mumbled, trying to catch my breath. This thing would match any chilli pepper on the Scoville scale.

"Just take the whole tin. You probably need them more than I do," Deborah said good-naturedly, and I tucked the incendiary tin into my blazer pocket.

Someone groaned behind me. "How long is this going to take, miss? Are you trying to rent the entire lot?"

"Don't rush us, sir." Without taking her eyes off me, Deborah took out a pad of paper.

I fought to suppress a smile. I knew it. Five hundred pounds would do the trick for anyone. She scrawled something on the pad, tore off a page, and shoved it towards me.

747 9:25 p.m. HAL

I looked up, confused. "What does that mean?"

She chewed on the last remnants of her peppermint. "That's the bus to Halbeath. It leaves from the terminal entrance. You get off at the last station and change to the bus to Inverness. If you prefer, you could get a taxi—hellishly expensive, though. Hurry, miss. Shouldn't waste time in matters of life and death."

My cheeks still burning with shame, I headed for the terminal exit.

Scotland welcomed me exactly as I had feared—with rain. And not just any kind of rain. The water pouring down reminded me of a shower-head turned to "Massage." I would have been fascinated by the eerie sight of the control tower, which pointed to the storm clouds with a bright-blue fist—fascinated under different circumstances, that is, beneath a starry sky and in temperatures appropriate to my clothing. The damp air, smelling of soil and exhaust fumes, penetrated my blazer within seconds. Shivering, I pulled the zip up to my chin.

It was at that moment that I realised I had never travelled by myself before. I felt lost and incredibly lonely, like a pebble in a stream of humanity, innumerable bodies swirling around me, chins down, hurrying to taxis or the car park. Rather than heeding Deborah's suggestion and heading straight to the buses, I retreated to a sheltered alcove next to the exit door. Two men in work clothes stood there, smoking. I turned my back to them and sat down on my suitcase. So this was where my journey was going to end. I squinted into the rain and swallowed hard. *No,* I told myself. *You can't burst into tears now.*

Maybe this was how it was supposed to be. First the horrible flight, and then the humiliation at the car rental counter. How could I even start looking for Charlie without a car? And now, this torrential rain. Omens. Scotland was showing me the door.

The men stomped out their cigarettes and climbed into a white van that pulled out with a screech and manoeuvred past a row of waiting taxis. A blue Vauxhall approached far too fast and stopped right in front of the covered crossing. A slender woman with curly red hair got out and looked around. Her freckled face lit up with a radiant smile as she waved.

"Aidan, over here!" she called in a strong voice, as if she were used to talking at that volume. It was deeper than I would have expected of such a delicate woman.

The man strode towards her casually, collar turned up, as if out for a stroll on a balmy spring evening. Remaining seated on my suitcase, I rolled myself deeper into the alcove to avoid being seen, and almost fell when my vehicle caught on a loose cobblestone. I righted myself, straightened my skirt, and caught the eye of a grinning taxi driver.

Meanwhile, Aidan Murray had reached the redhead, who locked him in a boisterous embrace. Was it Jennifer? Maisie? No, according to his call, it wouldn't be Maisie's turn until the day after tomorrow.

He opened the boot of the car and tossed in his bag. I held my breath as he glanced in my direction for a moment before closing the boot.

"Let's go, Vicky." He tapped on the top of the car and got in. The engine roared to life.

Vicky. Number four in Murray's harem if you counted Candy Dee. I snorted and decided to write Aidan Murray off once and for all.

I looked back into the terminal. My best bet would probably be to hop on the next plane back to Frankfurt, even though the thought made me nauseous. On the other hand . . . I turned and looked at the Vauxhall's disappearing taillights. I was here, wasn't I? Assuming my assistant hadn't messed up, a pleasant room awaited me in a trendy Edinburgh hotel, where I was sure to find both warm water and a minibar.

I pulled out the envelope with the reservation even though, thanks to Mama, I already knew the name and address by heart. Once she had understood that nothing could keep me from going on this trip, she'd wanted to know exactly where I was staying. She'd called me twice about it and, displaying a maternal anxiety that was not like her at all, had made me spell out the necessary information. *Eden Rock Lodge.* Sounded promising.

The grinning taxi driver nodded and beckoned me over.

I had never been one to give up easily. Never. Why should I start now? I could always ask my mother to have my driver's licence sent to the hotel. What else was express mail for? I would await the delivery in the cushy hotel lobby, comfortably ensconced in front of the fireplace, with a cup of Earl Grey and a good book. Or I could go shopping and take in the sights of Edinburgh.

I lifted my chin and recalled my grandmother's words—"But of course, the choice, dear Josefine, is yours to make."

"I won't disappoint you," I whispered, and imagined her stern expression morphing into the smile that had always made me feel special as a little girl.

I hurried to the taxi as fast as my pumps could carry me.

4

Jonathan Fraser had lived in Edinburgh all his life and, if you believed him, had driven a taxi for just as long.

"Just as ma father and his father," he assured me.

When Jonathan laughed, he pulled on his blond beard as if he wanted to stretch it straight. This would have been impossible, since his beard was as unruly as the curly hair that peaked out from under his thick woollen cap.

"Alpaca?" I asked.

"Virgin wool, miss. From good Highland sheep, of course."

"Of course." I grinned, looking at him in the mirror. He had rosy cheeks and a bulbous nose that was crisscrossed by tiny veins.

"So what do you do on your days off?"

I didn't usually make small talk with strangers, but it was already dark and all that was visible through the rain-battered windows were the brown silhouettes of buildings and the gleam of blurred traffic lights—it could have been any city out there. Admiring the sights of Edinburgh was not an option at the moment.

"You really want to know?" Jonathan sought my eyes in the rear-view mirror. "Usually, tourists want me to tell them a bit about the city. As a rule, they're not interested in the driver."

"Well, then, I'm not a normal tourist."

"I saw you." He briefly turned his head. I could see a row of teeth edged in brown. "You were lookin' quite lost sitting there on your suitcase."

"And you didn't answer my question."

His booming laugh sounded like a poorly tuned contrabass.

"My real vocation is that of a storyteller."

"A storyteller? But that's not an actual occupation, is it?"

"It is in Scotland." He winked at me. "A well-paid one at that if ya find the right location."

"Like where?" I leaned forward.

"Have you ever heard of the subterranean corridors in Mary King's Close? In that old district of our city, all kinds of curious things are afoot." He hissed quietly.

"You tell ghost stories?" I laughed, but suddenly felt uneasy. "And people actually pay for such nonsense?"

"I wouldn't call it nonsense," Jonathan said with a mysterious air. "Not at all. As the saying goes, there are more things in heaven and earth than are dreamt of in your philosophy. For us Scots, just because they're in a story doesn't mean ghosts don't exist."

My eyebrows shot up. "Is there any scientific proof of what's supposedly happening at Mary King's Close?"

"Aye. There are eyewitness accounts," Jonathan said seriously.

"Ah. And what exactly have these people seen?"

"A tall lady in a long black garment. An old man with a sad face who fades into the walls. And a little girl who plays with dolls left for her by tourists from all over the world."

The taxi left the paved road, rambled along over cobblestones, and came to a halt soon after. I peeked out of the window and saw that we were in a cul-de-sac with a grassy side strip and a few parked cars.

"Where are we?" My heart raced. Had I got into the wrong taxi?

"Hadfast Road is a dead-end street. Over there is a path that leads you to Eden Rock Lodge. It's no more than a hundred yards from here." Jonathan glanced at my shoes. "It's not the most comfortable accommodation you've selected."

"Looks like it," I said, silently cursing my assistant.

"Do you have an umbrella?" He didn't even wait for an answer before reaching into the glove compartment and handing me a collapsible one.

"You're an angel."

"Sometimes that, too." He started the car with a grin.

I got half out of the car, but then slid back into my seat. "Forgive me, I didn't mean to offend you before, Jonathan. I am sure you tell wonderful fairy tales."

"They aren't fairy tales." He frowned.

"I know. There are eyewitness reports."

"So you don't believe in the supernatural at all? What about fate? What about coincidences that are really no such thing?"

"Guess I've seen too much to still believe in fate."

"Oh, is that right?" Jonathan gave me a pitying look over his shoulder. "We Scots believe that reality is always intertwined with matters we cannot explain. That makes quite a few things easier—not to have to feel so guilty when things turn out different from what you expected."

"Sounds great for people who don't want to accept responsibility."

"Honestly, miss, the way you were sitting on your suitcase before— it looked as if you really could do without taking responsibility for every last thing for once." It seemed that he wanted to say something more, but he just tipped his cap with a grin. "Anyway, I wish you a good time in our lovely country, miss. I'll be waiting here a quarter of an hour before I leave, just in case you want to do the same thing my last passenger coming to this place ended up doing."

I got out of the car with an uneasy feeling and opened the umbrella. It was half-broken and so tiny that it barely protected my head and shoulders from the rain. Jonathan put on the high beams and pointed to a narrow gravel path. Maybe I should have been suspicious when Lara proudly showed me the low room rate she'd found.

"What did your last customer do?" I called through the passenger window while looking at the tin sign attached to a pole proclaiming, "Welcome to God's Country. Eden Rock Lodge."

"Insisted I take him to a proper hotel."

About two hundred yards later, I learned what had made Jonathan's previous passenger get back into the taxi. Eden Rock Lodge was as far from a proper hotel as a barn was from King Ludwig's castle. Blinded by night and rain, I almost pulled my little valise right past the dimly lit building. The entryway's concrete slabs were cracked, and they jutted up from the soil as if trying to escape. *That has to be a code violation,* I thought, and then looked up at the weather-beaten stone façade. It was only a little past 10 p.m., but all of the shutters were closed. A copper ship's bell hung next to a wooden door. Nothing suggested that a hotel was hiding within these walls.

But wait—there was another tin shingle like the one at the trail-head. Several letters had long since fallen from the sign, and the gappy remains read "Eden Ro Lo ."

For some strange reason, I didn't follow the example of my predecessor who had turned on his heel. Maybe it was because I was soaked to the skin. All I wanted at that moment was a dry spot—even a goat pen would have sufficed. I thought of Jonathan and his taxi, engine still running, just a few hundred yards away. Then I cautiously pulled on a rope to ring the bell.

Not a sound. I pulled a little harder—and the rope came free in my hand.

"Just perfect," I mumbled between chattering teeth.

I sensed more than saw movement in the shadows cast by the anaemic light, freezing in terror at the thought of what might be lurking there. It was probably only a cat, but my instincts took over, and I launched my shoulder into the door.

The door gave immediately and I stumbled into a brightly lit hallway. Warmth!

I lifted my head and looked into the angry face of a Scottish soldier, high up on a horse. His comrades were assembled around him in other gold-framed paintings. An entire Highlander army in oils—brandishing bayonets, playing bagpipes—guided me down the corridor to a room with an enormous fireplace and a reception desk. It may have smelled of mothballs and mould, but it was undeniably a hotel lobby. Thank god!

I looked towards the cosy fire in the fireplace and—

Impossible! I stood glued to the spot, my mouth hanging open, clutching the ripped-off bell rope in my fist, and tried to convince myself that I wasn't seeing ghosts sitting in two Chippendale chairs next to a tea table, playing rummy.

"There she is. Yoo-hoo, Josie! Is this a surprise or what?" Aunt Li was beaming and waving. "Come here, child."

Aunt Bri looked up from her cards with a tiny frown. "Did you swim here? You look awful."

What the hell were my aunts doing here? My knees went wobbly and, a few heartbeats later, I found myself lying on the carpet like a beetle in shock.

"Damn it, Li. You scared her so much she fainted." Bri's voice seemed to come from far away.

"Why is it my fault? She only keeled over after your . . . honestly . . . snide remark," Li said in a huff.

I half opened my eyes and inspected the two pairs of legs next to me. I could easily guess who wore the woollen tights and flats and who the elegant furry boots. I groaned. These two were all I needed right now.

"What did she say?" Li asked.

"Probably wants to know why in the world we're here," was Bri's dry reply.

"Tell her Mathilde sent us."

"Why don't you tell her?"

"She's unconscious."

"Good god, Li, her eyes are open."

"Would you two be kind enough to help me up when you're done arguing?" Exasperated, I looked at the ceiling, which featured an exceptionally ugly chandelier made of deer antlers.

"But Josie, we aren't arguing. Your great-aunt and I just have a difference of opinion." Li clucked her tongue.

"What else is new?" I said, using my elbows to try to sit up.

I was still dizzy, but Bri had returned to her chair to scowl at her cards, and Li simply stood there next to me.

"You *are* happy to see us, aren't you, dear?"

"Of course, Aunt Li. I'm delighted," I replied, unsteadily getting to my feet. Li immediately caught me in an embrace. She smelled strongly of calendula salve.

"The girl lies as badly as her mother." Bri tossed a card onto the discard pile and leaned back with a pleased expression. "Your turn, Li."

"What do you mean?" I asked.

"I mean it only took me a few minutes to get the truth out of her when you didn't show up for the cake tasting. By the way, we decided to go with buttercream—a purely strategic decision to keep your grandmother happy."

"It's sweet of you to be so worried about your cousin that you'd neglect the preparations for your own wedding. We absolutely agree with Mathilde—it's our duty to support you in any way we can in your search for Charlie," Li added cheerfully, pulling me towards the fireplace. "Augh, you're dripping wet, child. Take care you don't get the sniffles."

"A little cold is the least of her concerns right now," mumbled Bri, picking up a crystal decanter containing an amber-coloured liquid. She poured out half a glass and offered it to me. "You might not like the stuff, but it'll warm you."

Even the tiny sip I took burned like fire. I returned the whisky to Bri.

It sounded like Mama hadn't shared the true reason for my hasty departure. Worried about Charlie, hah! For all I cared, the little monster could drown in Loch Ness—after she handed over the ring. What was more worrisome was that Li and Bri apparently planned to accompany me.

"Are you sure you know what you're getting yourself into?" I asked.

"Are you?" Bri retorted. She looked me up and down before evaluating my suitcase. "What's in that tiny thing? A few pairs of sandals and a sundress?"

"Don't listen to her, Josie. I'm very excited about our Highlands adventure," Li said, squeezing my arm.

"Highlands, Shmilands." Bri scowled. "Have you looked outside? They're predicting nonstop rain and a storm for the next two weeks. This isn't an adventure—it's boot camp."

"Why don't you just wait in the car for the next few days?" Li said, pursing her lips. "Besides—"

"You have a car?" I interrupted.

"Of course," Bri snapped. "Were you planning to take a bus into the wilderness?"

"I forgot my driver's licence."

Bri grinned and I could feel myself blushing. It had never been easy for me to admit to a mistake.

"What a lovely coincidence! I guess from now on we'll just have to keep an eye on you." Li's eyes sparkled. "Let's ring for Trish. You need a hot shower."

I opened my mouth to protest, but then realised that I really was stuck with these two and their car.

"Yes, Josefine?" Bri asked so sternly that I lowered my eyes.

"Nothing, Aunt Bri. I'm so glad you're here," I mumbled.

"Like I said, the girl's a lousy liar."

Apart from a faint odour of dusty textiles and dampness, my room was a pleasant surprise. A loving hand had tried to create a genuine Victorian atmosphere. A stately four-poster bed held court, everything was clean, and yellow miniature roses welcomed me on the desk. They were arranged in a porcelain vase that most likely had served as a chamber pot in previous centuries.

Trish leaned against the door frame, watching me anxiously. She was probably used to derogatory remarks about the well-worn velvet upholstery of the chairs or the faded bedspread. The young woman inspired the same ambivalent feelings in me as Lara did. On the one hand, I wanted her to make herself scarce as soon as possible, but on the other hand, I felt like protecting her from this cruel world. To resolve this dilemma, I rummaged in my purse and gave her a generous five-pound tip. The expression on her porcelain doll face went from apprehension to surprise to bliss.

"Breakfast is served from seven till nine." She gave me the key and, with a breathless "*Oidhche mhath*—goodnight, Miss Sonnenthal," hurried out of the room before I could change my mind.

The door had hardly closed before I stripped off my wet clothes and padded, naked and shivering, to the bathroom, where I was astonished to find wall-to-wall carpeting. A lukewarm and weak stream of water gurgled from the rusty showerhead, but I hummed happily while lathering up. For a brief moment, I even believed that my streak of bad luck was over. Not only was the rental car problem solved, but I was strangely calmed by the fact that I was no longer alone. Li and Bri were often quite amusing—when they weren't at each other's throats.

It's difficult to reconstruct at what point I lost my nerve. It started with an ominous banging in the pipes, which soon grew deafening. The water waned to an icy-cold trickle before quickly running dry. Jumping out of the knee-high tub, I banged my ankle, reducing me to a whimpering wreck. I rinsed the shampoo out of my hair in the antique sink. Then I opened my suitcase and had to admit that Bri had been right. There wasn't a single article of clothing that was appropriate for this country and its freakish weather. Finally, I knelt with my dying mobile phone and charger in front of the funny British outlet—and burst into tears. How was I ever going to find Charlie when I couldn't even manage to bring a plug adapter?

I awoke with a pounding heart and a raging thirst. I had planned just to rest my eyes for a few minutes, but hadn't reckoned with the powers of the king-size four-poster bed and its down-filled pillows. The bed swallowed me up and carried me off into an uneasy sleep peopled with ghosts who all looked like seven-year-old Charlie and who ran away from me, giggling. I almost caught the last one, but then Justus suddenly stood in front of me in his navy-blue wedding suit. I reached for him, but he pointed sadly to the floor. There it was at my feet—the ring. I got down on my knees, but it had disappeared. I moaned in despair and stood up, only to find myself looking straight into the green eyes of Aidan Murray.

I fumbled for my glasses on the nightstand, and then just sat there staring at my dark mobile phone. I wished I could call Justus, even though it would mean a long sermon about why this trip was ridiculous. Calling my friend Claire, who worked at a food magazine in Berlin, would also have helped. She had a dry sense of humour and wouldn't have minded either the late hour or my gloomy mood. I would even have settled for Mama's sleepy voice, although I was mad at her for setting Li and Bri onto me. She could at least have warned me.

I put the phone down with a sigh. It was clear that I was on my own. First things first, then. I vaguely remembered a soft drinks machine in the lobby.

I snuck down the staircase in my nightgown, trying not to make much noise on the carpeted wooden steps. When I was almost down to ground level, I heard muted laughter from the lobby.

"What are you two still doing up?" My crazy aunts were sitting by the now-cold fireplace.

"We could ask you the same thing," Bri replied and laid down a card. "All right, Li, now you've lost round twenty-nine. So, you owe me"—she pursed her red lips—"six pounds and twenty-four pence."

"You've always been a disaster at maths, my dear." Li adjusted her gold-rimmed glasses. "It's six pounds and eighteen pence."

"Twenty-four."

"Eighteen."

"Twen—"

"Quit it!" I raised my hands. "Do you have any idea how late it is? Shouldn't you be in bed by now?"

Li was about to say something, but a look from Bri stopped her.

After a while, Li said with a yawn, "It's your turn, Bri."

I went to the vending machine and put in a coin. The mechanism was stuck. I rattled the worn metal handle, but the bottle of water remained where it was, thumbing its nose at me through the glass.

"The thing's broken," said Bri.

"Why am I not surprised? Could one of you tell me what's going on here?"

With a quick glance at Bri, Li said, "It's not my fault."

"Whatever," replied Bri.

"I told you, I put the room key in my left jacket pocket. What am I to do when it suddenly isn't there anymore?"

"If you stopped to think every now and then, you wouldn't constantly lose things."

"I put it in my jacket pocket, the left one!" Li repeated, her chin held high.

"What's all this about?" I was ready to explode.

Bri scrutinised me, raising an eyebrow at the low neckline of my nightgown. "Li mislaid our room key. Nice nightgown, by the way. I always pictured you as the flannel pyjama type."

"They have very cute flannel pyjamas these days," Li chirped.

It was a valiant effort on Li's part, but Bri's mocking laugh drowned her out. I decided to ignore Bri's remark.

"Why don't you ring for Trish and get a spare key?" I suggested.

"We can't wake the poor girl in the middle of the night," Li answered.

"No? So instead you plan to sit here until breakfast, is that right?" I asked.

Bri shifted her weight and straightened her back, which made her resemble my grandmother to an alarming degree. "It's simply good manners. Anyway, this chair is quite comfortable," she said grandly and closed her eyes, signalling that she considered the conversation over.

"But it's Trish's job to look after guests, even if it's"—I glanced at the big grandfather clock—". . . three in the morning. Dear god."

I went to the reception desk and reached for the bell, but Li's insistent "Nooo!" stopped me.

"You can't spend the night down here."

"We don't mind! We're actually not tired at all. At our age, you don't need that much sleep," Li assured me, but undermined her credibility by yawning loudly. "Excuse me!" She looked to her sister for support and gave a start. Aunt Bri's chin rested on her chest. Her pheasant-feathered hat had slid forward and was in danger of falling to the floor, and it could not be denied—she was snoring.

"Bri?"

My aunt's head shot up—the hat fell back and revealed a red page-boy haircut. "Josefine?"

The words tumbled out before I could stop them. "Why don't you both come to my room? I have to warn you, though, the shower's broken."

"Not a problem at all!" Bri was out of her chair so fast I wondered if she had counted on my making the offer all along.

"Not a problem," echoed Li, allowing me to help her up.

A loud thump made me spin around. To my surprise, Bri held a water bottle in her hand.

"So you don't have to drink that metallic tap water, child." She handed me the bottle with a thin smile and strutted up the stairs to the second floor.

"Sorry, honey." Li put a hand on my shoulder. "You know she's hard on the people she really cares about."

I did know that, only too well. What I was grappling with now was the fact that my seventy-three-year-old great-aunt not only sported flapper hair, but had also just kicked a jammed drinks machine like a spoiled teenager.

5

"Cheer up, Josefine."

"It's itching," I complained, fumbling with the turtleneck of the loose-knit woollen pullover until Aunt Li's pout made me stop. I slouched.

Jammed between snoring Bri and thrashing Li, I had hardly slept a wink the night before. Then, at breakfast, I'd made the mistake of telling the two of them about my lack of appropriate clothing for the Scottish climate. Li had insisted on a shopping trip, which had not only wasted valuable time, but also resulted in this mustard-yellow monstrosity, which made my behind look humongous and my breasts non-existent.

Bri, who had waited outside the upscale department store, stomped out her cigarette and scrutinised me from under her umbrella. She blinked at the ridiculous Border collie face on my chest. The jumper was so bulky I couldn't even hide it under my jacket.

"You picked that?"

I nodded in Li's direction and sighed.

Next to Bri in her elegant breeches and tailored tweed jacket, my new wardrobe made me feel like a country bumpkin. Li had insisted I also wear the lined rubber boots she'd found in the store's basement.

"Why in the world must you always say yes to everything, Josefine?" Bri teased before turning to Li. "We know that you have impeccable taste, dear sis, but you should really acknowledge that the girl is old enough to select her own duds by now."

But Li was entranced by a young street musician who sat cross-legged in front of a fast-food stand, plucking his guitar. His eyes were closed and he sang as if nothing else existed—not the drizzle and not the tourists roaming George Street and walking so close by that they trampled on his mat.

"Poor boy," Li said, pulling out her wallet.

Bri sighed. "If you continue in this fashion, Mother Teresa, you'll have spent our entire budget for the trip by this evening."

"Since when have we been so poor that we cannot spare a few pence for someone in need?" Li replied, and she crossed to leave a five-pound bill in the man's crumpled cap.

The young man didn't even notice the donation.

"I don't mind if you write him a cheque, dearest, as long as you still have cash in your purse—I urgently need a cup of coffee. I wouldn't say no to a piece of cake either, after the scare that thing gave me." She gestured to the Border collie jumper and laughed when I stuck out my tongue.

Li clapped her hands. "Cake—what a wonderful idea! I saw a lovely little pastry shop on the corner of St. Andrew Square, where they sell Scottish pastries." She linked arms with me and nudged the snout on my stomach. "Come along, Josie, let's feed your pretty new friend some butter scones." Giggling, she dragged me along the cobblestones, not missing a single puddle.

To my surprise, I loved plodding through the water in my boots instead of navigating around them in pumps. I trudged as heavily as I could to make the water splash. I had a herding dog on my chest, so why not act like a twelve-year-old?

Bri followed us with a pinched expression on her face. "Great shape we'll be in if the Scots bake as badly as they knit."

Li's powers of observation always astonished me. She may often have seemed a bit spaced out, but she seldom missed small details that the rest of us would overlook. The bakery was not only tiny, but also inconspicuous. The building was set back from the main drag, nestled against a corner house on a small side street. I wouldn't even have spotted it if Li hadn't led the way. Behind a display window filled with cakes, the interior looked dim, so I figured the shop was closed. But then the crimson door opened and released a group of elderly men, all in identical raincoats embossed with the logo of a French travel agency. A tall man with a tan face and a meticulously trimmed white beard tipped his cap and held the door open for us. He glanced at Bri and looked at Li a little longer.

"*Enchanté, mesdames.*"

With a hint of a bow, he didn't for a moment take his remarkably blue eyes off Li, who self-consciously studied the amateurish paint job on the door frame.

Bri sashayed past the gentleman without acknowledging his gallant greeting. I had to nudge Li to bring her out of her reverie. Head lowered, whispering "Most kind," she stumbled into the shop.

"A pleasure!" the gentleman called after her in German, tipping his cap again. Turning to me, he said, "You must try the caramel shortcakes, *Mademoiselle.* They give even our French patisseries a run for their money."

"We shall, *Monsieur.*" I thanked him with a smile.

It was very warm inside, and as my glasses soon fogged up, I had to squint to make out the counter and shelves covered with all kinds of pastries in cellophane bags with handwritten labels. A boy, maybe ten years old, sat drawing at one of the bistro tables. The pastry shop looked like any of its kind, though surprisingly quaint and un-touristy for being so close to a busy shopping street.

Then I recognised it—my chest rose and fell, and I felt as if I'd just returned home after a long spell abroad. It was the aroma—the unmistakable scent of sugar and cinnamon in melted butter. I had a vision of doughy fingers disappearing into greedy children's mouths whenever Grandmother looked away. And then, two hours later, the taste of warm apple cake—the delicious tartness making our lips pucker.

In those days, we weren't just big, reasonable Josefine and a little monster bent on mischief. We were so much more than that.

I looked up to meet the curious gaze of the boy. Bri and Li, their heads together, were chattering excitedly and leaving blissful fingerprints on the display case. There wasn't a huge assortment, but each torte and each cake was lovingly decorated with marzipan roses, chocolate garnishes, or caramel grids. The cakes on one tray were even decorated with the Scottish flag in blue and white icing, making me regret my choice of wedding cake, with its simple buttercream and crumbly praline topping. Maybe I should reconsider the order.

A saleslady had appeared and waited with a patient smile for my aunts to make a decision. She seemed vaguely familiar, but I couldn't place the delicate, freckled face, as I was still distracted by memories of Grandmother's kitchen.

"Oooh, is this real cheesecake?" Li cooed and poked me in the ribs. "Doesn't it look sumptuous, Josie? But look at that one over there . . . good god, I can't make up my mind."

"Yes, it's cheesecake, baked according to a traditional Scottish family recipe," the saleslady confirmed, at the same time signalling with a nod that she had seen Bri pointing to the chocolate cake and coffee machine. "Next to it is carrot cake with candied ginger. If you like, I could prepare a tasting plate."

"You could do that?" Li was in heaven.

"Not a problem at all, madam."

I had heard that strong voice before. I was sure of it. I wiped my glasses and put them back on. The young woman had a white scarf tied around her head. A red curl peeped out from underneath.

"Can you manage, Vicky?" a male voice called from the back.

My pulse skyrocketed. Was this some kind of joke?

"Good afternoon, ladies. What can I do for—? Woah!"

In front of me stood Aidan Murray, flour in his dishevelled hair.

"You're wearing an apron."

"And you're wearing a collie." He smiled.

"Hrm," I grumbled, and turned to see Bri staring at Aidan.

Last night's dream washed back over me and my face felt hot.

Vicky—now I recognised her from the airport—sized up Aidan and his hypnotised staring at my jumper. After a short pause, she turned and said with a smile, "Maybe you'd like to try an assortment of our cookies, miss? The lucky stars are very popular."

"That's all right, Vicky. I'll help this customer," Aidan chimed in. "You're late as it is. And we don't want to disappoint Mike's new girlfriend!"

He grinned at the boy, who immediately packed up his art supplies. The little guy was meticulous—every crayon seemed to have its very own spot in his threadbare pencil case. Vicky took off her apron. The way she now looked at me was quite different from her previous professional friendliness. She wrapped her arms around Aidan's neck and whispered something in his ear. I quickly turned away. I can't stand public displays of affection. I mean, get a room.

Li stood in front of one of the pastry shelves with her reading glasses on, studying each label intently. I headed towards Bri, who sat at the little window table, nearly obscured by her giant pheasant-feather hat, pretending to read an issue of the *Scotsman*. I plopped down on a chair that—strategic planning on my part—had its back to the counter. Bri's paper rustled.

"A handsome young man."

"You're holding that paper upside down."

"Answer my question." The feather bobbed demandingly.

"There was a question?"

Bri snorted, folded the paper, and squinted towards the counter where Aidan most likely was still cuddling with his girlfriend.

I arched an eyebrow. It was fun messing with Bri, especially after I had been the target of her sharp tongue for the last few hours. Unfortunately, Li arrived at the table with a plate piled high with cake, derailing my game.

"How do you know this nice gentleman, Josefine?" She took a seat, looking happy and slightly stressed. Scots, apparently, had a unique definition of "tasting." "Who's going to eat all of this?" she moaned, before shaking out a napkin and tucking one end into her ruffled collar.

"You should have thought about that before ordering the entire display case," Bri replied caustically. Her eyes were still on me.

"He's actually not nice," I said. "That man is the worst kind of womaniser."

"Really?" Surprised, Li turned to look at the counter and I did, too—I couldn't help it.

Vicky and the little Picasso were gone. Aidan was firing up the coffee maker. I hadn't noticed on the plane how broad his shoulders were. I felt a grudging fascination as I watched him expertly pull espresso shots and steam milk. It seemed so effortless—he probably could have read a book while doing it.

He looked over his shoulder at me and smiled. I turned away quickly and was met by Bri's inquisitive eyes.

"We met on the plane," I said defensively. "And like I said, the jerk has more than one iron in the fire, not that I care. After all, I'm practically married, and he's not the kind of man I—" I suddenly realised how I sounded.

"I thought he was a pastry chef," Li said, her mouth full. "What iron are you talking about?"

"Oh, Li, it's just a saying. She means the man chases lots of women." Bri rested her chin on her hands and focused her pale-blue eyes on me. "What Josefine really means is that she . . ."

To my chagrin, I felt myself blushing again. I stubbornly stared at the feather sticking out of Bri's hat. It no longer bobbed up and down, but drooped slightly to the left.

". . . likes him." Bri basked in her cleverness, and that was probably what pushed me over the edge.

"Oh, come on, Aunt Bri! The man's a baker."

I realised too late why Li had stopped chewing and Bri's eyes opened wide. A plate clattered down in front of me.

"I thought the young miss might like our chocolate cake." Aidan's frosty voice trickled down my spine like ice water. His tone of voice made clear that he not only had heard my condescending words, but, due to his excellent German, had also understood them. "With rich dark chocolate icing and, most of all . . . not too sweet."

My heart was pounding and I began to perspire. How could I be such a snob? Apologetic words sat on my tongue like bitter pills, but I couldn't get them out.

Aidan accepted my mumbled "Thanks" with a blank expression and served Bri's coffee. Her chocolate cake was placed on the table much more gently than mine had been. He wished my aunts *bon appétit* and left without so much as looking at me.

I leaned back in my chair defiantly and crossed my arms. So what if Aidan Murray thought I was a snooty goose? After all, I had figured him out from the start. Casanova was an amateur next to this man.

Bri took a deep breath.

"Not one more word," I said.

She shrugged and leaned over to Li, who was making a valiant attempt to conquer her tasting plate, though the portions on her fork became smaller and smaller.

"Like I told you, she likes him," Bri declared without even attempting to lower her voice.

Chewing, Li nodded. "He likes her, too."

I threw up my hands and walked out, leaving them to their sweets. The shop's awning offered little protection against the rain, but I was grateful for the drops on my face. I closed my eyes and listened to my aunts' cheerful voices and Aidan's deep laughter.

Everything felt wrong—Grandmother's demand that I bring back the ring, giving in instead of standing up to Adele von Meeseberg, the flight, this dreadful country with its dreadful rain, and last but not least, my horrible cousin, the cause of this entire disaster, who made me forget my manners and insult someone who had been kind—more than kind, helpful—to me all along.

I should go back in and apologise . . . after blowing my nose. I pulled out the napkin I had pocketed and stared at the blue cursive script.

A taste of Scotland since 1830. Murray & Sons Ltd.

The man's a baker, I had told Bri, the sentence dripping with condescension even without an added "only." I hated it when Justus acted like he was above other people, but I was just as bad. I cringed, recalling Grandmother's admonition when she had settled a dispute between Charlie and me years ago.

You can't take back a bad word—you can only regret it. Realising your mistake and apologising doesn't make you a better person, but at least it shows that you have some backbone.

I straightened up and opened the shop's door—almost bumping into my two aunts.

"Forgot something?" Bri mocked, but she was immediately grabbed at her tweedy sleeve and pulled outside.

"Leave her alone," Li said with unusual vigour, winking at me before the door shut behind them.

I squared my shoulders at the counter, but there was no sign of Aidan Murray.

"Hello?" I said hoarsely. I cleared my throat and tried again. "Mr. Murray?"

No response.

Not sure what to do, I timidly stepped behind the counter, crossing an invisible barrier into Aidan Murray's life.

The dirty cups and plates from our order were piled next to the sink. I caught myself rubbing Bri's lipstick from her coffee cup with my thumb. My untouched chocolate cake was still on its plate. Aidan had selected it for me. What a sweet gesture.

I broke off a little piece and put it in my mouth. Mmm, incredible. Taking another bite, I tiptoed to the double-leafed swinging door to the bakery and peeked through the little window. I couldn't help myself.

Aidan Murray was leaning against a floured working counter. He was on the phone, shock evident on his face.

This was clearly the point at which I should have made myself scarce. However, my foot seemed to nudge the door of its own accord. I could now hear Aidan's voice so clearly that I understood his English without a problem.

"I don't know what to say . . ." He grabbed the back of his neck as if his head were suddenly too heavy. "Since when? Why didn't you ever—?" He was obviously struggling to sound calm. "That's not a problem . . . No, really . . . Ian? Why him of all people?"

I shifted from one foot to the other and made sure the shop was still empty. When I looked through the window again, Aidan was pacing.

"How do you figure? I haven't heard from him in more than a year. How am I going to . . . on such short notice . . . ?" He stopped. "Got it. I'll try my best . . . No idea. I'll think of something. He's got to be somewhere."

He stopped in front of a gigantic mixer. Grabbing a big bag of flour with his free hand, he dumped it in without noticing that half ended up on the floor. Then he looked at the empty bag as if unsure what to do with it.

"We're doing great! Ever since we removed the sign outside, tourists flock here because they think they're in on a secret. So don't worry about—" He snorted. "Dad, honestly, I don't feel like talking business right now. I'll come up as soon as I can, okay? We can talk then . . . You're not serious, are you? . . . Vicky will manage . . . Yes . . . No . . . Yes! I promised, didn't I? If need be, I'll beat the living daylights out of him or knock him out cold with whisky, or both." With a scornful laugh, Aidan closed his eyes for a moment. "Don't let it get to you, old man. I love you—*Mo gràdh ort, athair.*"

Aidan hung up, his head falling forward onto his chest. I held my breath as his gaze wandered around the room. Then he looked at his phone and smashed it against the wall with a roar. To my horror, Aidan Murray crouched down, hiding his face in his hands.

"Earlier on, did you manage to do what you wanted to do?" Bri finally asked after I'd trailed them silently from one shop to another for more than an hour, listening to them quarrel and chatter about trivialities. I managed a glum nod in reply.

"She didn't settle it," Bri declared while examining the cowboy hat on a mannequin in a shop window, which also sported a sexy interpretation of a Scottish kilt.

"You don't think so?" Li scrutinised the doll as well. "Quite pretty," she mumbled, and I hoped she was talking about the hat and not the obscene mini-kilt.

"That he was," mumbled Bri. "And such a manly man; quite a change from—"

"Manly? But this is a lady's hat," Li objected, pointing to the mannequin. She could barely lift her arm, so many shopping bags dangled from it.

I stared at the little bag from Murray & Sons and forgot the tart comment I was about to make. Instead, I saw Aidan crouched on the linoleum floor like a devastated little boy. Of course, I had silently slipped away to save us both from embarrassment. I'd just have to live with my remorse by myself and make sure never to commit such a terrible faux pas again. That was not the Josefine I wanted to be.

"I got cookies." Li proudly held up the bag. "Lucky stars, a Murray specialty. Mr. Murray told us that you—"

"Please, Aunt Li," I said firmly. "I don't want to talk about that man any more. That goes also for you, Bri."

"All I meant was—"

"Enough."

"Fine." Bri shrugged and headed to the store on our right. A hat shop—god help us.

"Aunt Bri?"

She stopped. "Yes, child?"

"Don't you think we should go back to the hotel and pack? Unless we get going soon, we'll have to drive in the dark."

"Where are we going?" Li asked innocently, earning a poke in the ribs from her sister.

"Why can't you ever listen? As Mathilde explained, Josefine got this postcard from Charlie. The girl is staying at some sort of bed and breakfast in the Highlands."

"I wouldn't mind an excursion to the Highlands at all, but what makes you think that Charlie is still there?" Li sounded insulted.

"We have to start somewhere," Bri replied. "Unless you have a better idea."

I turned away with a sigh. If I'd had my own car, I'd have left these two at Eden Rock Lodge in a heartbeat, where they could play rummy and bicker with each other to their hearts' content. I looked up and froze.

It was just for a split second. I craned my neck to follow the two figures I thought I had seen among umbrellas and rain parkas. We were back at the mat where the young man had played guitar a few hours ago. It was deserted, covered with footprints.

"Are you all right, Josefine?" Li called, but my rubber boots had awoken with a life of their own.

I'd never been a good runner, even back when I was trying to lose a few pounds to please Justus. I had soon realised I was in over my head—both with 6 a.m. wake-ups and the speed at which Justus ran. Eventually, a torn muscle ended my half-hearted ambition, and my fiancé admitted that I was impeding his marathon training. Since then, he had made his peace with my love handles, and the only time I ever ran was to catch the subway.

Now I wished I had more stamina. I felt a stabbing pain in my ribs after just a few hundred yards and had to slow down. I stopped on a side street, gasping for air, desperate not to let the young man and woman out of my sight.

"Charlie!"

My shout echoed hollowly off the row of identical brown houses with bluish doors. With my hands on my hips, I straightened up and exhaled noisily, disappointed. They were gone.

"What was that about?" someone panted behind me. "Next time you feel like running a race, let me know, will you?"

"Aunt Bri! You ran after me?"

"No, I took a taxi," she shot back, plopping down red-faced on the steps in front of number 67.

Worried, I crouched down next to her. "Are you all right?"

"I'm no porcelain doll. And I won't be pushing up your grandmother's daisies anytime soon. It's my plan to survive the whole lot of you and make off with the von Meeseberg fortune."

"I can believe it! What's your secret, Super-Bri?"

"Yoga three times a week and a lover who's thirty-five," she replied in such a serious tone that I believed it for a fraction of a second, until the hint of a grin betrayed her.

"That's what I suspected."

We smiled at each other and shared a rare, peaceful moment there on the wet stairs. My relationship with Bri had always been complicated, mostly because she used to steer clear of us kids. Her disinterest probably made Charlie and me cling to her even more, no matter how often she claimed that we got on her nerves. After all, who else in our upright family liked to spit cherry pits across the room or collected tadpoles?

"I saw Charlie. At least, the girl looked just like her."

"If my eyes didn't deceive me, the pair you were after went in there." Bri pointed to a green, wood-panelled house at the end of the little street. It was probably a bar or a pub.

I jumped up, but she grabbed my sleeve.

"Hold up. I'm all for a cold beer, but we should look for your aunt Li first. I gave her the slip back on George Street. Who knows where she's got to by now. I wouldn't want her to fall prey to some Scottish Casanova who claims to be the great-grandson of Sir Walter Scott."

6

Bennet's Inn was not one of those pubs where you go to read the paper or play backgammon with a friend. We stepped into a cacophony of voices and were hit with the sour, humid odour of people who've had too much to drink and are crammed together in a small space.

I pressed ahead of Li, who held on to her sister's arm and looked around curiously. We had found her on George Street in the company of an elderly gentleman who turned out to be quite harmless. The suspected swindler sold bratwurst and other cholesterol-rich delicacies at a stand. Li had sulked as Bri tossed her deep-fried Mars bar into the nearest garbage can.

I scanned the room anxiously. I hadn't made up my mind on whether to embrace Charlie or slap her first.

I pointed to an open table by the window. "Wait there while I look around."

The sound of someone playing guitar came from the next room.

"Get a beer for me, Josefine, and some herbal tea of the digestive variety for your aunt Li. She needs one after that heart attack–inducing snack," Bri shouted after me while Li scowled at her.

I gave her a thumbs-up and dived into the crowd.

It took forever to make my way to the bar, being either elbowed, leered at, or complimented with every step. At first I responded to the compliments with a polite smile, but I quickly learned to studiously ignore them.

The adjacent room had no windows. A motley group of old and young musicians was gathered around the only table, drinking dark beer out of pint glasses. When one struck up a melody, the others joined in on their flutes, stringed instruments, and harmonicas.

I honed in on the young, red-haired guitar player and his companion. The song they were playing was familiar. Charlie used to play The Corrs on repeat, the Irish band blasting through the house as I tried to practice Debussy études on Aunt Li's piano. My heart started to beat faster, marking time with "At Your Side." The girl's head was leaning against the guitar player's shoulder. She gazed into space while her knees bounced to the beat.

She was the spitting image of Charlie—the same boyish figure in jeans and sneakers, the same unruly, dyed-black hair, which contrasted strangely with her delicate, elfin face and light eyebrows. But this girl had a thinner mouth, not the full lips that Charlie constantly smeared with shiny lip gloss. Her eyes, shadowed by long, thick eyelashes, were slightly too close together, making her look a little naïve.

I was disappointed, but not surprised. The past few days had shown that nothing about this trip was going to be easy. Someone else might have seen meaning in this doppelgäanger, this strange coincidence—but not me. I was not one of those people who would see rabbits and flying horses in cloud formations. Clouds were clouds—no more, no less. All I had done was mistake a stranger for my cousin, wasting time in the process.

I walked back to the bar, but then a crack appeared in my smug rationalism.

"If I didn't know your opinion of guys like me, I might think you're stalking me," Aidan grumbled into his glass.

I shifted nervously from one foot to the other. "Listen, Mr. Murray—"

"Why so formal all of the sudden?"

Maybe running into Aidan Murray for the third time meant something after all. If nothing else, it was an opportunity to apologise for my outrageous remark in the pastry shop.

"Aidan, I'm sorry that you had to overhear my conversation with my aunts."

The words sounded lame even before they were out of my mouth. Aidan set down his glass, hard.

"Are you sorry that I heard you, or do you regret saying what you said?"

"I . . . both. What I said about you wasn't fair . . ." I stopped, confused.

Straight-faced, he returned to his beer. "You can think whatever you want." Lifting the half-full glass, he emptied it in one gulp. He gestured to the bartender, who looked like a member of a biker gang with his beard and tattooed arms. "Gavin, get me another ale and also a Glenmorangie. That way, my stomach might be able to tolerate your horrible Scotch pies. Why don't you shoot the butcher who sells them to you?"

"Aidan, *mo charaid*—my friend. Playing the tough guy, are ya? Did you burn a tray of scones, or are you out to prove something to the pretty German lassie?" Gavin pulled the tap handle with a roaring laugh.

I wasn't sure what bothered me more—this grouchy man who bore little resemblance to the lady-killer from the plane, or his melancholy eyes, which made him look soft, almost feminine. Yet nothing about Aidan Murray was . . . My thoughts turned to mush and the words refused to come.

He looked at me wearily. "Was that all, Mrs. Stone?"

"That's not my . . ." My nose twitched. "Did you just call me your teacher's name?"

"Well, you look like her and you're both know-it-alls. The word-play's not bad either. You are a bit like a stone—a pretty stone, but a stone nonetheless."

"A stone?"

"Mhm," he said with closed eyes.

"That's not a compliment."

"I had no intention of paying you one."

He seemed to inhale rather than drink the honey-coloured brew. Ugh. For me, the peaty aroma of Scotch always conjured up visions of smoked, dead animals.

"I guess I deserve that," I said.

"You do."

"Fine." I nodded as regally as I could. "We're even, then. I wish you continued success with your bakery. Your cakes are terrific, by the way. Good-bye, Aidan."

At least I had tried.

"Josefine?"

I stopped. Aidan looked me over from my face down to below my breasts. Super! I had momentarily forgotten about my hideous jumper.

"Have you ever tasted a real single malt?"

But reconciliation over shots was not to be. Before I could respond, a sudden ruckus broke out a few steps away, near the restrooms. I caught a glimpse of a wildly bobbing pheasant feather in the middle of the commotion.

"Bri? Aunt Bri?"

My heart was pounding when I finally got close enough to see— and then I stopped short, thunderstruck.

A stout, short man, bald and bull-necked, had planted himself in front of another man and was unloading a battery of unintelligible Gaelic invectives. Two heads shorter than his opponent, his bluster seemed almost ridiculous at first. But then I registered the dangerous flicker in his eyes and the fact that Bri was within the reach of his meaty arms. Her face was pale with anger. She pushed past the tall man, who was apparently trying to protect her.

"You're a very rude fellow and possess not an ounce of decency!" Her finger wagged like a metronome in front of the Scotsman's nose.

"*Madame*, my name is Antoine Barneau. Please allow me to settle this unpleasant matter," said the tall man and, to Bri's clear displeasure, he stepped back in front of her.

It was the charming Frenchman who had held the door to Aidan's shop for us.

The entire situation was beyond strange. Edinburgh is a city of four hundred and fifty thousand, but at that moment, it seemed like a claustrophobic village in which one constantly stumbled across the same people.

"If you excuse my saying so, Monsieur Barneau, there's no need for you to play musketeer." My aunt thrust past the helpful man like a belligerent child.

Oh, Bri! I felt a shove from behind and almost stumbled, but someone else caught me by the arm. I smelled alcohol and clean, manly sweat.

"Sorry," Aidan whispered in my ear.

"What are you doing?"

I don't know why I whispered, too, especially since two women next to me were now singing "La Marseillaise" to egg on the Frenchman. Just a couple more yards to reach Bri.

"I'll take care of this. You can go back to your schnapps," I said over my shoulder and took a few more steps. "And take your bad mood with you."

"Touché," Aidan said, following me. "But I'm drinking Scotch— miles from the hooch your German potato farmers secretly distil in their sheds."

"Beat it," I hissed.

But Aidan pushed me aside and stepped between the two men like a referee in a boxing ring.

Monsieur Barneau had handed his cap to Bri and was rolling up his sleeves. He did so meticulously, but kept his eyes fixed on his opponent. The Scotsman danced to and fro with raised fists, swaying a little. The spectators hooted, stamped their feet, and clapped, while my aunt looked at the cap as if it were a hot potato.

"What the hell is going on here?" Aidan thundered.

The element of surprise was on his side. Barneau stopped adjusting his sleeves and the Scotsman forgot to bob and weave like a prize fighter. I noticed that Gavin returned the baseball bat he had been brandishing to its place on the wall and stood behind the bar, watching, his muscled arms crossed. Bri was the only one who was not impressed by Aidan's interference.

"Heavens, did women's lib pass this country by?" Bri ranted in German. "This is the twenty-first century, gentlemen. Women earn black belts in judo and preside as judges. Step aside, please, and I'll deal with the drunkard." She drew a deep breath and continued in a dignified tone, "I refuse to move from this spot until he apologises for spilling beer on my Barbour jacket—even if I have to spank him. His mother apparently failed to do so."

Aidan raised his eyebrows while the Scotsman stared at her without understanding a word. Monsieur Barneau rolled down his sleeves with a smile, making some female onlookers sigh with disappointment.

"She didn't mean that," I said quickly, finally managing to grab Bri's arm. "Our apologies! My aunt is a little—"

"Furious!" She violently pulled away from me.

"Confused." I pointed meaningfully to my forehead and grabbed her wrist as firmly as I could.

"Ouch," complained Bri. "You're hurting me."

"I haven't even got started," I hissed, and dragged her out of the strike zone.

Aidan had placed an arm around the shoulder of his countryman and was talking to him quietly. From a safe distance, still holding on to Bri, who squirmed to escape my grip, I looked on in amazement. The combatant's expression went from anger to astonishment, and he ended up looking almost guilty.

He pointed to Bri, raised his hands—palms up—and shook his head. Aidan patted his back and winked, which made the other man laugh out loud. He turned around. I stepped forward to block his way, but the Frenchman was faster.

The talk that followed consisted only of gestures and grimaces, but it resulted in a handshake. Grinning, Monsieur Barneau ceded the ring. The short Scotsman now stood in front of my aunt like a sheepish schoolboy. Her furious expression was unchanging as he showered her with a stream of strange words that sounded something like English. He finished with an awkward bow.

"Dudley says that he's very sorry he spilled beer on your lovely jacket," Aidan translated. "He would consider it an honour if the lady accepted his coat as recompense. He deeply regrets the misunderstanding. Unfortunately, he only speaks a dialect we call broad Scots, which can be a bit tough to understand."

Bri was unimpressed, even when Dudley peeled off his grubby raincoat and offered it to her with outstretched arms.

"You should accept his gift, ma'am," Aidan urged. "It is a genuine Mackintosh, very popular with shepherds in the Highlands. These coats are the best you'll find in the United Kingdom—expensive, too."

"Do you have a part-time job as an auctioneer, Mr. Murray? And stop calling me ma'am—I'm not a hundred years old," Bri replied, keeping her eyes on Dudley.

Dudley in turn seemed to recognise that more effort on his part was needed. Amid the crowd's hooting, he bent forward and, putting on an expression of deepest remorse, pointed to his behind.

"I don't suppose I have to translate *that*," said Aidan, trying to keep a straight face.

Dudley closed his eyes in resignation and awaited his spanking. New hoots all around.

"Tell Mr. Dudley that I accept his gift for my grandniece, who mistook our vacation in Scotland with one on the island of Ibiza," Bri said solemnly. "She could use a proper raincoat."

Blood rushed to my cheeks. After Aidan had translated Bri's proclamation with obvious amusement, all eyes turned to me and my Border collie pullover.

"As to the additional offer"—Bri cast a critical glance at Dudley's derrière—"I'll make do with a glass of dark beer."

"No, thanks, I'll stick with water," I said as Gavin offered me the whisky bottle. Sipping without much enthusiasm, I snuck a look at the table where the former adversaries were peacefully sitting together, toasting harmony and understanding among nations with their fourth pints.

There was no hope of leaving for the Highlands before the next morning. Bri had been sloshed since her third pint and was obviously unfit to drive. No more proof was needed than her much-too-loud laughter when Dudley tried to empty his glass in one gulp while holding his nose.

And Li? Her cheeks were rosy and her eyes glued on Monsieur Barneau's lips. He was expounding wittily on Mary Stuart and encouraging his listeners to raise their glasses yet again to the only French Scottish queen.

I spun on my stool and met Aidan Murray's eyes from the other end of the bar. Aidan signalled Gavin for another bottle of beer, then came and sat down next to me.

"Don't begrudge your aunts their fun. You could use a little laughter yourself. Do wonders to relax you," he said, pushing my mineral water away.

"Funny, you seemed the one in need of stress relief not so long ago," I replied, and reached for my glass.

Gavin laughed.

"Lassie gives as good as she gets, pal." He winked at me and stroked his beard. "This scumbag has waited far too long to meet a girl like you."

"Seems to me someone is waiting for a lukewarm pint over there," Aidan growled.

"I'm gone, ma love-birdies."

I followed the bartender with my eyes. "Why did he call you a scumbag?"

"That's the Scottish way of telling someone you like him," Aidan answered. He clicked his bottle against the one he had ordered for me. "*Slàinte mhath*, Mrs. Stone—to your health."

I stared at the label. "I don't like beer."

"I'll order a glass of Chardonnay for you, then."

"To be honest, I don't drink."

It was true. I disliked the taste of alcohol and hated feeling like my head was full of cotton balls—which inevitably happened after the second glass and invariably resulted in my losing control.

"Why are you like this?"

"I could ask you the same thing," I shot back.

"I thought you'd realised by now that you misjudged me. To my regret, even though it sounds kind of fun, I'm really not a womaniser, Josefine."

"Well, you misjudged me, too."

"That's completely different."

"Why?"

"I never pretended anything." The smile had left his face. "You, on the other hand, are trying very hard to be someone you're not."

"Fascinating. What am I supposedly pretending to be?"

"Happy." He shrugged. "As is expected from a soon-to-be-married woman."

I laughed out loud, knowing I sounded somewhat shrill. "Aidan Murray, you're an incredibly arrogant man."

"I haven't finished yet." Aidan took a sip of beer and wiped his lips with the back of his hand. "First of all, you're a very attractive woman, but you're not aware of your effect on men. This suggests that you either don't like yourself or that the man in your life doesn't tell you often enough how pretty you are. Second, you enjoy playing the successful, tough lawyer and probably do your best not to get emotionally involved with your clients. But your eyes tell me you'd prefer a job where you're judged on more than money or power. And third, you march through life in a straight line, like a pony with blinders on. Not out of conviction, but because you're afraid of the flowers on the side of the road."

I was taken aback, and could only think of justifications or insults. Either would have validated Aidan's assessment. So I just snorted, boiling inside.

"You asked and I answered." Aidan's smile was so utterly free of mockery or malice that my fury collapsed in on itself.

"Thanks for your assessment, Mr. Murray," I replied as casually as the frog in my throat allowed. "But don't give up your day job for psychology—because you're wrong." *Totally wrong.*

"I'd be glad for you if I was." He sat silently for a moment and then waved Gavin over.

I stared at the beer bottle. *Maybe I should take a sip. Maybe it would calm my nerves.*

"I'll settle up, Gavin. This lady's drinks are on me, as is whatever the table over there ordered," Aidan said with a wink. "Can't have Mrs. Dudley reading him the riot act because he spent all the housekeeping money on booze, can we?"

"Sounds good, pal." Gavin dried his humongous hands on his apron, grabbed one of the many notepads from a shelf, and removed a pencil nub from behind his ear. His hands, which would have been perfect for a biker, had difficulty controlling the tiny pencil.

"Will ya be paying your brother's tab as well? Poor guy was really broke last time. He said you'd take care of it."

Aidan jumped up and almost toppled the bottles. I grabbed them just in time.

"Ian was here? When?"

Gavin tried to decipher the handwritten tab.

"About two weeks ago. Had a lass with him, a pretty one."

He grinned at me and I couldn't help grinning back. Gavin was like a teddy bear who didn't realise he looked like a grizzly.

"Always with a girl, isn't he?" Aidan said. "Did he tell you where he's going?"

"Here's the total," Gavin said, ignoring the question.

Aidan glanced over the long tab with a sigh and piled some bills on the counter, but kept his hand pressed tight on top of them. Propping my elbows on the table, I rested my chin in my hands and pretended to be absorbed by the beer bottle. I thought about the phone conversation I'd overheard. So Ian was Aidan's brother. And if I understood correctly, Aidan was looking for him, which aroused a strange feeling in me—a closeness even. Was there something other than our mutual aversion we had in common?

"Gavin, I've got to find out where he is." Aidan sounded insistent, almost desperate.

"So you can beat him up like last time?"

His face closing up, Aidan replied, "I had my reasons."

Gavin crossed his arms again. "I'll bet. And I'm sure they're as convincing as Father McNeil's Sunday sermon. But I like the lad and don't want to be responsible if he can't play his next gig because you accidentally broke his arm."

"You got him a gig? Where?" Aidan raised two fingers, as if swearing an oath in court. "I won't deck him, I swear. All I want is a talk."

"Isn't that funny? That's just what you said the last time."

"Please, Gavin. It's . . . a family matter."

"Why don't you call him?"

"You seriously believe Ian can afford a mobile with the pittance he makes as a street musician?"

"How sad—especially when his brother's such a big shot."

"It was his choice, Gavin. C'mon now, stop wasting my time and tell me where the little Hendrix-wannabe is hiding."

"You really have no idea at all how good the lad is."

"Where, Gavin?"

"In Inverness." Gavin was not happy. "My cousin added him to the line-up at her place, the Hootanelly, for next Saturday. He planned to show the Cairngorms to his girl on the way there. But you didn't hear this from me—are we clear?"

"Clear as your shellfish chowder, pal." Aidan removed his hand from the bills and the bartender snatched the money like a Rottweiler grabbing a sausage.

"Keep the change," grumbled Aidan, earning him a glare from the grizzly.

"Sure will, Mr. Big Business."

Aidan got up. He looked content and determined. "I never knew you had a cousin in Inverness. Always thought your family was only made up of three exes and a bunch of kids."

"Get lost, Murray, before I remember that I don't have to serve a snotty guy like you, no matter how much dough you have."

Aidan cleared his throat and I looked up with pointed indifference.

"Mrs. Stone." Aidan saluted. "A pleasure, as always. When you have a moment, think about what I said. Stop and open those pretty eyes. You'll find some fantastic flowers waiting for you."

"Well, you are the expert on picking flowers." The sentence was out of my mouth before I had time to think, and I immediately regretted it. Never would I be so rash in court—it would weaken my position. Yet this man's mere presence was enough to make me botch my closing argument.

Aidan accepted the zinger with a grin. He put on his leather jacket and stretched out his hand. It felt cool and dry.

"Two to one—you win, Mrs. Stone. See ya."

Fortunately, he was gone so fast that I didn't have a chance to say out loud, *I hope not!* However, I was suddenly quite sure that this wouldn't be my last encounter with Aidan Murray.

I met Gavin's glance and raised my bottle to him. I took a gulp and grimaced.

Flowers on the side of the road. What nonsense!

I had looked forward to having the king-size bed to myself again, even though the extra night at Eden Rock Lodge messed up my schedule. But instead of restorative sleep, my night was filled with strange dreams and endless waking periods during which I pleaded with the alarm clock to finally give me a reason to get up.

I was wide awake by four in the morning, staring at the ceiling. At five, I gave in, took my phone off Bri's charger, and pushed the heavy velvet-upholstered chair to the window. Clutching the phone like a life raft, I watched daylight arrive.

In the online travel diary of a visitor to Scotland, there was one particular sentence in incredibly purple prose that I had quickly dismissed. But now, looking at the fog hanging over meadows from which trees seemed to claw at apricot-coloured clouds, it rushed back to me intact.

It is the light, this special, magical light somewhere between day and night that makes Scotland a place like no other in the world.

I am neither a nature lover nor prone to waxing poetic about spring mornings that resemble rainy November evenings. Yet there I sat, wrapped in a wool blanket, feeling that very same enchantment—as if I'd discovered a new planet. Better yet, it felt as if I'd travelled back in time, like the nurse in Aunt Li's novel who fell in love with the red-haired chief of a Highlands clan.

I turned on my phone since—distant planet or not—I had been unreachable for two days. Adjusting my glasses, I gaped in amazement.

Twenty-one missed calls and nine text messages, all from Mama. I ignored the brief stab of pain at finding nothing from Justus. We seldom texted, and called only if we had to. Besides, he didn't even know that I was in Scotland since he'd left his Blackberry at home when he set off for his macho retreat. I sighed and flipped through Mama's messages.

Dear Josefine. I hope you arrived safely. How's the weather? Love and kisses. Mama

BTW I heard that Li and Bri coincidentally travelled to Scotland, too, and I gave them the address of your hotel. Love and kisses Mama

I hope Bri and Li found you. Love Mama

Are you all right, Josefine? This is Mama. Please call me back.

Josefine, this is your mother. If you don't call immediately, I'm calling you.

Why is your phone turned off?

All right, so I probably should have asked you before giving them the address. But it really wasn't my idea.

Stop it, Josefine. This isn't funny anymore!

Fine. It was my idea for them to come. You should still call me.

That was my hypocritical mother for you! Claiming my aunts travelled to Scotland "coincidentally" when, in truth, she had set them on my trail. I briefly considered making her stew a little longer, even though I knew she'd meant well—and, as another coincidence, had actually ended up helping me.

Battery was dead, everything fine, all three alive, I typed.

I set the phone on the windowsill and touched the glass with my fingertips. There was a draft coming from somewhere and a layer of condensation had formed. I drew the outline of a small heart in it. The diffuse apricot light had turned to a deep lilac. A storm was approaching, driving grey, horse-like clouds before it.

I pulled in my knees and closed my eyes. I liked the image, even if it was only made of clouds.

7

"Rise and shine! Do you want to eat this horrible breakfast or should we hit the road?" Bri's rasping voice called from outside my door.

I sat up with a start and put on my glasses. Ten o'clock. Ten o'clock?!

"I'll meet you at the car," I shouted, jumping out of the chair and throwing off the blanket. My cramping legs wobbled beneath me.

"All right, we'll tell Trish to feed your porridge to the chickens. I think it was meant for them in the first place, the way it tasted." Bri cackled as I headed for the bathroom.

A frenzied ten minutes later, dragging my suitcase like an obstinate dog behind me, I passed Trish, who sleepily wished me a good trip. When I went to put a tip into the jar on the reception desk, her pale mouth made an O of surprise.

"Take one of the umbrellas in the lobby, miss."

"Huh?"

"Please take one. People always forget about them," Trish explained.

When I stepped outside, I understood. Pouring rain. What a country.

The path was muddy and full of potholes. I stumbled down the incline, cursing myself for having packed rather than worn the rubber boots. Just when I'd nearly reached the car, my feet went out from under me and I found myself on my behind while my suitcase careened onward before tipping over on the pavement.

"Oh, Josie. Did you hurt yourself?" Li cried out from the passenger seat of the dark-blue rental car.

I scrambled to my feet and stowed the filthy suitcase in the boot before dropping into the back seat. My cherished linen trousers were caked with mud. I caught Bri's gaze in the rear-view mirror. Her eyes showed compassion for a second, before resuming their usual mockery.

"Spare me your commentary, unless you want me to ask whether that hat was a DIY project," I said, looking for the seat belt. There was none.

Bri turned around and grinned. She had to lift her chin to look at me from under the brim of the abysmally ugly creation sitting on top of her head, loaded as it was with a silk rose the size of a hand. "We could, of course, just start driving, but it might work better if you gave me some sort of address."

"Are you in any condition to drive?"

"Listen, young lady! I already had a driver's licence when your mother was still playing naked under the cherry tree."

Li giggled and started to hiccup.

I bent forward and took Bri by the shoulders. "Let me smell your breath."

"To check for minty freshness?"

I raised an eyebrow, which made Li giggle even more. "Are you sure you're not still drunk from last night?"

Bri wriggled away haughtily. "I'm sober as a newborn calf—something that cannot be claimed for your great-aunt Lieselotte. She's been reciting toasts in French."

"Have not!" Li huffed, her gleeful smile belying her protestation.

"Have too," Bri said. "The moment any old womaniser with an accent woos her, she loses her mind—and her memory. She raised her cup of tea to the couple at the next table this morning, shouting, '*À votre santé.*' The nice people were more than a little confused, I can tell you. Probably thought they'd landed in Brittany by mistake."

"Don't talk nonsense, dearest sister." Li's eyes narrowed. "Besides, Antoine is neither a womaniser nor wooing me. Both of us are much too old for such things."

"There we are. An . . . toi . . . ne." Bri stretched out the name as if it referred to a slimy sea creature.

"You're just upset because a man prefers talking with me instead of devouring you with his eyes." Li was hurt. "Incidentally, our conversation last night was very sophisticated. Antoine was a physician before his retirement and his wife owned a second-hand bookstore in Strasbourg. She carried all of Sir Walter Scott's books, and even had an original edition of—"

"God!" Bri snorted. "And you don't find it suspect that he shared all of that immediately after you told him you spend all day reading—and crocheting those hideous covers."

"At least I'm doing something to keep my mind sharp. As for matters of aesthetic taste, let's start with the pink tracksuit with which you embarrass yourself at your fitness club."

"At least I fit into a tracksuit, Li."

"Stop it!" I barked, covering my ears. "You're acting like twelve-year-olds."

"Does that mean that you'll finally give me an address so I can enter it into this contraption?" Bri asked, while Li, grumbling, opened her book.

That's how arguments between the two usually ended—sharp-tongued virtuoso Bri, who cared little about what others thought of her, would get her way, and gentle Li, who shied away from conflict, would disappear into a printed world of fantasy, where it was up to her to say who won an argument.

Sighing, I rummaged for Charlie's now-tattered postcard in my handbag.

"Kincraig—a *k* at the beginning and a *c* in the middle," I mumbled, looking at the little heart Charlie had used to replace the dot on the *i* in my name.

While Bri typed our destination into the GPS with surprising speed, I leaned back and frowned out of the window. The rain had grown stronger over the course of the morning and the sky was almost black. Squalls of rain drove all kinds of trash across the road. Apparently, tourists didn't show much respect for the Scottish landscape they enthused about online. I watched a particularly capricious gust of air playing with a soft drink can, tossing it into the air and rolling it down the street until it disappeared.

Bri started the engine, or tried to.

We yelped in horror as the car lurched forward.

"Oops," Bri said, adjusting her hat.

"Aunt Bri?" My hands were clammy. "You have to push the clutch before you turn the key."

"Right you are." She fumbled around until the car started.

"This is how she always does it," Li explained, an edge to her voice. "It's how she teaches people humility. And it works. When you get out of the car after a drive with Bri, you're fully aware of how precious life is."

"Be quiet, Li. I have to concentrate."

I groped for something to hold on to as the car started to roll forward at walking speed.

Humility. What an auspicious beginning.

To my surprise, Bri—impatient and quick-tempered—turned out to be a fairly decent driver, even though she wasn't used to driving on the left. I didn't mind crawling through Edinburgh's heavy traffic at twenty miles an hour, but that changed once we got on the freeway to Perth.

I was about to point out to Bri where she could locate the accelerator when I noticed her white knuckles.

"Aunt Bri, are you all right?"

"Why shouldn't I be?" She was breathing hard and her eyes were fixed on the middle of the two-lane motorway. Honking belligerently, a cattle truck veered around us, sending a wall of water at our windscreen.

I checked the side-view mirror. "I think you have to drive a little faster."

Li laughed and turned a page. It wasn't clear whether she was amused by her Highlander romance or my request.

"I'm driving plenty fast, Josefine," Bri said. "Why don't you just relax? Dream about your fiancé or about someone more exciting." Her eyes flicked nervously to the traffic building up behind us. "How about the handsome Scottish baker?"

"You're terrible!"

"And you are alarmingly dried out for your thirty years, young lady. There's nothing wrong with adding a little butter to the dough before you tie yourself to a dullard for the rest of your life."

"I won't allow you to talk about Justus that way."

"At least I have the decency to tell you what everyone thinks."

"What the hell do you mean by that?" Furiously, I tapped Li's shoulder. "Aunt Li, what is she talking about?"

Li peeled her eyes from her book reluctantly, but her sister leapt to her aid.

"You're a clever woman, Josefine. I'm sure you understand just fine without interrogating my poor sister. Let it go for now, before I drive us into a ditch. Enjoy the view."

"Oh, we're crossing the Firth of Forth," Li exclaimed.

Even I allowed myself to be distracted by the two majestic bridges spanning the sparkling, silvery estuary that links the Firth of Forth with the North Sea. Other drivers seemed equally impressed. As we rolled across the mile-and-a-half-long bridge in rapt silence, all the regular lane changing and honking ever so briefly fell away.

I was about to grab Li's shoulder to demand the confession she still owed me when, for a moment, I thought I saw Aidan Murray in one of the cars that overtook us. The taillights of the truck quickly dissolved in the mist at the northern end of the bridge.

So it had come to that. I was not only having nightmares, but actually hallucinating. What was going on with this country?

The car careened onto the shoulder, screeching to a halt. I was hurled forward and got wedged between the two front seats. Bri's hat lay on the dashboard and Li whined while fishing for her book on the floor. Flushed with anger, Bri rolled down the window and shook a fist into the rain—not that this impressed the motorcyclist who had cut us off.

"Hoodlum!" my aunt screamed. She killed the engine.

Li sighed and smoothed the pages of her book while I tried, unsuccessfully, to extract myself from between the front seats. Bri closed the window and calmly put her hat back on before taking notice of my struggle.

"What are you doing up here?"

We stared at each other for a few seconds. Throughout my life, I had often tried to hold Bri's ice-queen gaze. I couldn't do it this time either. So I sucked in my stomach and tore myself lose from the mousetrap into which I had fallen. *I really should lose a few pounds so the bodice of my wedding dress won't rip.*

"I need a cigarette," Bri griped.

"A cup of tea would be lovely," Li replied. "With milk and a tiny spoonful of honey. It's much healthier than sugar."

I closed my eyes and silently counted to ten. Bri interrupted me at eight.

"Nothing to say, young lady?"

I quickly looked at the fuel gauge. "Petrol? Restrooms?"

"Two words sounding like hallelujah." Bri started the car. "Let's find a petrol station."

The next lesson I learned was that rest stops are nearly unheard of on Scottish motorways. We were forced to relieve ourselves in the bushes of a small parking area, and then drove almost twenty miles before spotting a sign for a petrol station. Shortly afterward, Bri turned down a winding drive flanked by yellow broom bushes. Two blue petrol pumps stood in front of a little wooden building.

I had never been so happy to get out of a car. I stretched out my arms and raised my face to the drizzle. The soothing scent of peat and the ocean filled my lungs. Umbrella and cigarette case in hand, Aunt Bri headed for the broom bush–covered hills. Aunt Li had stayed in the car with her book, eyes shining and mouth half-open. It was obviously a thrilling passage—perhaps an R-rated one.

I fished my mobile phone out of my bag—no new messages—and then opened the fuel cap of the car.

Bri was perched on a bench on the hill, enjoying a cigarette and taking in the view. Straight-backed and still, and with the umbrella unfurled over her hat, she looked like Mary Poppins come to life—even though not a soul on earth was less similar to that cheerful nanny than Aunt Bri.

I looked around idly. There were several other cars, a few buses, and a camper van in the car park. One family was picnicking, the father grilling sausages while his noisy children played in the bushes.

A dark-green, four-door pickup truck was half-hidden behind one of the buses, so I hadn't noticed it at first. Upon spotting it, however, the fuel cap dropped out of my hand and rolled under the car. Cursing,

I knelt down to retrieve it, and when I got up again, Aidan Murray was leaning against his truck with crossed arms, grinning right at me.

At least I wasn't hallucinating. On the other hand . . . I squinted. Yes, it really was him. He picked up the paper cup he'd balanced on his truck's roof and raised it to me as a toast. I turned my back. Maybe if I ignored him, he would disappear.

I studied the display on the pump, watching the numbers roll over in slow motion.

"Hello, Mrs. Stone," said a cheerful voice behind me.

My hands became clammy. Why was I such a wreck around him? "You again?" I said without taking my eyes off the display.

"I'm equally pleased to see you." His voice told me that he was smiling.

I threw him a reluctant look. "How small is this country that I can't get rid of you?"

"Well, there's only one motorway from Edinburgh to Inverness, Mrs. Stone. But you're right, it's a funny coincidence. Maybe fate has something planned for us." He winked.

"The only motorway, huh," I snarled. "And you had to make a stop at exactly this service area. What are you doing here anyway? Shouldn't you be selling cakes with your girlfriend Vicky?"

"The womaniser thing again?" Aidan narrowed his eyes.

"You tell me."

"What about you? What are you and your aunties doing in Inverness? Is your cousin living there?"

"We're going to Kincraig, for your information. My cousin is staying at O'Farrell's Guesthouse. Any more questions?" I bit my lip. Why in the world did I tell him all that?

"Kincraig?" He seemed puzzled.

Had I not been sure that embarrassment wasn't part of Aidan Murray's emotional repertoire, I might actually have believed his ruffled act. He quickly caught himself and studied the fuel display, which had finally stopped streaming numbers. I put the nozzle back on the pump, screwed on the fuel cap, and tapped on Li's window.

"Aunt Li, I'm going in to pay. Should I get you some tea?"

She flashed a thumbs-up without looking up from her reading. Her cheeks were flushed. So it *was* an erotic passage.

"Mrs. Stone, I'm afraid you won't get to Kincraig as easily as—"

I spun around. "Why can't you just leave me alone, Mr. Murray?"

"All right! I'll back off. But you really should make sure you got the right fuel."

This man was incredibly stubborn—unfortunately, he was also incredibly attractive, leaning against the pump and gazing at me curiously as if I was an exotic animal. But I would never become part of his trophy zoo.

"Please. Just go your way and let me go mine," I said as kindly as I could.

He raised his hands. "It's up to you, Mrs. Stone."

"Goodbye, Mr. Murray."

The green pickup was still there when I came out with two coffees and Li's tea. Aidan sat in the driver's seat, making a phone call. To avoid having to meet his gaze again, I focused on balancing the hot drinks. Bri wasn't back yet, so I sat down in the driver's seat and handed Li her tea.

"You're an angel, Josie." She put her book on the dashboard and sniffed at the cup. She was the only one in my family who called me Josie, and each time she did I felt warm inside.

"Unfortunately, they didn't have honey, so I added some sugar," I told her, fighting the urge to look across the car park.

"I see your Mr. Murray has turned up again. He really is a good-looking man," Li said casually, sipping her tea.

"You think so?"

"I do, indeed. Above all, he's a gentleman—polite, helpful, well bred. A little like Mr. Darcy, but funnier. You seldom find such a combination in men."

I laughed. Aidan had about as much in common with Jane Austin's seductively brooding hero as a log of wood with a bar of gold. Poor Aunt Li. As far as I was aware, she had never known a man outside the pages of a book.

"Don't you find it odd that your paths keep crossing?"

"Not you, too, Aunt Li! Fate and all that! Listen, I'm engaged and not interested in Aidan Murray."

"But you are interested in him. Why else would he bother you so much?"

"He doesn't bother me at all."

Li's next question blindsided me. "What are we doing here, Josie?"

She said it with the same understanding smile she had worn many years ago when she'd freed me from the principal's office, where I was accused of cheating on a maths test. To this day, nobody knew that Charlie had secreted the crumpled scrap of paper into my pencil box to help me with formulas I couldn't remember no matter how hard I tried.

Just like then, I could neither bring myself to confess nor to hold Li's affectionate gaze. Instead, I stared at the wet windscreen and thought of Charlie, Grandmother, and the ring that had to be on my finger when Justus and I exchanged vows. Li's question had opened a door in my mind and, inside, snippets of lost memories swirled around like dust. In this room lurked not only my fear of disappointing Adele von Meeseberg, but also long-suppressed rage, resentment, and a dull feeling of worthlessness.

"You know why we're here," I said.

"I know that you and Charlie have, unfortunately, not been the best of friends. So I'm asking myself why it's suddenly so important she be a part of your wedding party, as Mathilde claims. I'm quite sure you have enough pretty friends who would look good in Charlie's bridesmaid dress."

I could feel myself blush.

"So tell me, Josie. What is this all about?"

I had yet again underestimated this old lady in her thick glasses and old-fashioned pantyhose. Hidden behind her gracious, often quirky demeanour, there was at least as much of the keen Markwitz family wit as Bri so loved to display.

"Charlie stole the wedding ring from Mama's safe," I whispered.

"The bride's ring?" Bri looked shocked. "That is a problem."

I managed something like a smile. "Do you understand now why I have to find Charlie?"

"It's not important whether I understand or approve of your actions, Josie. The question is where your search will lead you. The ring just shows the way."

"I don't understand," I replied, disappointed she hadn't given me the answer I wanted to hear.

"I didn't either, for a long time—for quite a long time."

"What about the curse? All those tragedies when the bride didn't wear the ring? Do you believe it? Or is Grandmother the only one who clings to this superstition and I'm making myself crazy for nothing?"

"Let me put it this way—the mythos of the ring made sure I chose the right path."

"But you never got married."

"Right." She smiled and seemed sad for a moment.

I almost regretted my words, but was too confused to change topics. "Neither did Bri."

"You don't seriously believe your aunt would let some curse keep her from doing whatever she pleases, do you? Bri made a conscious decision, and she believes that her life without a husband works out beautifully. But we're talking about you right now. And what I want you to remember is that it doesn't matter whether you believe in the curse or whether you just made the trip because of Adele's stubbornness. What is important is that you recognise the opportunity."

"What opportunity?"

"The chance to question what you want to do with the rest of your life."

"But—"

"I assure you, Josie, you'll understand sooner or later. Let's fetch your aunt before she has to be admitted to hospital with smoke poisoning."

"Absolutely not!" Bri hid her hands behind her back.

"Bri," I said. "Just give them to me."

"Who do you think I am, to let a little brat take away my car keys? Besides, you don't have a driver's licence. I'm sure the police won't like that."

"First of all, I most certainly do have a driver's license—I just don't have it on me. And second, have you seen a single police car in the past three hours? We're more likely to be stopped because your snail's pace is holding up traffic."

"You're a lawyer. You mustn't do anything illegal."

Bri pouted and looked, as she so often did, like an angry little girl. However, with at least a hundred more miles to drive, I was not willing to back down.

"Didn't you say I should do something inappropriate for once? Well, I'm ready."

I held out my hand to show her that I meant business, and it worked—Bri surrendered the keys and climbed into the backseat. Settling into the passenger seat, Li patted my knee as I started the car.

"Project Wedding Ring has begun," she whispered, opening her book.

"Mm," I said, engaging the clutch.

It took a few miles to get accustomed to driving on the left side, but traffic was running smoothly and the drizzle had let up, so visibility was good. Soon, I even dared to overtake a car, making Bri, who had sulked in the back for ten minutes, pipe up.

"You're going too fast."

"Just close your eyes and think about something exciting." I grinned into the rear-view mirror.

"Dear grandniece," Bri drawled. "You greatly overestimate my repertoire of thrilling events."

"Hear, hear," mumbled Li, opening the glove compartment.

To my amazement, she pulled out the latest version of a fancy smartphone. She held it close to her thick glasses and wiped the display.

"Wasn't that your handsome baker back at the rest stop?" Bri asked with a strange undertone.

"A meaningless intermezzo, dear aunt," I replied calmly. "Mr. Murray is headed to Inverness. So you'll have to make do with Justus, even if you think he's boring."

"And we're going to Kincraig—big *k* and small *c*," Li mumbled, absorbed in something on her phone.

Bri whistled. "So the dark-green pickup truck that's been following us for twenty minutes doesn't belong to your pastry chef?"

"Stop it, Bri! He's not my . . . What?"

I braked so abruptly I almost caused an accident. A sports car had to veer to the side to avoid us—racing by me, the driver honked violently. My heart was pounding as I adjusted the side mirror to get a better view. It was true. Aidan's car was three vehicles back.

"That tops everything," I said in a flat voice.

Without signalling, I merged into the right lane, squeezing between a minivan and a camper. After overtaking two cars, I switched lanes again, and then, my heart pounding, sped off the next exit.

The triumphant feeling of having shaken off Aidan Murray, Hollywood style, lasted only a few moments, until the car began to buck and cough like an asthmatic chain-smoker. The engine died and the car rolled downhill for about twenty yards before coming to a halt on the shoulder. I turned the key with dogged determination, but a croaking sound was all I got in return.

Silence settled over us. Li stared out the window. Then Bri giggled and adjusted her hat.

"Let's hope your Scottish admirer has a tow rope."

A few short minutes later, someone knocked at the window. Stony faced, I rolled it down.

"Mrs. Stone. Ladies." Aidan tipped an imaginary hat.

"Mr. Murray, you couldn't have come at a better time." Li was beaming.

Even Bri looked at him with approval—her eyes lingering too long below his belt for my taste.

"You're driving a diesel," he said with a smile, his elbows on the windowsill and thus disturbingly near me. He smelled of shampoo and a freshly ironed shirt. He had also shaved, which I hadn't noticed earlier.

"You could have told me that before," I mumbled.

"Don't tell me you put in petrol!" Bri laughed.

"I did try to warn you—you might remember," Aidan replied.

I scowled.

There was no use trying to defend myself. He was right. What bothered me most was that he had anticipated our distress and followed us like some kind of knight in shining armour.

"Now how are we supposed to get to Kincraig?" Li asked, and began to clean her glasses.

I leaned back and crossed my arms. "I'm sure Mr. Murray has an idea."

"That I do."

I sat up. The dangerous glimmer in his green eyes should have warned me, but a condescending "So?" slipped out of my mouth before I could stop it.

Aidan gave me a blank look. "Only if you ask for my help."

"Forget it."

"Josefine!" Bri objected.

Li took my hand. "I'm sure he won't walk out on us, darling. He's too . . . chivalrous for that."

I turned to him with a haughty look, but all I saw were the inquisitive heads of some Blackface sheep traipsing about in the opposite lane. In my side-view mirror, I saw Aidan hop into his truck and turn it around in three energetic manoeuvres, seemingly getting ready to drive away.

"Well, you handled that beautifully." Bri puckered her lips.

"Like great-aunt like grandniece, I'd say," Li sighed.

I fumbled with the seat belt and almost tripped over my own feet. "Hey! Stop! Wait a sec!"

The truck began to move and I broke into a run. Even when I caught up and trotted alongside, Aidan didn't stop.

"You can't do this! My aunts are over seventy!" I shouted.

Aidan accelerated. I ran faster.

"Okay, okay! I'm sorry."

The truck slowed down.

"So?" Aidan echoed the condescending tone I had used.

A sharp pain shot through my ribs. "What else do you want?" I huffed, trying to keep up, even as Aidan had begun speeding up mercilessly again. I gritted my teeth and ran faster.

"Honestly, I don't think an apology's going to do it this time."

"Okay . . . What then?" My lungs were burning and the pain in my side made breathing difficult. I really would have liked to have stopped running, but I had no choice. I couldn't leave Li and Bri stranded out here.

"I want an explanation."

"What . . . kind of . . . explanation?" I panted.

"It's eighty miles to Kincraig. That should give you enough time to figure it out."

"You . . . you are . . ."

"Breathe, Mrs. Stone. Twice in, twice out—that way you might manage another mile."

I closed my eyes. The pain in my left side was so intense that all I wanted was to curl up in the foetal position in the wet pasture. To my enormous relief, the truck slowed down. I grabbed the window frame, my legs moving under me like defective gears of a clock.

Aidan scrutinised me and slowed down some more. "I'm waiting."

My knees felt like butter. I wouldn't last another fifty yards.

"You're right. I've been arrogant and rude and"—I gritted my teeth—"I don't know why I behave the way I do. Every time you . . ."

I was shocked to feel a lump in my throat. My fingers let go of the window frame and the truck left me behind. Huffing, wheezing, and clenching my fists, I stopped in the middle of the road.

"You make me act crazy!" I screamed after the taillights. "And I hate it when you call me Mrs. Stone!" Tears of rage, despair, and shame ran down my face. And for some strange reason, I didn't care.

The truck stopped. Aidan put it in reverse and inched back to where I was standing.

We looked at each other silently. When I took off my glasses and wiped my eyes, a tiny smile appeared on his angular face.

"What's the matter with you, Josefine?" He motioned to the passenger seat with his chin. "Get in. Or should I collect your aunts by myself?"

8

"You'll have to leave the rental car here." Aidan shook his head. "There's nothing we can do. The tank has to be emptied and cleaned at a proper repair shop."

"But we're supposed to go to Kincraig."

Li was sitting on a boundary stone, knees pressed together, handbag clutched to her breast. She looked so desperate that it touched my heart. It was really sweet that she now wanted to find Charlie as urgently as I did.

Aidan closed the hood and wiped his hands on his jeans. "I'll drive you." With a glance at me, he added, "Kincraig is more or less on my way."

Bri had been pacing in front of our car. Now she stopped and squinted at me. "That's very kind of you, Mr. Murray. But we're going to take a taxi," she said, pulling out her phone.

I wanted to hug my aunt right then. True, her tongue was sharper than the cacti in my father's stone garden, and she was an incorrigible pessimist, but when it really mattered, she made completely selfless decisions. And until that point, I had made it clear how much I hated being near Mr. Murray.

Li moaned. "A taxi? It'll take forever to come . . . Have you looked up, by any chance?"

She was right. An army of clouds was lining up for war against an unnamed opponent.

"They predicted heavy rain on the radio, ladies. It might be a good idea to find a dry spot before it begins. It's quite common for roads to be flooded and impassable even for trucks like mine."

Bri gave Aidan a dismissive look. "Nonsense. A little bit of rain won't kill anyone."

"Don't underestimate our Scottish April storms, ma'am."

"Mr. Murray," she said. "The Markwitz family walked all the way from Silesia to Frankfurt, in snowstorms. Do you really believe that your drizzle can impress me?"

"Didn't we escape in a horse-drawn carriage?" Li asked, and was the immediate recipient of a reproachful sidelong glance.

"Aunt Bri," I cautiously cut in. "I think we should accept Mr. Murray's kind offer."

She raised an eyebrow in offence. "I thought I was doing you a favour."

"It's better this way."

My smile for Aidan was shy. I had avoided looking at him on the short drive back and was tongue-tied even now. "Thank you, Mr. Murray. We appreciate your help very much."

"What's this, then?" Bri mumbled, watching with a frown as Li removed her travel bag from our boot and scurried happily to the truck.

Aidan placed her bag in the truck bed and gallantly opened the door for her. She climbed into the high back seat with the agility of a young girl, knocked on the window, and gestured that we should follow suit before our knight changed his mind. Aidan turned to retrieve Bri's and my suitcases.

"You can call the car rental agency once we're on our way. I'm sure they'll take care of your car," he said to me over his shoulder. "We can arrange for a new one in Kincraig. I know a few people there who'll be happy to help."

My aunt watched as Aidan bent over the luggage and said warily, "Seems you know people all over the place."

"Bri!" I exclaimed, and reached for my suitcase just as Aidan did.

Our hands touched for a moment and I jumped as if I'd touched a live wire. For a fraction of a second, Aidan paused too, but then continued moving the luggage to his truck and covering it with a tarp.

"Sorry, ma'am, not everywhere. But I certainly do have friends in my own village."

"Your family is from Kincraig?" I blinked, an uneasy feeling coming over me. "In that case . . . you probably know the O'Farrell Guesthouse?"

"Would you mind if I did?"

"I certainly wouldn't," Li called from inside. "I could use a nice hot Earl Grey with just a dash of cream. They do serve tea there, don't they, Mr. Murray?"

He waited for my response.

"No, it's no problem," I said, and looked at my feet.

"Good." Aidan turned to Li. "Frau Markwitz, you'll be surprised at what else awaits you there besides an excellent cup of tea. Finola O'Farrell is famous for her Scottish cuisine. And she exemplifies hospitality."

Li clapped her hands. "What are we waiting for?"

"My thoughts exactly," Bri grumbled, before getting into the truck on the passenger side.

Feeling a little queasy, I climbed in next to Li. The back seat was covered with stains and dog hair.

Just as Aidan started the truck, the first heavy drops of rain splashed on the road. Trying to ignore the strong smell of wet dog, I stared at the back of Aidan's neck. The pale skin below his hairline looked soft and incredibly vulnerable, and I had to fight the urge to stroke it. I firmly folded my hands on my lap and watched the rain streaking across the window.

It was difficult for me to focus on the imminent meeting with Charlie. Maybe thinking about Justus would help. But I realised that I could hardly remember my fiancé's face.

I woke up with a jolt. Li's head had fallen on my shoulder and she was snoring, her mouth hanging open. Bri and Aidan were talking quietly up front. The amusement showing around my aunt's mouth told me that they had buried the hatchet. Careful not to wake Li, I sat up straight—and was surprised by what I saw.

We had left the motorway and were on a one-lane road from which vehicle passing places jutted out every fifty yards. Aidan deftly weaved in and out of them to let oncoming traffic pass.

He had apparently succeeded in driving us through the fearful April storm. The clouds stood higher now and no longer glowed with colours that could convince even sworn atheists that the last judgement was afoot. A ray of sunshine courageously broke through. Soft, almost biblical light illuminated the hills, gilding the boulders scattered like primeval animals. We moved past the ruins of a castle, and I felt my chest swell in awe. No wonder people were enthralled by this strange country.

Even Bri fell silent and watched a fishing boat rolling gently on the waves. Above the distant shore rose a snow-covered mountain range. The panorama was almost too surreal—as if a cheesy graphic artist had applied every known Photoshop trick to one single landscape image.

Aidan caught my eyes in the rear-view mirror.

"Welcome to the Cairngorms," he said softly, his voice husky.

I was moved by the thought that Aidan Murray was homesick. I wondered what kind of child he had been—wild, no doubt, with torn trousers and dirty knees. I stared at the back of his head so intently he could probably feel it.

Stop it! I admonished myself, and looked out again at the moss-green moorland that, I was sure, didn't smell of dog and subtle masculine musk.

Very soon, I would be able to wring Charlie's swan-like neck. Stammering apologies, embarrassed, she would hand over the bride's ring—and my job would be done. Maybe I could even fly back tonight, resume a life as predictable as a Swiss clock—a life that moored me, gave me the stability I so desperately missed. Sure, a hasty departure would disappoint my aunts. But they were welcome to continue this Scottish adventure on their own. I had had enough.

"Are we there yet?" Li mumbled sleepily, sitting up. "Oh. It's so beautiful here."

Aidan turned the truck towards the lake, following an old wooden fence lined by birch trees. My stomach tensed up in anticipation. He finally stopped in front of a Victorian brick building that sported zinc dormers and transom windows. It definitely was the house from Charlie's postcard.

"Oh! Just look at this enchanting garden—almost like in the south of England," Li exclaimed.

"Don't say that to our Scottish hostess, or she might slam the door in our faces," said Bri with a hoarse cackle.

We heard a sudden sound like claws screeching over metal, and the head of a panting dog appeared at the rear window. It bore a striking resemblance to the one on my jumper.

"Ooh." Bri's eyes were huge.

"Yiff," said the Border collie, seeming to smile at us.

Aidan slid from his seat. "Hank! Down!"

The dog disappeared from the window.

"What kind of way is that to welcome guests, you bad boy?"

Aidan's voice was affectionate but also exasperated, reminding me of Mama with her poor whippet. Li grabbed my sleeve.

"I'm sure he's already had breakfast," I told her.

My grandmother and both of my aunts shared a strange fear of dogs. Li would actually cross the street to avoid dangerous-looking specimens. Pragmatic Bri, wont to ignore whatever bothered her, pushed the car door open.

Aidan was crouched on the gravel path petting the dog, whose tail wagged adoringly. It seemed he had a male fan for a change. It was fascinating how this man appealed almost magically to everyone in his orbit. I was ashamed to admit that I was jealous. I could do so much good in the courtroom with such a gift.

Smiling widely, I bent down to the dog—and quickly pulled my hand back when he growled a warning.

"I guess Hank doesn't want to be my friend," I said, giggling to hide my shock.

Aidan looked at each of us pensively. "Oh, he does. But he likes to be the one who determines when."

"Is that a Scottish thing?"

I was upset about sounding upset. Thanks to Mama, I knew all about four-legged creatures, especially traumatised ones. But this collie seemed to be pondering whether or not I was edible. I thought of the chocolate cookies in Li's suitcase, but Hank, most likely, couldn't be bribed.

Aidan got up and stuck a hand in the pocket of his jeans. "It's more of a Hank thing," he said. "He's basically a friendly guy, but it takes a little while for him to show it."

"So a Scottish thing after all," I said, and Aidan laughed.

Frowning, Bri pointed to Hank, who was now watching her.

"Will he stay here while I get my suitcase?"

"Just ignore him, ma'am," Aidan said, opening the boot of the truck.

"That was my intention," Bri replied. She walked past deliberately, looking elegant even while stumbling in her heels over a few innocent daffodils.

Hank watched as we dragged our suitcases over the cobblestones towards the house. Aidan brought up the rear.

Before we reached the house's green door, I turned around. Hank sat on the gravel path like a statue, his head turned almost one hundred and eighty degrees. I could have sworn that he was laughing at me.

It was immediately clear that the O'Farrell Guesthouse was unusual. The sign on the door bore no name, just an ornate, etched *"Fáilte!"* There was no doorbell next to the Gaelic welcome, and no door knocker. Instead, we were met by the inquisitive faces of several porcelain geese, lined up on the windowsill of what appeared to be a guest bathroom.

I exchanged uneasy glances with Bri and Li. At any moment, I would face Charlie—assuming she hadn't moved on.

"The door's open. Just follow the scent of food," Aidan said.

"When in Rome . . ." muttered Bri, and she pushed against the coffered door, which swung inward with a screech.

But it was Hank who entered first. Squeezing past my calf, he trotted into the hallway and stopped, as if asking himself what the heck we were waiting for. I left my suitcase behind and followed the dog, who continued down the dark hall and disappeared through a door that was ajar.

The aroma of cake and fresh coffee grew stronger as I continued down the hallway. It was the same scent that had transported me to Grandmother's kitchen from Aidan's pastry shop.

I almost tripped over Hank when I entered the kitchen. He hunkered next to an empty bowl, staring at it as if he could miraculously make it fill itself with food.

"Have you brought me my new guests, Hank?"

I guesstimated that the woman was in her fifties, but it was impossible to say for sure. Her flour-dusted face was smooth, yet it exuded a wisdom exclusive to the very old. She was small, almost tiny, and her floor-length skirt intensified this impression. Her brown eyes were the kindest I had ever seen.

"You must be Josefine." The woman wiped her hands on her apron and rushed towards me.

Taken aback that she knew who I was, I let her embrace me.

"I'm Finola. Finola O'Farrell. I hope you like chocolate cake made with beetroot. Aidan couldn't tell me whether you'd feel like having tea and cake or hot broth. So I made both."

I felt my whole body relax. There was nothing in Finola, nothing at all, of the forced friendliness so common to professional hosts.

"I love chocolate cake . . . with beetroot," I replied politely, determined to ask about Charlie right then and there. But someone gave a little cough, reminding me that I hadn't come alone.

Finola's smile grew even warmer still. Li was greeted with a hug while Bri received a firm handshake, as if Finola sensed her innate stand-offishness.

Chatting amiably, she led the twins to the kitchen table where a large-bellied teapot and a beautiful cake were waiting. She told them to make themselves at home, and my aunts did exactly that. Li poured herself tea and reached for the cream with a contented sigh. Bri served herself a piece of cake.

Then Finola turned to Aidan, who lingered at the door. She kissed him on the cheek, then looked down at Hank. The dog had abandoned his hope for food and was staring at Aidan's boots.

"This crazy animal knows exactly when it's Friday afternoon. He's been waiting for you in front of the house for two hours. Angus is mad as hell because he wouldn't stay in the shed with the others. Twice he ran off and was nowhere to be found—and we had such important guests here from Ireland today," she said with a *tsk*.

"Hank truly appreciates me, Aunt Finola." Aidan smiled. "It's probably just as well he wasn't around to scare away another buyer for

Mable's litter. If he continues acting like a Doberman, it might affect Angus's reputation."

Finola sighed. "You know your uncle. He wants to show people the best specimen of the breed, even if Hank's a little . . . special."

The dog pricked up his ears.

"Aunt? Uncle?" I was flabbergasted.

Aidan shrugged his shoulders with exaggerated nonchalance. "It's not my fault you picked O'Farrell's Guesthouse of all places!"

"Some coincidences are nothing of the kind," Li declared from the kitchen table, her mouth filled with cake. Apparently, chocolate and beetroot was a winning combination.

"Nobody's saying it was your fault," I said brusquely. "But it would've been nice if you'd mentioned that you live here."

"I don't live here," Aidan replied, narrowing his eyes.

My mood swings were starting to get on his nerves—mine too, so I couldn't blame him. But I had a lot on my mind, and somehow couldn't make myself ask the question that was burning the tip of my tongue. *Is the little monster here?*

"Speaking of accommodations . . ." Bri dabbed her mouth with a floral napkin that matched the tablecloth. "We just showed up without even calling to ask if you have room for us!"

Finola waved her concern away. "Oh, there's always room for more. The large room with two beds opened up yesterday. If you don't mind sharing, we can easily fit in an extra bed. Unless"—she gave me a side-long glance—"you'd prefer the guestroom in Aidan's boathouse."

Boathouse. My eyes widened and Aidan exhaled audibly. Luckily, Bri stepped in before I could blurt out something rude.

"We are quite used to sharing, dear Mrs. O'Farrell. I doubt Josefine will need a room of her own."

"And I'm not even sure whether I'll stay tonight," I added.

"I do enjoy having the place to myself," Aidan said pointedly.

"Don't be rude, dear nephew," Finola snapped. Even annoyed, she still looked like Cinderella's fairy godmother.

"Do you have many other guests here at the moment?" Li asked slyly, studying the roses on the teapot.

"Or other family members?" Aidan was very alert.

"What are you talking about, lad?" Finola said warily. "That reminds me—you must have a serious talk with your father. He fired Mrs. Clouchester, and I'm running out of candidates from the village who're willing to keep house for the pig-headed man. He's grown very gaunt because all he eats is frozen food from the supermarket." She turned to Li with an apologetic smile. "Right now, three couples from Cambridge are staying with us. They're friends and came here to hike. They're gone all day and go to bed early at night. So the house is all yours, including the library and the room with the fireplace. It would also be my pleasure if you joined us later for dinner—assuming you like trout. Angus had a very good haul this morning."

"Oh, that sounds lovely." Li looked to me for help.

I cleared my throat and stepped forward. "Mrs. O'Farrell, we—"

"How about telling me where Ian is, Aunt Finola?"

"Pardon me, Mr. Murray—you interrupted me."

"Please continue, Mrs. Stone," he said, eyes fixed on Finola.

Hank got up and padded outside, as if anxious to avoid the confrontation.

I pulled Charlie's postcard out of my handbag. It trembled in my hand. "I believe that my cousin, Charlotte von Meeseberg, stayed here with you. It's very important that I find her."

"I know Ian's supposed to play at Hootanelly's in Inverness tomorrow night. Not hard to guess where he brought his lazy behind to get a warm bed and a free meal on the way. So, where are you hiding Ian and his little girlfriend?"

"Excuse me—my cousin?" I fought to be heard. "She also goes by Charlie?"

Finola looked back and forth between Aidan and me. Then she pressed her arms to her chest and groaned, "*O mo chreach!* Good heavens! I think I'd better sit down."

Aunt Bri jumped up and offered her a chair, and we waited eagerly while Finola fanned herself with a gardening broadsheet.

"Ian. What a lovely name. I just remembered—Charlie's friend is also called Ian," Li mumbled, fussing with her mobile phone. She patted the display as if attempting to wake up a little sleeping animal.

For a moment, there was absolute silence in the kitchen. Only the ticking of the pendulum clock and the swishing of Finola's paper could be heard.

"No." Aidan turned to me. "Ian's new friend is . . . your cousin?"

Bri chuckled into her teacup.

Li was beaming. "What a riot! Ian is Aidan's brother! Could you ever have imagined it, Josie?"

I no longer cared what my expression might reveal. I just sat there, unable to answer.

Finola sighed. "Fine, yes, Ian was here." She folded her paper slowly, painstakingly. "With Charlie. A sweet child. An incredibly caring and very talented young woman."

Bri laughed. "Are you sure you're talking about our Charlie?"

"She suspected someone from her family might show up." Finola's smile was somewhat lopsided. "She always talked about you, but she called you Jo. That's why I didn't immediately put two and two together."

"Where is she?" I whispered. My heart was pounding against my ribcage so violently that I thought it might burst.

"They caught a bus this morning to go hiking in the Grampians," Finola answered, regret in her voice.

"To the mountains! With the weather we're having? Typical of that wannabe Casanova."

I watched Aidan storm around the table several times before stopping in front of his aunt with clenched fists.

"May I speak with you briefly—alone? There's something about Dad we have to discuss," he said, composed, changing the subject out of the blue.

Finola turned pale and jumped to her feet.

"Just a second," I said. "Where are the Grampians? How do I get there?"

"You can't today," Finola said. "It's already way too late. Besides, the storm front from the south they've been talking about is almost here. It would be suicidal to go up the mountains now."

"But I need to see Charlie!" I cried desperately. "Today! She has something of mine."

"The Grampian Mountains are no joke, Josefine. Even experienced mountaineers wouldn't risk it in a storm," Aidan said, raising an eyebrow at my muddy pumps. "And we don't even know for sure they're up there."

"A storm? Is Charlie in danger?" Bri asked.

"They've plenty of mountain bothies for hikers. I can assure you that Ian knows quite a few romantic mountain huts with beds and fireplaces," Aidan replied.

He glared at me as if it was my fault that his brother had slipped through his fingers.

"Well, I'm not going to any mountains tonight. I have a date," Li declared and held up her phone. "A dinner date at"—she squinted to read the name on the display—"the Castle Hotel."

Bri's dessert fork clanked onto her plate. "You have a *what*?"

I couldn't bear it any longer. Tears spilled from my eyes as I ran outside.

"This is the voice mailbox of Dr. Justus Grüning. Since I am away on a business trip, I cannot take your call. In case of an emergency, please contact lawyer Arnulf Bender at the law offices of Maibach, Roeding &

Partners. He will give your concern his full attention. If this is a private matter, please leave a short message." *Beep.*

The phone display dissolved in front of my eyes. I put it away and rushed down the path—head down, jacket collar turned up—while the wind whistled around my ears and tears of disappointment streamed down my cheeks.

I had almost made it. Almost! If only I had insisted on driving to Kincraig yesterday. Damn you, Aidan Murray! If he hadn't settled the dispute in that stupid pub, Bri would never in her life have got drunk with pig-eyed Dudley. Not only would she have been able to drive, but we'd still have a car—I definitely wouldn't have filled up with the wrong fuel if Aidan hadn't shown up yet again to rattle me. Nothing was going the way it was supposed to, and it was all Aidan's fault.

Irate, I kicked a stone into a puddle that shone like molten gold. I tilted back my head and gasped. The afternoon sun was being swallowed up by a pitch-black wall of clouds.

It wasn't until then that I realised I'd left O'Farrell's Guesthouse far behind and had reached the first few houses of the village. Under normal circumstances, I would have been delighted by the cute houses with peaked roofs and freshly painted picket fences, but I was too upset to pay attention to the charming gardens.

I saw a bus stop a few yards ahead and headed towards it. To my amazement, it held not only a timetable, but also a pay phone, a table strewn with travel brochures, and even an old sofa. A girl of about seven—in overalls, her schoolbag between her knees—sat on the sofa working on a maths problem. There was a huge clap of thunder, and heavy raindrops splashed against the corrugated tin roof.

"Hi," I said awkwardly, and turned to study the bus schedule. I was cold.

"Back at ya," she answered in a high, clear voice.

I sighed. The timetable was wet and illegible despite the protective glass.

"Are you sad?"

Surprised, I looked down at her mousy little face, but the girl didn't seem to expect an answer. I was struck by her dirty fingers and chewed nails. Somehow, they didn't match the speed with which she scribbled three-digit numbers in her notebook. When I was her age, I could barely add five and two.

"Are you waiting for the bus?" I asked, ignoring her question.

After a pause, she nodded.

"Is it coming soon?"

She shrugged.

Perfect! I love this country. Disgruntled, I stared into the rain and tried not to shiver. "Does it ever stop raining around here?"

"I don't know." She grinned. "I'm only seven."

"You're funny."

"That's what Mum says, too."

"Do you have a name, funny girl?"

"Maisie," said a deep voice behind me.

I turned around with a start. Aidan's green truck stood in front of the bus stop with its motor running. He had rolled down the window, and now gave the girl a stern look.

"How many times has your mum told you to do your homework at home and not at the bus stop?"

"Aidan!" Maisie's face lit up like a hundred-watt bulb. "Did you bring me the chocolate that's wrapped in red and white? You promised."

Maisie . . . From the phone call on the plane. I could feel myself blushing. His alleged lover was a seven-year-old girl. But I thought . . . Obviously, I should stop thinking.

"Was there ever a promise I didn't keep, my lady?" Aidan pointed down the road. "The storm's almost here—I'm sure your mum's worried. I'll bring the chocolate tomorrow so you can share it with your brothers. Home you go, now."

"Aye, sir." She crammed her notebook into her satchel and pulled a bright-green cap over her blonde locks.

Maisie flashed me a sassy grin and then she was off, hopscotching through the puddles. My heart skipped a beat. *Just like Charlie.*

Aidan leaned a bit farther out the window.

"And you, Mrs. Stone? Do you plan to stay here overnight?"

"I'm taking the bus." I made a show of plopping down on the bus stop's upholstered bench, but its broken slats afforded me no dignity—my knees rose up practically to eye level.

Aidan turned off the engine, climbed out of the truck, and sat down next to me. "There's no bus today," he said calmly.

"Then I'll wait till tomorrow. Right here." I bobbed my feet up and down angrily, but stopped when the old sofa bounced in time.

"The bus only runs Mondays to Fridays."

"Why doesn't that surprise me?" I snarled at him.

"You'll have to get used to the fact that time is a flexible entity in Scotland."

"Got any more clichés in your repertory?"

Aidan chuckled. "It depends on what you want to talk about."

"How the hell do I get to the Gramp-whatevers?"

"What in the world has your cousin done that it's so important you find her?"

"I could ask you the same about your brother." I moved away from him—a futile attempt due to the sagging middle of the sofa.

"My brother hasn't done anything." Aidan twisted his mouth.

"That may be, but you're pretty mad at him."

"Some people cause a lot of damage when they don't do what they're supposed to—when they think rules and obligations don't apply to them. Nobody's better at leaving his family in the lurch than Ian," he said with a sneer.

"My cousin is rule-breaking personified. As for family obligations . . . I'd say she doesn't even know what that means."

Aidan silently took off his leather jacket and draped it around my shoulders.

"That's really not necessary," I protested, but he waved me off.

I surreptitiously snuggled into the comforting warmth of the jacket. The leather smelled of waterproofing agent and the woodsy musk that would probably remind me of Aidan all my life, whether I wanted it to or not.

"I'll tell you something about family obligations, Josefine." He sighed and leaned back, slouching comfortably on the bench. "Murray & Sons has been around for over a hundred years. My great-great-grandfather opened the first village bakery in Kincraig with fifty pounds of seed money. Everyone said he was crazy. In 1896, country people didn't go to a store to buy bread or cakes. But Joseph Murray was obsessed with producing the best Scottish baked goods based on old family recipes."

A tiny smile played across his face. He closed his eyes, speaking more to himself than to me.

"Good old Joseph spent almost two years perfecting his baking skills. He came up with several varieties of shortbread and butter scones, even though he wasn't very good at writing or arithmetic. He measured the ingredients with an old coffee cup, which he called his good-luck cup. It's still on display in our main store, by the way."

My body leaned in the wrong direction—closer to Aidan. "What happened to Joseph?"

"His hunch was right. Within a year, people were coming from all the neighbouring villages to buy his cookies and cakes. He opened a second shop in Aviemore and, after the First World War, his grandson Hamish founded Murray & Sons, Limited. That's how it started."

Aidan got up and paced around the tiny bus shelter. He had to raise his voice over the wind rattling the tin roof.

"When margarine swept the nation in the fifties, Hamish, who was famously stubborn, clung to good Scottish butter. That's what made our company what it is today—a family business dedicated for generations to the art of traditional Scottish baking. To this day, we still use Joseph Murray's recipes—not measured with the old cup, but still baked with love, and butter from Scottish Highland cows."

I realised my mouth was hanging open. Aidan had stopped pacing and now looked down at me, his eyes shining like stars.

I've never seen a more attractive man.

The thought set off fireworks in my head—and other places, too. Guiltily, I dropped my head and stared at my engagement ring.

"That's an amazing story, but I don't see what it has to do with your brother."

"Ian has decided to leave the family business."

"That's it? Your brother didn't want to be a baker and so your family treats him like a criminal?"

"He's destined for it—not just because of his background. Finola once said that no dough can resist the music in his hands. He's an incredibly gifted pastry chef, but he throws his talent away." With a morose grunt, Aidan added, "Ian is an unpredictable dreamer, unwilling to compromise. He's terrified of making an effort."

"Are you jealous of your little brother? Maybe just a little bit?"

"God, you don't understand anything." The disappointment in his voice stung.

"Why don't you explain it to me?" I said.

"My father has cancer, Josefine."

"I'm so sorry." I fought the impulse to take his hand.

"He supposedly retired several years ago, but he couldn't stay away. His meddling didn't bother me much since I was mainly off at the Edinburgh branch. But Ian had to deal with it on a daily basis. My father hated Ian experimenting with the old recipes, despite the fact that whatever Ian pulled out of the oven was delicious. I mean, who'd ever have thought of infusing oatmeal cookies with currants and saffron. Dad was throwing fits, and one day—"

"Ian took off." I almost laughed out loud at the familiar tale. Charlie had obviously found her counterpart.

"He grabbed his damn guitar and disappeared. I have to admit I was relieved. Finally, some peace and quiet. That changed two days ago." Aidan put a hand over his eyes. "My father wants me to bring Ian back so he can make up with him. And anyone who knows Malcolm Murray knows that the stubborn old donkey would never do that unless he's in really bad shape." He put his head in his hands and groaned.

"Wouldn't it be a good thing if Ian and your father worked things out?" I ventured.

"Ian's going to bring the business down with him. He only works when he feels like it. Half the time he's off busking for a few pence." He groaned some more. "Yes, I'm mad at my brother. But I promised my father I'd bring him home."

Aidan's suppressed rage mirrored mine when I thought of Charlie.

We watched the rain for a while. It blew sideways and beat against the acrylic glass of the bus stop. Then Aidan turned and put a hand on my knee.

"I'm sure you're wondering why I'm telling you all this," he said solemnly. "Whatever's going on with your cousin, Josefine, I can tell that you're as desperate to find her as I am to find Ian. That said, we can't do anything about it today." He gestured to the storm. "Higher powers are dead set on delaying our search."

"Higher powers, huh?" I sighed.

It was stressful being constantly forced to make decisions—especially when people kept telling me that mysterious powers were in charge anyway. I thought of Jonathan, the storytelling taxi driver. It would be so much easier to just give in and unload the responsibility for the so-far-failed recovery of the stolen ring onto fate or some other nonsense.

"Ian's playing in Inverness tomorrow night. We'll drive there together and, if needs be, I'll drag him from the stage myself while you confront that cousin of yours. That's the plan, so get used to it." He got up and smiled. "It's just one more day, Josefine. Your aunts will appreciate the rest and, honestly, you look like you could use a hot shower."

"One more day." When I sighed, the dimples in Aidan's cheeks grew deeper. He had won and he knew it. I quickly looked away from that infectious smile. "Why are you doing this?"

"Doing what?"

"Being nice to me even though I've behaved atrociously towards you." I looked at him. "What's in it for you?"

His eyes went to my ring finger and, for a moment, I forgot to breathe.

"I guess I'd like to find out how much rational, proper Josefine actually resembles the girl in the dog jumper."

9

Our room at the guesthouse was large and airy. It had floral wallpaper and a cream-coloured micro-fibre carpet that felt strangely like grass under my bare feet. There were two twin beds and an air mattress waiting to be inflated. The room faced south, so you could stand at the open window without getting soaked. I could see all the way to the opposite shore of Loch Insh, and the Grampians—their peaks shrouded in clouds—seemed close enough to touch. Somewhere up there was Charlie.

I pulled my robe tighter against the chill, worried—but, for the first time, not about the bride's ring. What if she and Ian hadn't managed to find shelter before the storm hit?

My cousin had always been fragile, and she was sick a lot when we were little. Either her nose was running or she had a nasty cough, which she sometimes faked to get more of Bri's special cherry cough syrup.

It made me uneasy to imagine Charlie loaded with a backpack heavier than she was, hiking a treacherous mountain trail. No matter how crazy she drove me, she was still my little cousin.

Right now, though, I had another family member to worry about. Li stood next to her open suitcase, dolefully inspecting its contents.

"Anything I can do, Aunt Li?"

She tossed aside the last scrap of clothing in disgust. "I've got nothing to wear for tonight. Not a thing."

I grinned, but she frowned.

"It's not funny, Josie."

"Of course not. Sorry." I sounded not even half as contrite as I should have.

"I'll have to cancel my date with Antoine."

"Don't be silly."

"He'll be embarrassed to be seen with me! Besides, I really don't know how it works . . . a date," she mumbled glumly. "It's been such a long time."

I studied her face with its soft, brown eyes. I had always seen Li as a kindly, calendula salve–scented old lady with arms wide enough to press two children against her. Though I had seen a few old photographs of her and Bri in their youth, I found it difficult to imagine Li as a young woman—and impossible to picture a man at her side.

"Why didn't it work out . . . with the man you were seeing back then?" I asked gently.

"He married someone else." Li took off her glasses and smiled the dreamy, melancholy smile that signalled no further questions would be entertained.

"Honestly, Li." I pushed away the pile of clothes and sat down beside her on the bed. "I'm sure Monsieur Barneau would be thrilled even if you showed up in a burlap sack."

"You're making fun of me."

"Not at all. Monsieur Barneau likes you. And I think he's nice."

"He's no Mr. Darcy, but at my age, it's time to compromise. A cheerful French doctor is an acceptable alternative to a moody aristocrat, don't you think?"

I stroked her hand. It was crisscrossed by tiny veins and looked incredibly fragile. A wave of tenderness washed over me.

"Dating is like riding a bike. Maybe you'll wobble a little at first, but after a few yards, it'll all come back. You'll have a wonderful evening." I plucked a simple, fir-green knitted dress from the discard pile. "Tell me, how did this date with Antoine come about? Isn't he travelling with a group?" I asked, walking over to Bri's suitcase that stood in the middle of the room, still unopened.

"Antoine told me that no physician who was passionate about his work finds retirement easy. In order not to feel useless, he began organising group tours for seniors. So he's more or less a private tour guide and could . . . change their itinerary to come to Kincraig." Li blushed and added quickly, "Because of the severe weather, you know."

"And you're worried he might be embarrassed by your outfit!" Smiling, I shook my head. "By the way, where's Bri?"

"She went for a walk—at least, that's what she said she was going to do. She's actually sitting in Mr. Murray's truck, sulking. I saw smoke wafting out of it. She's not happy that Antoine and I . . . What are you doing?" Li watched warily as I opened Bri's suitcase and quickly found what I was looking for.

"Making sure Monsieur Barneau is the envy of every man in the restaurant when he arrives with you on his arm."

I strolled proudly into Finola's kitchen at seven on the dot. I'd changed for dinner myself and had just deposited a very chic Aunt Li in a taxi. My aunt was deathly pale and could hardly tell the friendly driver which restaurant to take her to, but I was sure she'd relax after an aperitif or two. Even though I'd only met her French admirer twice, I was confident that the old-school gentleman would know how to treat a woman like Li. I hoped with all my heart she could enjoy being the centre of attention for once.

I hoped to solve the next problem over dinner with Bri. She simply had to stop telling everyone how much Monsieur Barneau's interest in her sister displeased her.

Not only was Bri's behaviour childish, it also baffled me—despite the fact that I knew the legend of the wardrobe. Family lore had it that, when they were little girls, the sisters had sworn a blood oath to get married on the same day and only realised as adults that they couldn't both wear the bride's ring during the ceremony. Since apparently neither was willing to break the oath or risk disaster, they made a logical, outrageous decision—neither Bri nor Li were ever to get married.

This moving story underlined the importance of the ring, but even so, it was never quite convincing enough to quell wild speculations about the sisters' marital status. Uncle Carl liked to claim that Li had missed meeting the right man simply because she never looked up long enough from her romance novels. And it was no secret that he thought Bri was a lesbian.

The truth was, it was nobody's business why my great-aunts had decided to spend their lives like a pair of old slippers. But I couldn't let Bri hurt Li or her chance at happiness by acting like a ten-year-old who is scared of losing her playmate.

The dinner table was set with tasteful Wedgewood china, but Bri's chair was empty. Finola had braided wildflowers into napkin holders and arranged a large bouquet in an azure vase. A few bright petals lay sprinkled on the tablecloth. I spotted a clay pot resting in the oven, most likely filled with Angus's trout.

Loving attention to detail was clearly the selling point of O'Farrell's Guesthouse, but I wasn't sure whether I liked it or found it cloying. Justus and I favoured minimalism. We'd never decorate a windowsill with porcelain geese. Yet this kitschy surrounding somehow made me feel that I was . . . in good hands?

I went to the window. Outside, the budding April garden was drowning in rain.

No sign of Bri. Had she really been brooding in Aidan's truck for two whole hours? It wasn't like her at all. Unless . . . With a growing sense of foreboding, I rushed to the front door and nearly ran into Hank, who was curled up on the geese-adorned mat like a furry pretzel.

"Hey, Hank. How about letting me pass?"

The dog opened one eye and immediately closed it again. He had apparently seen enough. I frowned.

"*Move*, Hank," I said more sternly.

His ear twitched, but that was the extent of his reaction. At a loss, I looked at the motionless animal and tried to remember Mama's lectures. With normal dogs, a firm voice and confident body language were enough to make them obey. But Hank wasn't a normal dog. By chance, I put my hand in my pocket and touched the peppermint candy from Deborah at the car rental desk.

I stared at Hank. It was worth a try and, by the time he'd realise I had tricked him, I would be out the door.

"Look, Hank," I said sweetly, rattling the tin.

His nose twitched.

I took out one of the mints and waved it in front of him. "Mmm, smells taaasty."

His eyes followed with interest.

Grinning, I wound up for a throw. "Go get it, you little bugger."

The mint slid across the polished floor like an ice hockey puck, finally coming to rest in front of the staircase.

After what felt like an eternity, the dog took his eyes off the mint. He studied me like a lab technician analyses an especially bizarre specimen. Then he sighed and dropped his head back onto his paws.

"Trying to teach Hank how to fetch in his old age?" I heard an amused voice behind me.

Embarrassed, I turned around—and almost dropped Deborah's mint tin. The man leaning against the railing of the staircase wore a jacket over a shirt with an open collar—and a skirt.

"Or do you want to poison the poor animal with the strongest peppermints in all of Scotland?" Aidan's dimples were deeper than ever, his cheeks dark with five o'clock shadow.

"I just need to step outside for a moment," I stuttered, forcing myself not to ogle Aidan's muscular calves in dark-blue, knee-length socks. I had always wondered why some women found men in kilts sexy. But Aidan Murray looked neither ridiculous nor effeminate in the blue-green kilt that ended just above his knees. Was he wearing . . . ?

God! I really don't want to know that.

"Penny for your thoughts, Mrs. Stone." He smirked.

"Have you seen my aunt?" I could feel my cheeks glowing. "I heard that she was hiding out in your truck." I spoke fast, trying to paper over the inappropriate images in my head with words.

Aidan looked at Hank, clicked his tongue, and pointed to the kitchen with his chin. The dog got up and scampered by without so much as glancing at me.

"Your aunt? I drove her to the village half an hour ago. She wanted to get something in the souvenir shop and was going to take a taxi back. Since I was going to see my dad anyway—"

"A souvenir shop? Bri?"

I stared at the door. If there was anything Bri hated more than crocheted book covers, it was tourist tchotchkes. It would never enter her mind to visit such a shop, let alone spend a single British penny on a silver-plated spoon embossed with a coat of arms. I kneaded my lips with my fingers.

Aidan looked guilty. "Did I do something wrong?"

Think, Josefine. What is the crazy old bat up to?

"By any chance, did you drop my great-aunt near the Castle Hotel?" I asked. "My other great-aunt is there now on her first date since god-knows-when."

The expression on Aidan's face changed from trepidation to horror. "You don't think—"

"Will Finola be terribly upset if we miss dinner?"

He shook his head slowly, seeming irritated by my cool, matter-of-fact tone—my lawyer voice.

"In that case, I hope you don't mind accompanying me to a fancy restaurant in that get-up, Mr. Murray."

He answered my pointed look at his knee socks with a mysterious smile and took the key to his truck off a hook by the door.

"No, I don't mind. And for the record, my *get-up* is perfectly appropriate for the Castle. We Scots wear our kilts with pride, always and everywhere. Remember that, Mrs. Stone." His hand already on the door handle, he stopped suddenly, bent down, and whispered in my ear, "And to answer what your eyes were asking before, a Scotsman never tells what he's wearing underneath."

There was a reason the hotel towering on a hill above Kincraig bore its majestic name.

Aidan told me on the short drive over that the Castle Hotel had been the dilapidated manor of an impoverished *laird*, as owners of large estates are called in Scotland, until a retired Englishman fell in love with it. He had bought the estate and spent his entire fortune restoring it, planning to establish one of Scotland's best restaurants. Sadly, the fruit of his labour was reaped by his heirs—the man died just before the restoration was completed.

"Another man with a grand vision—even if he was just an Englishman." Aidan pointed out the stylised emblem on the glass door, as proud as if he had earned the award himself.

I found it difficult to make small talk with him. No matter how many Michelin stars the restaurant had, I wasn't on a date with Aidan Murray. It was strange enough to enter a restaurant with a man who was not Justus Grüning, let alone one who looked like the hero of a trashy Highlands romance novel.

To my surprise, Aidan's kilt was indeed appropriate in this historic building, where chandeliers floated like glittering balloons in the entrance hall. We did attract attention, but not the sort I feared, when Aidan guided me nonchalantly past groups of chatting guests clutching champagne flutes. The men reflexively made way, while the ladies craned their bejewelled necks and overtly appraised my companion. I shuffled beside him, feeling awkward and invisible. For a moment, I thought I'd spotted Bri. But even though the wide-brimmed hat would have fitted my aunt to a tee, the face beneath was younger and rounder.

Our rescue mission ended abruptly at the double doors leading to the inner sanctum of this temple of gastronomy.

"Does madam have a reservation?"

The waiter's hair was slicked down, the parting razor sharp. He wore a tailcoat, he smiled like a hired killer, and it was obvious that no one could make it into the dining room alive without his consent.

"I am looking for someone," I replied with a friendly smile, stretching to peer over his shoulder.

"Of course, madam. Isn't everyone?"

He pressed his lips together and used every inch of his tiny body to fill the door frame.

"Unfortunately, we don't have a single unoccupied table tonight." He motioned to the reception desk, presided over by a woman in half-moon glasses and a saccharine smile. "You might make a reservation for next week."

Aidan snorted behind me.

"What's so funny?" I hissed, shooting him an angry look before turning back to the waiter. "Could you at least tell me if one of your guests is an elderly lady with a hat, sitting by herself, probably drinking?"

"I'm unfortunately not at liberty to discuss our guests, madam."

"Now you listen to me!" I gasped for air, hearing the words come out of my mouth two octaves too high. "It is not only against the law but absolutely ridiculous for you to deny me access to your restaurant—as if William Wallace or Robert the Bruce, or some other Scottish grandee, was sitting in there. I have dined in far grander establishments than your one-star kitchen can pretend to be and—"

"Of course we have a reservation."

Aidan squeezed my upper arm so hard I almost cried out. The host looked him up and down.

"Under what name?"

"If you can't even remember that, Callum, I'll have to let your wife know that you've been guzzling too much moonshine," Aidan replied. "A cosy table for two will be perfect."

"I can't do it, Murray," he said nervously, glancing at the reception desk. "I've got strict instructions only to seat people with reservations."

Suddenly, he looked not impressive at all. He stuck out his lower lip like a schoolboy getting sent to detention. Aidan must have sensed that I was about to burst into undiplomatic laughter, so he dug his fingers even harder into my arm. I grimaced.

"You owe me, pal. Or have you forgotten?"

I peered at Aidan, then Callum. What was he referring to?

"It's a matter of principle," grumbled Callum, bobbing on his heels.

"And for me, it's this wonderful young lady who matters. I'd like to impress her with a nice dinner." He nudged me forward.

Callum scrutinised us silently, his gaze pausing on the arm Aidan had wrapped proprietarily around my waist. I tried not to squirm.

"You really want to dine here?"

I almost shook my head. The warmth of Aidan's arm climbed up my spine and made the back of my neck tingle. I tried to picture Justus, but couldn't bring him into focus, as if I couldn't find the right camera setting. That was not good, not good at all.

Callum went to the reception desk and glared at the woman until she dropped her sugary smile and strutted away. He sulkily scribbled something in the reservation book, then slammed it shut.

"Mr. Murray and companion." He glowered at Aidan. "Please follow me."

"So you're familiar with William Wallace and Robert the Bruce?" Aidan grinned, placing his elbows on the table.

I lifted the leather-bound menu a little higher to hide my embarrassment and tried to concentrate on my mission.

Our table was perfectly situated behind a marble column, only a few yards from Li and Monsieur Barneau. I was tremendously relieved, since Bri didn't seem to be there. Not yet, anyway.

I peered over the edge of the menu. My aunt and her companion were deep in conversation. Li looked relaxed and cheerful—her pink, round cheeks shone in the candlelight. Antoine Barneau talked nonstop, made faces that made my aunt laugh, and picked up the napkin that had slid from her lap. Li tucked an imaginary strand of hair behind her ear every now and then, an involuntary gesture that moved me deeply. When she was young, my aunt had had beautiful long hair.

"Is everything all right?" Aidan was watching me.

I nodded and scanned the large hall, its walls covered with tapestries depicting hunting scenes. A couple was holding hands at a window table while the food on their plates grew cold. Next to the fireplace, a waitress served a dessert decorated with colourful pennants to two prim little girls, who displayed a subdued delight that I knew only too well from my own childhood.

No sign of Bri. Thank god!

I caught a doubtful glance from our waiter.

"I guess we'll have to order more than just appetisers," I sighed. The entrée prices were astronomical.

"You should take advantage of the opportunity."

There it was again, that silly tingling sensation between my shoulder blades.

"What opportunity?" I said stiffly, playing with my fork. I could hear Bri's hoarse voice calling me dried-out dough that needed Aidan to butter up.

In reality, I'd had lots of sex, sufficient sex. Justus was actually a good lover, in my opinion. Affectionate. Very considerate. Okay, lately we'd been really busy with work and too tired to . . . But that was nothing we couldn't change.

Aidan leaned back, stretching out his legs. His foot brushed my calf.

"Well, I'm hungry." He pulled back his foot without apologising. "They cook well here and since I'm wearing a kilt, dinner's my treat—old Scottish tradition. So make the most of it."

"You really take this Scottish stuff seriously." I took off my glasses and reached for the whisky Aidan had ordered for me, without asking.

"This Scottish 'stuff' *is* serious," he replied. Then he picked up my glasses and handed them to me. "Indulge me. Put them back on."

I didn't get it.

"You look good with your glasses—I like it."

Stunned, I did what he asked, blinking through the lenses that had earned me the nickname "Owl" in school. These glasses elicited a pained expression from Justus whenever I wore them outside the office or the car.

"Let's take a real look at the menu. Take your time."

Aidan looked at my hand, which suddenly seemed to have a mind of its own. Instead of staying on the table, engagement ring clearly visible, it slid to my lap and anxiously tugged on my napkin.

Traitor, I heard a voice whisper.

I hastily lifted the glass of whisky to my lips and drained it in one gulp. Aidan raised his eyebrows.

My eyes watered—I coughed and gasped for air.

"God, that was awful!"

Aidan looked aghast. "No, it was heartbreaking, as if you smoked—no, inhaled—fifty of the finest Cuban cigars in two minutes flat."

Before I knew what was happening, he took my hands in his and gently wrapped them around his whisky tumbler—all the while looking at me with his green, speckled eyes.

"Smell it."

Slowly, I stuck my nose into the glass while my heartbeat somehow . . . slowed down? Aidan's hypnotic voice was now so close that I could feel the warmth of his breath against my ear.

"Breathe," he whispered.

"I am breathing," I hissed.

"Close your eyes. *Uisge beatha*—it's Gaelic for 'water of life.' Imagine the taste as a series of pictures—deep and expressive like our lochs, sublime like the snow-covered mountain tops of the Cairngorms, damp and aromatic like the moors, smoky and warm like a peat fire, cool and invigorating like a brook in the glens. . ."

I slowly brought the glass to my lips and took a tiny sip, swishing it around in my mouth and letting it dissolve on my tongue like a bonbon.

A wave of almond and honey crashed over me. I could sense Aidan's triumphant smile even behind my closed eyes.

"I just don't think we'll be friends, Mr. Murray, this witches' brew and I."

I opened my eyes and, for a long moment, we just smiled at each other.

"Oh, we'll see about that. It's just like with this entire country. Once the spark is lit, it doesn't take much to fan the flames."

"Do you find that also applies to matters of the heart?"

Why the hell did I say that? I forced my hand with the engagement ring back onto the table, hoping the narrow silver band would lend me its usual feeling of security, but in vain. Aunt Li's carefree laughter drifted over as I looked at the hand that seemed to belong to a stranger.

"Of course," Aidan said, unfazed. I should have known that he would return the ball to my court.

"Are you on fire, Mrs. Stone?"

I almost choked on my second sip of whisky.

"You don't seriously expect me to answer that, do you?"

"Because you don't know? Or because you're afraid what the answer would reveal about you—or him?"

I clenched my fist so hard that the ring cut into my skin.

"You deserve to be on fire, Josefine."

The silence bit into my skin like ice water. I wanted to squirm, but I pressed my back against the backrest of my chair and my feet against the floor.

"By the way, I'm willing to reconsider the 'Mrs. Stone' matter." He casually put a piece of bread into his mouth. "You aren't really a stone. You're too delicate for that. What's the German word? Too highly strung—*bespannt*."

I stared at him, at a complete loss.

Fortunately, I was saved by the waiter's arrival. His expression did not bode well.

"Maybe you're like a thistle," Aidan said, chewing.

Callum tapped his foot impatiently.

"A very beautiful thistle, to be precise."

"Ahem," said Callum. "Madam, you asked me before about an elderly lady with a hat." His eyelid was twitching.

"Is my aunt here?"

I shot a glance at happy Aunt Li, who was offering Antoine a taste of her soup, and then looked around the dining room like a panicky mouse. Callum came closer and whispered to me conspiratorially.

"I'm afraid there's a slight problem."

I thought Callum would lead me to the hotel bar or the billiard room, but instead he indicated that I should follow him to the kitchen.

It was strange to enter the noisy kitchen, smelling of roasting meat and frying oil, after the genteel hush of the dining room. The hotel kitchen was surprisingly small, but about ten people were rushing around, their faces flushed. I sucked in my stomach to make way for a sturdy woman carrying a salad bowl the size of a tyre. Chaotic chopping, sizzling, and shouting followed an order that only those working there understood.

I rushed after Callum past gas stoves with whirring extractor fans until we reached the dishwashing station. A young man with a ponytail stood awkwardly in front of an open broom cupboard.

And there she sat—on a plastic stool, knees pressed together, chin jutting out. Her white trilby hat sat so snugly on her head that it was in line with her ramrod-straight back.

"Bri! What are you doing here?"

The dishwasher, relieved from his unwanted babysitting duty, returned to a tub piled high with dirty plates.

My aunt made a pinched face as if the sight of me gave her a toothache.

"I could ask you the same thing, girlie." She looked behind me with narrowed eyes and grinned. "Ah, yer Scotsman. I shoulda guessed."

Aidan, who had followed us, was leaning against a sink.

"You're drunk." I eyed the empty glass that my aunt protected with arthritic fingers.

"Yippee ki-yay! Happens in the best of—*hiccup*—families." She ogled Aidan's legs and actually licked her lips. "Mm. Looks good on him, the little Scottish skirt."

With a hint of a bow, Aidan didn't miss a beat. "Thank you, ma'am. Your hat's not half bad either."

"Don't pull my leg, laddie," mumbled Bri, examining her glass. "Iss empty, so I can't toasss the love birds." She pointed to the dishwasher. "He wuz watching me . . . like I'm some kinda dangerous criminal."

"We don't usually treat intoxicated guests like this, but she stole an apron and snuck into the kitchen. The maître d' caught her trying to pour something into the vinaigrette." Callum sounded upset, but his shining eyes betrayed how much he enjoyed the scandalous commotion.

"Is that true, Aunt Bri?" I was horrified, already considering all of the legal implications of such an offence. Unfortunately, I was neither a criminal lawyer nor familiar with British law. Would they press charges?

Bri puckered her lips. "I didn't *sneak* into anywhere, young man. I went through the door."

"Just imagine if every Tom, Dick, and Harry waltzed in wherever he pleased! And you can explain to Officer Bell why you tried to poison our food. He'll be here any second." Callum stopped short. "Wait a second, were you sent by the Duke of Lachlan Hotel in Aviemore?"

"Poison?" Bri laughed out loud. "A lil touch of a laxative issn't hurting anyone. You'll see when you're my age. I shoulda charged for it . . ." She was laughing so hard tears filled her eyes, but rather than sounding joyful it was more like listening to someone under too much pressure.

I squatted in front of Bri and carefully peeled her fingers from the glass she clung to as if it contained the remnants of her dignity.

"I'll take another Scotch with lotsa ice. Stirred, not shaken!" She giggled, hiccupping again.

For the first time in my life, I won a staring contest with my aunt. Under normal circumstances, this would have made me feel triumphant, but I felt nothing of the sort.

"Why?" I asked.

Bri's face fell. For quite a long time, she just sat there, hiccupping dolefully. I could feel all eyes in the room on my back.

"Could I have a few minutes alone with my aunt?"

But Callum just looked pointedly at his watch to remind me that the police officer's arrival was imminent.

Once again, Aidan intervened before I could make a serious error. He put his arm around Callum's shoulders and whispered to him until they were out of earshot. Bri squinted at the lightbulb on the ceiling as if it were an especially ugly work of art in a gallery.

"Outside hooey, inside phooey," she murmured. When she saw that I didn't get it, she added, "This restaurant seems all hoity-toity, but there's spider webs all over back here!"

"Fine," I said calmly. "So you don't want to talk. But you're going to listen, even if you don't like what I have to say." I leaned forward. "You have two choices, Aunt Bri—you either wait for the policeman, who not only will hit you with a substantial fine, but will also throw you in the drunk tank"—Bri's pupils had shrunk to the size of pinheads—"or we discreetly sneak out the back door right now. Li has every right to enjoy herself. She doesn't need a babysitter."

"I did her a favour," Bri declared grandly. Her left eye was twitching, but her speech had begun to regain its usual clarity.

"A favour." I bit my lip. "By giving everyone diarrhoea?"

"As far as men are concerned, my sister is as clueless as Red Riding Hood. This French cad isn't good for her—I can smell it straight through his cloud of cologne."

Bri's expression of defiance and guilt reminded me of Frau Ziegelow when she'd confessed to breaking into her husband's salon and swapping around all the hair dye.

"Let's leave your questionable motives aside for the time being and discuss the offence itself, which might result in a criminal record," I said in my most professional voice.

"Spare me the lawyer routine, Josefine. It doesn't impress me." Her eyes were flashing. "How about we talk about your questionable motives for marrying a man who sees you merely as a cute little value-added asset."

"My relationship with Justus is not relevant here!" It was just like Bri to turn the tables and attack me.

"But it's the reason we're here, isn't it?" Bri looked around the broom cupboard, and briefly lost her balance on the little stool. "Give me a break—hasn't anybody stashed a bottle of booze around here?"

"What do you mean?"

"I can't discuss this tiresome topic without alcohol." She burped and rummaged through a box.

The mouldy odour of old dishrags wafted towards me. "You aren't answering my question."

"Aren't you a lawyer? Maybe figure it out. Or simply listen to your own nether regions for a change instead of trying to please everyone. For crying out loud, nobody's demanding you play the upright von Meeseberg woman, giving up your own life just to live up to the expectations of generations of frustrated wives."

"Why are you trying to ruin everything?" I nearly shrieked, trying to make Bri's words stop ringing in my ear.

Justus loved me. He said so.

I was living my own life.

And I was more than a damn value-added asset.

Bri stopped her fruitless search for liquor and folded her hands in her lap. "Josefine, I've known you since before you realised that legs are made for walking. Do you seriously believe I would cause you any harm?" Her expression softened. "Or that Li would?"

"No. But sometimes you don't understand that there are boundaries, even when you love someone."

Something deep and unsettling shimmered in Bri's ice-queen eyes, something that ran deeper than a few glasses of Scotch. "True love isn't a cow penned in a pasture, Josefine. It can't be fenced in, much less controlled," she said, sounding completely sober. "I hope the right man will show you that one day—even if he turns out to be wearing a kilt."

She got to her feet and stumbled, looking surprised when I didn't reach out to steady her. Instead, I crossed my arms in front of my chest.

She clicked her tongue and grimaced. "We'd best leave now before they find out I added the laxative to the soup as well."

With a sly grin, the dishwasher helped us make our escape out the back.

Callum and Aidan had disappeared, probably to toast their old friendship. To my surprise, I felt a twinge of regret about my aborted date. Still, I had accomplished my mission, if only partially successfully. I shuddered to remember how Li had offered Antoine a taste of her soup. Before long, she would be forced to beat a hasty retreat to O'Farrell's Guesthouse.

Bri's medicine chest was both famous and infamous, containing drops, salves, and pills for any malady known to man. To me, it had always seemed like a magician's closet, but for Charlie, it was confirmation that Bri was really a witch who flew over Frankfurt each night while we slept. It seemed to me now that eight-year-old Charlie hadn't been too far wrong.

We cautiously stepped outside into a dimly lit backyard. Rain fell in sheets. The wind had knocked over several dustbins and was whipping across the pavement, as if intending to clear up the mess it had made with a celestial high-pressure cleaner. The awning offered no protection at all against the icy downpour. All I wanted was to return inside at once, police or no.

I spun around, but the door had locked behind us.

"Shoot!"

I rattled the doorknob in desperation. Bri hung heavily on my arm while at the same time trying to light a cigarette. Within seconds, my composure collapsed like a house of cards.

"Bri! Lose the cig and stand on your own goddamn feet before I let this storm blow you all the way to Shanghai."

"Good for you! I never knew you could curse," my aunt cackled over the howling wind. She waved a soggy cigarette in front of my nose. "This one's had it anyway."

Staring at the sad slug of tobacco, I wished Aidan was there—Aidan, who knew how to handle things, who made me feel safe.

But he was off distracting Callum, maybe even sweet-talking the police officer, and our only choice was to hike down to the village and hope to find a charitable soul. I closed my eyes, trying desperately not to cry, and heard Bri's voice as if it was coming from far away.

"What do you say we get in Mr. Murray's car before we drown out here?"

I squinted into the rubbish-strewn backyard, and indeed, there was the green truck—lights on, engine running. Aidan jumped out and ran towards us, leather jacket pulled over his head.

"Miladies ordered a taxi?"

Something happened to me in that moment. Aidan took Bri's arm and helped her to the truck while I huddled against the building, paralysed with surprise at the fluttering in my stomach. So that's what everyone was always talking about.

He gives me butterflies, Josefine, hundreds of them, an entire army! I could hear Charlie's voice, see her arms thrown wide like one of those idiots who jump out of planes for fun—Charlie with an otherworldly smile on her face. She was fearless, sure she'd live and love forever. She was like this every time she fell in love. But Charlie's romances were like clockwork. Heartbreak would follow, sure as Grandmother's five o'clock tea. Each and every time.

"Josefine? Are you coming?"

I looked up in a daze. Aidan was patiently waiting, oblivious to the rain that glued his shirt to his chest. He was freezing—I saw it in the way he tensed his shoulders—but didn't seem to care. I was all that mattered to him at that moment.

As soon as we were in the truck, I impulsively reached for Aidan's hand, but let go just as soon as I'd grasped it. His skin felt warm despite the cold.

"We should probably wait for the police officer," I said in a low voice and turned to the back seat, where Bri was already snoring, her mouth hanging open. "I don't want you getting into trouble for helping us."

"The policeman already left." Aidan's face gave nothing away.

"Why?" I asked, surprised.

"Well, good old Officer Bell owed me a favour."

He looked almost sheepish sitting there with his strong hands wrapped around the steering wheel. How could I ever have assumed he didn't work with his hands?

Because you're a lousy judge of character, Josefine—especially when you're personally involved.

"I'll find out one of these days what kind of shady business you're involved in, Mr. Murray. All of Kincraig seems to owe you," I said. He just shrugged. "Come on, what's your secret? Did you divide a lottery win among the populace? Do you bribe them all with baked goods?"

"No, Mrs. Stone. It's just that I was the boy in school who was really good at maths," Aidan replied, putting the car into first gear.

We were soon greeted by the warm light of the O'Farrell Guesthouse. Hank, his ears pricked up, sat waiting for us on the top step of the porch. He didn't bark, but his brethren in the shed started up a racket when they heard the truck. A man shouted something and the dogs immediately fell silent. A window slammed shut and an almost magical quiet spread across the front garden.

"That'd be Uncle Angus," Aidan explained. He rested his arms on the steering wheel and gazed at the dashboard.

"The one with the trout?"

"Trout, dogs, geese—creatures great and small."

We were silent for a few moments before I hesitantly unbuckled my seat belt. "Well . . . thank you very much for helping us. I don't know what I would have done without you."

"My pleasure!" His voice was warm, but he avoided my eyes.

My heart beat faster. Was it possible that cocky Aidan Murray felt self-conscious—because of me? I stared at his lips and felt a wild urge to kiss him.

"All right. So, then, I'm going to haul my trashed aunt upstairs." I groped for the door handle.

I had to get out of this car pronto before I did anything I would regret. It was bad enough that the thought of kissing him had crossed my mind!

"I stay in the boathouse down by the lake, about two hundred yards from here," Aidan said calmly. "If you take the trail behind the shed, you can't miss it." He looked up. "Just in case you need me."

Just in case I needed him. His words reverberated in my ears, morphing into a salacious offer that made me blush.

"You're too kind, Mr. Murray," I stammered, and had to avert my eyes. I touched my ring, desperate for support. "I don't think I—"

"For crying out loud, can't you speed it up a tad? I need to go to the little girls' room. And by the way, I am not trashed, Frau Solicitor—a little tipsy at most."

At that moment, I would gladly have stepped into a snowstorm to create a mile-wide distance as fast as possible between Aidan Murray and my wildly beating heart. I breathed a panicked "Goodnight," leapt from the car, dragging Bri from the back seat, and stumbled up the staircase with her.

This time, Hank mercifully let us pass.

One look was enough for Finola to know what was going on. She gracefully helped me lead Bri to the second floor, guided her to her bed, turned on the heater, and asked whether we needed anything. When I shook my head, unable to say a word, Finola just patted my arm gently and dragged Hank behind her, who had followed us and settled next to Bri's feet.

My aunt slumped on the edge of the bed while I changed her out of her wet clothes.

"Li looked so happy," she mumbled, screwing up her face as if she was about to cry.

Just seconds later, curled up like a puppy, she was fast asleep.

I ran the entire way. I ran until I stood in front of the porch of the warped wooden boathouse and remembered that I had to breathe. My heart was beating much too fast and my ribcage hurt. Rain streamed off my hair, over my chest, down my back, and into my one remaining shoe. I had lost the other somewhere on the slippery trail—maybe that was the first price I had to pay.

Aidan knew I would come. I realised this when he stepped out of the darkness of the porch, crushing the soda can he had nursed while he waited. He left it on the porch and edged towards me like you would approach a shy woodland creature. He stopped a few respectful yards away, in case I needed to flee.

And I wanted to. I wanted to escape from the silent statement in his eyes that pierced my skin.

You are here.

My chest expanded to make room for my heart. If this sensation shattered me, I would never be able to reassemble the parts into a safe and sound whole.

Yes, I'm here.

"The thing is . . ." I shouted against the wind, pulling frantically at my rain-soaked dress.

"You've lost a shoe, Cinderella." For the first time, he used the informal *"du"* in our German conversation.

"What's happening is . . ." I tried again, even louder, in the absurd hope that volume would hide my nervousness. "I really don't know why I'm here, but you"—after starting with *"du"* I switched to the formal *"Sie"*—"I . . . Aidan . . . Mr. Murray . . . God!" I stamped my shoeless foot and grimaced.

Pebbles. Small, sharp pebbles cut into my soles to punish me for coming here.

"The least formal works for me," he chuckled.

"It's not fair!" I yelled, raising my hand with Justus's ring. "I'm engaged. I'm here looking for my cousin because she stole a family ring I have to wear when I walk down the aisle because of my grandmother, who . . . Oh, it doesn't matter!" I had a feeling that my face was as big a mess as my words. "Anyway, I need the ring to get married. And then you . . . then you show up . . . and you aren't only handsome, oh no!" My voice cracked. "You're also kind and funny and helpful and give me compliments. So, okay, at first I found you insufferable. And, actually, not everything you say is nice. I'll probably never forgive you for that stunt you pulled when you drove away from me, but . . . you like my glasses. You call me a thistle—whatever that means. When you look at me, it makes my head spin. I'm supposed to be on fire? I mean, who talks like that to a stranger? Are you saying I'm not capable of . . . Because, if I want to, then . . ."

I am here and I don't care what happens tomorrow.

Aidan was standing directly in front of me, so close I would only have to reach out to touch the irresistible dimples hidden beneath his stubble.

"What exactly do you want, Josefine?"

I knew that he already had the answer to that question. I finally dared to look him in the eye and chose to pretend that Aidan was as insecure and afraid as I. Yes, Aidan, the ladykiller who'd undoubtedly stood right here in the rain with countless other eager women. To imagine he was scared too made everything easier.

Butterflies.

You were wrong, Charlie. There aren't hundreds of them.

There are thousands.

Our fingers intertwined and I let him pull me towards him, tenderly.

"Show me how to catch fire," I whispered.

"No, *mo chridhe*—my heart," he said. "I'll show you what it means never to let the flame die."

That's when I lifted my chin to be kissed by Aidan Murray.

Just got home and found your note on the kitchen table. What the hell are you doing in Scotland? Call me immediately or at least text. Tried your phone and pager. Justus. P.S.: I love you.

10

If I'd had my wish, I would have kept reality out of that room forever, locking the door with chains and padlocks so it could never get
in. Behind my closed eyelids, I replayed vivid snapshots of the night
before.

Aidan's skin, golden in the light of an oil lamp—the dragon tattoo
writhing on his back as we struggled to get even closer than we already
were—sweat, gasps, stammered words . . . I meticulously stored each
memory. Every sound, every touch, every kiss. I even memorised my
sore lips and the exhausted ache between my thighs. They, too, were
parting gifts.

I knew that Aidan was no longer there even before opening my eyes
to the sunlight that fell through the shutters and threw wrinkled circles
of light on the sheets. I should have been disorientated, waking up in
a strange place, a strange bed. But I knew exactly where I was—exactly
where I shouldn't be.

I stared at the white ceiling for a few minutes as reality crept in
slowly but relentlessly, bringing along with it unwelcome friends.

Guilt. Shame.

I had cheated on Justus, and my treacherous body had enjoyed it like stolen fruit from a forbidden garden. What was worse, I would do it again, over and over if possible.

I scoured myself for the expected remorse, but found none. How was that possible? And how could I feel so dejected and so outrageously happy at the same time?

I turned on my side and winced. Something had stung me. A small thistle was sticking up between the pushed-together mattresses. Aidan had left a folded note on his pillow. The handwriting was undeniably beautiful.

You looked so peaceful that I didn't want to wake you. I went to see my old man. The coffee maker is on and milk is in the fridge.

P.S.: At the risk of getting slapped, you look almost prettier when you're asleep—even though you sleep with your mouth open.

I dropped the note like it was hot, then stared at it from a safe distance. What was I going to do? I felt like a passenger who had just missed the last flight home from an airport at the end of the world.

Home. What was my home? Where was it? Was it the sky-blue townhouse in Frankfurt's West End, with the designer kitchen I had almost never used?

Was it Villa Meeseberg, the family homestead, which I loved dearly, but where I couldn't seem to breathe anymore?

Was it the chaotic house in Bad Homburg where I'd grown up, but which felt as distant from me as my parents did? It had been that way since elementary school, when they looked at each other in amazement because the ambitious little person I was seemed almost not to belong to them.

I went to the boathouse's tiny kitchenette, rifled through the cabinets, and found a mug adorned with a bellowing stag. Pulling the bedsheet tighter around me, I listened to the coffee machine gurgle, feeling as if a trapdoor had opened under my feet.

Why did I feel this way when I had accomplished so much? My life spread out in front of me like one of my bulleted to-do lists, a stellar portfolio of competence that I could proudly present to the von Meeseberg family. Look—here is your model daughter, showpiece granddaughter, pride and joy of a grandniece. I always had excellent grades and graduated with honours on more than one occasion. My lawyerly behind sat in an ergonomic leather desk chair from which I earned a six-figure salary. I had savings, investments, and several life insurance policies.

And very soon I would marry a sensible, successful man who wanted a family and who was my equal in navigating polite society, where, over drinks, you established business friendships and made important small talk and donations to charitable organisations while a nameless server circulated with hors d'oeuvres.

I sipped my coffee and walked through the apartment. The coffee tasted just like it should—hot, black, and bitter.

Framed photos were lined up on the sideboard that stretched along a window overlooking the lake. When I picked up the first, I had to smile. It wasn't difficult to recognise the boy, splattered with dirt and missing an incisor, proudly hunched on an old motorbike, his arms barely long enough to reach the handlebars. Another photo showed Aidan, about twenty, next to a much younger, slighter version of himself. I turned the frame around and read the smudgy note.

"Aidan and Ian, 2002."

"So you're Ian," I muttered, scrutinising the pale face with soulful, dark-brown eyes. I felt strangely close to Aidan's brother right away.

In a larger family photo, I recognised Finola O'Farrell. She was flanked by two men who towered over her like protective giants. One of them, a bearded, serious-looking man in dungarees, held her hand. The other was wearing a suit and had an air of great dignity about him. His hand rested on Aidan's shoulder, paternal and possessive at the same time. Ian stood to the side and seemed to be looking at something beyond the frame. One got the impression they'd begged him to smile for the photographer—only to find out later that he hadn't.

Maybe I was wrong. After all, it was a photo, not a personality test. But I couldn't help thinking of our own family portrait that hung in Grandmother's sitting room. Charlie's funereal expression was a perfect match for Ian's.

"A young, great love, so full of hope. The two are made for each other," Li had said at the family meeting about Charlie's disappearance. Suddenly, it felt like an entire lifetime had passed since then, not just a week.

A love so full of hope.

It had sounded like a meaningless cliché. But then Aidan came into my life.

Should I really risk it?

My heart was pounding in my chest and I started to sweat.

The mere thought of abandoning what I had worked towards for years and completely changing my life knocked the wind out of me. Charlie's face appeared in front of my eyes. I was sure that she hadn't hesitated for a second. She gave up her studies and turned her back on Frankfurt to be with the man who apparently loved her as much as she loved him. I, on the other hand . . .

I gently put back the family photo and picked up a frame that was lying face down.

It took a few seconds before I understood what I was looking at, seconds during which reality found its way through the locked door and slapped me across the face.

After what felt like an eternity, I raised my head and looked through the picture window. The pier dissolved in the distance, where sunlight glittered on the lake. The rain had gone at last.

I slowly counted to twenty and forced myself to breathe while I let go of the previous night—for good. Then I finished my coffee, left the mug in the sink, and got dressed.

I left Aidan's note on his pillow, but in an inexplicable fit of sentimentality, stuck the little thistle into my pocket. It pricked my finger again, as if in protest. Before I closed the front door, I cast one last look at the photo gallery and felt almost relieved.

The essential difference between my cousin and me was that she would have known the name of the waitress serving hors d'oeuvres. And that was why some part of me had always wanted to be more like open-hearted, vulnerable Charlie.

But I wasn't like her, and now I knew that for sure.

The wedding photo on the sideboard proved that Aidan wasn't like that either.

I took the path back to the main house, walking barefoot, without feeling the cold. On the way, I found my lost shoe. It was wet and dirty.

Just before reaching O'Farrell's Guesthouse, I turned onto the flagstone path leading to the lakeshore. I sat down on a bench shadowed by an old pine tree that looked like a small, hunched woman contemplating her reflection in the water. I pulled up my legs and wrapped my arms around my knees.

It was quiet here, and peaceful. A few ducks waddled by, and up in the now almost cloudless sky, a bird of prey wheeled in forbidding circles. Without thinking, I stuck my hand in my pocket and cried out. What a stubborn little thing this thistle was.

"Seems to me you could use a blanket and a hot cup o' tea," someone said behind me.

I immediately put my feet on the ground and brushed my hair out of my face, dropping Aidan's prickly present.

Finola ignored my dirty shoes and damp dress. The wool blanket she laid over my shoulders smelled of sheep and dog. She then handed me a cup of tea, sat down next to me, and silently watched as I breathed in its soothing steam. It might have been sunny by now, but I really would not advise anyone to visit Scotland in the spring. I realised I was shivering.

"So kind of you," I whispered awkwardly, unaccustomed to people who didn't ask questions.

Finola leaned back and looked out at the lake with half-closed eyes.

"The view's stunning, isn't it?"

She had stuck a pencil into her chignon, which slightly resembled an empty bird's nest. Her knitted jumper was far too large and matted from years of washing—obviously an old favourite. Finola O'Farrell was a simple woman, but there was something about her fading beauty that intimidated me.

"It's a very special flower, you know. It's even immortalised on the Scottish coat of arms."

"Sorry?"

"The thistle."

She turned to me. Nothing seemed to escape her yellow-green eyes. I quickly scooped up the thistle as though I hadn't meant to throw it away.

"They usually bloom much later," Finola added with a smile. "You seem to have found a particularly ambitious specimen."

"What's so special about thistles?" I asked.

"There are many legends involving thistles. First and foremost, it's the emblem of the royal clan, the Stuarts, and that's most likely why the thistle became the symbol of Scotland." Finola took the flower from me and gently touched the purple blossom. "I myself am partial to the story of the Norsemen who landed on our shores in the twelfth century, planning a night-time attack. To approach without being heard, they took off their armour and shoes—and walked right into a field of thistles. Their screaming woke up our men, who easily routed the barefoot barbarians." Finola opened my hand and gently placed the thistle on it. "It's a wee little plant that knows how to defend itself, that stands for courage and deep conviction. In matters of the heart"—she paused—"one single blossom means more than an entire bouquet of red roses."

My stomach contracted. "What a lovely story," I stammered with burning cheeks.

Finola nodded and returned her attention to the snow-covered mountains.

I couldn't hold it in any longer. Words tumbled out of my mouth like the crumbling stones of a badly constructed barricade.

"I saw some photos in the boathouse . . . a wedding picture, a pretty photo with a very . . . happy couple. I mean, Aidan . . . looks very happy." I had never been so relieved to finish a sentence in my life.

Finola's expression softened. "It was a wonderful day for all of us," she sighed.

"She was a stunningly beautiful bride." I swallowed. Aidan's expression was forever etched into my retinas—the warm smile, the sparkling eyes resting on Vicky, the auburn-haired beauty from the pastry shop. Delirious with happiness.

"She was, indeed. She had . . ." Her voice suddenly seemed to come from far away.

"Well, hello, you two. Girl talk?"

I jumped. Aidan was standing on the path, his hands in his pockets, grinning like the boy on the motorbike.

I had been so stupid. To believe that he . . . that it had been more than a brief interlude in which both of us forgot we belonged to someone else.

I clenched my fist, enjoying the pain, and buried the thistle in my pocket.

Aidan had been right about one thing, anyway. The thistle really was like me, a wee little thing able to stand up for herself. There wouldn't be a second time—I had too much to lose. Besides, I was not a woman who steals another woman's man, however loosely he treats his marriage vow. Aidan Murray was a womaniser after all, nothing more.

"Thank you again for the tea, Mrs. O'Farrell. It really made me feel better. Now I'd better go see whether my aunts have murdered each other."

I stood up with a smile, careful not to look at Aidan. Only after passing the rose bushes did I start to run.

"If your night was as awful as you look, you'd better forget all about it." Bri sounded amused.

Out of breath, I let the kitchen door slam behind me and stiffened when I saw the table. Pancakes! Finola had made pancakes with bacon and maple syrup. There was a fire in the woodstove and wildflowers all around. In a different life, I'd have killed for this breakfast. But right now, the idyllic scene was torture. I had to get out of here.

"Go and pack. We're leaving."

Li blinked and reached for her glasses next to a cup of tea and an open book. She looked bleary, her skin the colour of a dried leaf.

"Are you all right, Aunt Li?"

"Just slightly indisposed," she mumbled. "But I'm afraid you'll have to go on your little excursion without me since there probably won't be enough facilities . . ." She cleared her throat, embarrassed.

I scowled at Bri, who made large, innocent eyes and, true to form, counter-attacked.

"Li, at least, spent the night in her own bed." Bri smirked and continued petting Hank, who was leaning against her leg with closed eyes. This would have baffled me under normal circumstances, but now it generated just one thought—two really warped personalities had found each other.

"Yeah, great job, Bri. I hope you've got a hangover that doesn't quit," I snarled.

Shocked, Li covered her mouth with a hand.

"Josie, how dare you take that tone with your aunt Bri?"

"It's the tone that's fit for someone who—"

"Where are we going?" Bri asked calmly. "Or should I ask how fast and how far?" Hank's tail drummed on the floor. Bri smoothed her skirt. "Look what you've done, you monster dog—hair and drool stains all over. Auntie Bri can't leave the house like this."

"Who are you and what have you done to my aunt who hates dogs?" I exclaimed.

"They've become friends. Bri even took Hank for a walk. Isn't that nice, Josie?" Li looked at her sister as if she had tamed Cerberus, the hound of hell.

Bri rolled her eyes.

"He hasn't left her side since this morning and she purrs when she talks to him," Li stage-whispered, torn between amusement and awe. Then she stood up so fast she spilled her tea. "I'll be back in a sec."

Bri shrugged and leaned over to scratch Hank's belly while I stood there at a loss. We heard the toilet flushing and Li returned soon after.

"I think I'm getting a little better. Thank goodness for your charcoal tablets, Sis."

I crossed my arms and planted myself in front of my travel companions. My mouth was dry. "I'm driving to Inverness to look for Charlie. Are you coming or staying here?"

Li came over and put a hand on my shoulder. "Josie, is everything all right?"

"Everything's fine, Aunt Li," I lied, when all I wanted to do was throw myself into her arms, sobbing. "I just don't want to lose any more time. There's so much to do back home. After all, I want to get married in two weeks!"

Bri stopped stroking the blissful dog. "But is that really what you want?"

I nodded. It's uncomfortable to lie when one has a hunch that the other person knows the truth. The two sisters looked at each other.

"Anyway, we don't have a car," she added.

I exhaled and went to the kitchen window. Finola and Aidan still sat on the bench. Her head rested on his chest and Aidan had his arm around her shoulders. It was a moving, protective gesture that reminded me that their family was grappling with his father's cancer diagnosis. I'd been so preoccupied with my own problems I hadn't asked him about it once. I turned away quickly, feeling I had intruded on their privacy. Plus, the sight of Aidan's beautiful, deceitful back made every inch of my body want to flee.

I felt Li and Bri's eyes on me, anxious like a pair of blackbirds who have watched their chick fall out of the nest. I closed my fingers tighter around the keys to the truck that I'd taken from the hook in the hallway.

"Well, you do have to set priorities in life," Grandmother had said when Charlie missed the bus on the morning of her A-level exam and, without hesitation, had "borrowed" the mailman's bike. That stunt earned her a few hours of community service, but also saved her university career.

I held up the key ring and jingled it. "We have ten minutes to get packed."

Justus was just here and he was terribly upset. Could you call him? Papa is afraid your fiancé might pitch his tent in our tulip bed until we tell him where you are. I beg you—call him. Me too. Kisses, Mama

P.S.: Have you found Charlie?

"We stole a car," Bri giggled as I steered the truck down the gravel driveway and onto the street.

My hands were shaking and it took me three attempts to put the truck into gear. But as soon as the little Victorian bed and breakfast was out of sight, my guilty feelings were swept aside by immense relief, which continued while I drove through the village, rigidly obeying the posted speed limit. We passed the bus stop, where a motley crowd of backpackers had just been dropped off. So much for "buses only on weekdays." I wondered what other lies Aidan had told me.

With one hand on the steering wheel, I fumbled through my bag until I found my mobile phone. There was a message from Justus.

I opened the message, the phone jammed against the steering wheel, read it twice . . . and, with a lump in my throat, then a third time.

I love you.

These past nine years, I had only heard those magic words twice from my fiancé—first, after I got certified to practice family law, and second, after his bachelor party, when he slipped into bed with alcohol on his breath. Yet now, he'd written them for the second time.

No, mo chridhe, *I'll show you what it means never to let the flame die.*

Aidan Murray's hypnotic eyes appeared so suddenly in front of me that the phone fell from my hand and clattered to the floor. The noise jolted me from my brooding. Out of habit, I'd steered into the right lane. Fortunately, there was almost no one on the road, but my heart pounded as if I'd just looked death in the eye. I gripped the wheel, moved back to the left, and ground my teeth together so hard that I thought Bri and Li would hear. There was only one explanation for my situation—someone had cast a spell on me. Ever since I'd landed in this country, nothing had been the way it should be, neither in my head nor in my heart.

I checked the rear-view mirror. My aunts looked out of opposite windows, lost in thoughts of their own. Much to my chagrin, Bri appeared fresh and rested while Li still looked under the weather.

However, the gentle smile on her face transcended the discomfort her sister had caused. She pressed her phone, which was beeping incessantly, against her chest like a love letter she was saving for later. I silently cheered Monsieur Barneau's persistence. Bri had been too late with her laxative, it seemed.

After passing Kincraig, I sped up. There was only one path back to reality—the bride's ring. Everything would be all right once I had it. Aidan Murray would become a footnote in the story of my life, easily forgettable.

I should have anticipated that fate would throw me another curve.

The police officer was a tall man with dreamy, baby-blue eyes that seemed at odds with his uniform. Maybe that's why he immediately put on sunglasses after taking off his helmet. It couldn't be because of the sun, which, exhausted from its brief foray, was resting behind the clouds again.

The guardian of the law sauntered around the truck, then stopped in front of the bonnet and wrote down the number plate so slowly that it seemed like a joke. My stomach was acting up. I had immediately discarded the thought of switching seats with Bri, who at least had a driver's licence—there'd been no time, anyway. Worried, I stared at the police officer's name tag. This was a clear sign that god hated me.

Bell. It was the police officer who had been called to the Castle Hotel last night because of an old lady's crime against soup. Damn it, was there only one policeman in this stupid town? A ticket was one thing, but Officer Bell would probably suspend my driving privileges as soon as he found out that I was driving without a licence. I wasn't ready to even think about the matter of the "borrowed" car.

"Lock the doors and don't roll down the window, no matter what," Bri hissed behind me. "The best thing would be to step on the accelerator and scram."

I looked back in disbelief.

She jutted her chin forward. "What? The guy looks like a serial killer. How do we know that his uniform is even real?"

"Oh my god!" Li turned even paler.

"It's what they do, these sickos," Bri continued. "Pretend to be a cop so you'll follow them to a remote location and then—"

"Bri! Haven't you already done enough to make Li feel miserable? Do you have to scare her, too?"

A suspicious look appeared on Li's face. Bri's laughter sounded forced.

"What do you mean, Josie?" Li asked with big, fearful eyes.

I bit my lip and peeked at Bri. Li was looking at her sister, who had actually lost a little of her colour despite her pointedly casual expression.

"What does Josie mean, Bri, saying that you've done enough to make me feel miserable?"

Bri opened her mouth, but at that very moment, the policeman knocked on the window. I defied my aunt and rolled it down. My saccharine smile was reflected in Bell's mirrored sunglasses.

"Madam." Not a single muscle stirred in his face.

Fascinated, I stared at his pinched mouth that resembled the end of a tiny balloon.

"A wonderful morning to you, Officer. I must say, you Scots do wear handsome uniforms. Our men in blue could really learn something from you," Bri blurted from the back seat.

"And what gorgeous weather we're having today. Those lovely fleecy clouds," Li chimed in, matching Bri's best high school English. "Sheep clouds, you understand? They look like sheep—*baaa*." She waved her arms around.

Officer Bell remained straight-faced. Then he uttered the words I'd feared ever since the piercing siren almost stopped my heart.

"Licence and registration, please."

A list of excuses exploded like fireworks in my brain. "Just a moment," I said in as friendly a manner as I could and bent forward to rummage in the glove compartment—as if I might find a clever solution there among the sweet wrappers and crushed soft drink cans. My period of grace lasted barely half a minute, just long enough to reveal that Aidan liked liquorice. Bell cleared his throat and I looked up.

"It seems I forgot my driver's licence." With a guilty grin, I pushed forward to the next confession. Maybe I would get lucky and find that Scottish law enforcement took a more relaxed view of things. "As for the registration, I'm sure it's here—"

"I was driving," Bri interrupted from the back seat.

Bell took off his sunglasses, raised an eyebrow, and turned to my glowing face. He seemed like a confused boy who'd grown up too fast, but he had the power to throw us in jail. He completely ignored Bri as she climbed out of the truck and stood protectively next to my door.

"Is this your car, madam?" His child's eyes drilled a hole through me.

There it was. I wasn't just defeated, I was dead.

"The car belongs to a friend. It's on loan," I assured him. Then something amazing happened.

The tiny mouth opened and grew wider and wider. Officer Bell was laughing—a deep, unexpected laugh.

"Nice try, madam. But I just happen to know that the owner of this car would never loan it to anyone—and certainly not to a woman." He held up three fingers. "So we are talking about three offences here— driving without a licence, with no registration, and in a stolen vehicle!" He almost sounded amused.

Dumb jerk is probably just thrilled he gets to do something other than hand out parking tickets for once.

"Listen, sir, I already told you. I was the one driving. Here's my licence." Bri tugged on Bell's sleeve. She reached into her purse—and a little plastic baggie fell to the ground. "Oh, that's . . ."

She bent down, but the policeman was faster.

"That's nothing." Bri turned pale.

It's not easy to say who was more stunned, Officer Bell or I, as we realised what was in the bag he held between his thumb and index finger like a dead mouse.

"Offence number four," Bell said after an awed pause, reaching for his radio. "Possession of illegal drugs. I'm going to need all of you to get out of the car. I'm requesting a police car to take you to the station."

"Did he say drugs?" Li called out. "What drugs? Why would any-one have drugs?"

"I'd be interested to know the answer myself." Scowling, I pushed the door open and planted myself, hands on hips, in front of Bri.

My aunt looked down, without a response for once in her life. Li got out of the car and squinted at the little plastic bag that still dangled from Bell's fingers.

"But that's your tea, Bri!" she exclaimed. "The tea to calm your nerves that you got in the gift shop yesterday, when Antoine and I were having dinner."

"They have a gift shop in a place like the Castle—" I stopped, sud-denly remembering the young dishwasher who'd given Bri a conspirato-rial smile before helping us escape into the rain. "No way!"

"What? It *is* tea, isn't it?" Li's jaw dropped.

Bri turned to me with a condescending snort. "And you think my sister doesn't need a babysitter."

11

I thought several times about calling Justus. The first time was as we sat crammed like sardines in the back of the police car, while I counted the liver spots on the back of Bell's bald colleague's neck. The second time was when we sat on a bench in Kincraig's police station, where Li griped about a missing seat cushion for half an hour until Bri took off her felt hat and pushed it under her sister's behind. The third time, I didn't want to smudge my phone display with fingers inky from fingerprinting.

When we were finally left alone in a cell, my mobile and Li's precious iPhone had long since been taken from us. My aunt was allowed to keep her Highlands romance novel, but to show her outrage, she only leafed through it.

"Marijuana," she muttered, shaking her head. There was a rustling of pages, followed by sad sighs to show how far her estimation of Bri had fallen. "Marijuana!"

She had been repeating the word for two hours now, and I felt like I was slowly going mad. Bri, crumpled trilby back on her head, kept her eyes fixed on the light above the small sink.

"I didn't even get to smoke any of it!" Bri snapped.

Li paused her mantra for a second, and I turned away so they couldn't see my incredulous grin.

Apart from the lack of a door handle, the room didn't match my idea of a prison cell. It smelled of paint and cleaning products. The folding bed on which we sat was functional and clean—I remembered similar furnishings from various school trips. The space was small for three people, but it would have been tolerable if only my aunts didn't argue like an old married couple.

"I hope you realise that I'm missing dinner with Antoine because of you and can't even let him know! He's driving to Inverness just to see me." Li started the attack.

"And I hope you realise that a few grams of marijuana weren't the only reason we were arrested," Bri snarled, looking at me. "And why does this man want to buy you food again, anyway? Is the Frenchman into chubby women or can he just not think of anything better to do?"

Li grandly raised her chin. "We go out to dinner so we can have a nice conversation. That's how it's done, dearest sister, if you want to find out more about a man than the size of his underwear."

"You unfortunately underestimate the importance of a man's underwear size, dearest sister. But by all means, continue to feed your doctor onion soup and let him seduce you with his silly accent. Just don't come to me crying when he disappears back home, never to be heard from again."

The silence that followed slid down my spine like a cold, slippery eel.

"How could you know that?" Li asked calmly. "I didn't tell you that Antoine and I had onion soup."

"Li—" I interjected.

But she raised a hand and got up from the cot with surprising agility. She went to the sink, washed her hands, and dried them carefully. Then she looked at herself in the mirror, fixed her hair, and took a deep breath before turning around. The deep sorrow in her gaze was heartrending.

"What did you do, Bri?"

Her sister crossed her arms. "I saved you from doing something you'd regret. We both know how it ended for us last time."

"For *us*?" Li adjusted her glasses.

"That's right, for *us*. Need me to refresh your memory? Erich decided Irma Mellingstedt was the better choice for his bank account and dumped you. Too bad he got you pregnant first. Of course, I was the one who picked up the pieces and got you back on your feet."

"Pregnant?" I asked, my mouth agape.

Li stood there hugging herself as if she might crumble into a thousand tiny pieces.

"I lost the child," she whispered to herself.

I inhaled sharply, but the words of consolation stuck in my throat.

"And I almost lost my sister," Bri said, lifting her head. Tears shimmered in her cool eyes despite her attempts to blink them back. She suddenly looked as sad and fragile as Li, who had turned to support herself against the sink.

"Fifty-five years, Bri," Li said forlornly. "Will it ever stop hurting?"

"I'm sorry," Bri said in a flat voice. "I'm so very sorry." She got up with difficulty and slowly approached her sister. "You should have someone at your side who loves you the way you deserve to be loved. Yes, Lieselotte Markwitz, you were supposed to grow old and grey with the love of your life by your side. And though it sounds sappy and really not the way I usually . . . and even though I don't particularly . . . this Frenchman . . ." She stretched out her hands in supplication. "What I did was wrong, but I did it because I was afraid. I couldn't take it if your heart got broken again and you withdrew to that place where nobody can reach you. Not even me."

I listened, dumbfounded. Bri's face was already losing its vulnerability, swiftly being replaced by the acid aloofness befitting the role she played in our family.

"Tell me you forgive me, already—before my arm falls off."

Li scrutinised Bri for a long time. She took so long that I began chewing on a fingernail, afraid she would reject the awkward peace offering. But just before Bri could turn away, Li rushed to her and hugged her.

"You're a silly girl." Li held her sister at arm's length and stroked the deep furrows on Bri's forehead with her fingertips. "Have you forgotten? 'I, Lieselotte Markwitz, swear by everything I hold dear that I will never abandon my sister Brigitte.'" Tears flowed down her cheeks.

Bri swallowed a few times. Finally, she nodded and Li smiled.

"Besides, Bri, I *have* grown old and grey with the love of my life by my side."

Officer Bell didn't know what to do when he returned and found three sobbing women in his cell. He put on his best authority figure look, waved around some kind of official document, and announced in an exasperated voice, "Ladies, you're free to leave."

We looked at each other in amazement.

"We're a country that welcomes tourists," the policeman added with a grumpy glance in my direction. "But you better let your aunt drive until you have a valid licence with you. My colleagues from the city won't be so lenient."

"You're really letting us go? What about the truck? The marijuana?" I replied suspiciously.

"I don't know what you're talking about." The muscles of his jaw twitched.

"My grandniece is referring to the dried plant matter in the plastic bag, which . . . Ouch!" Li rubbed the spot where Bri's elbow had landed.

"He doesn't know what Josefine is talking about, Li," Bri repeated.

"That's why I wanted to explain . . . Oh." Her face lit up. "I see." She beamed beatifically at Bell. "That's so very helpful of you. You know, I'm sure my sister didn't put the weed in her purse on purpose. She has no idea how to roll a joint, let alone smoke—"

"We are leaving, Li. Now!"

I quickly retrieved our belongings from Bell. It was obvious that the police officer did not relish letting us go, but nothing would keep me from walking through the cell door as fast as possible—no matter what had opened them, or who.

My pulse quickened when I stepped into the hallway behind my aunts, who were holding hands like two excited little girls. What tiny hope I'd had that Finola O'Farrell might be behind this development crumbled like a dry scone when I saw Aidan get up from a wooden bench at the entrance. I could almost feel the blood draining from my face.

"Mr. Murray! Don't tell me you are once again our guardian angel," Li squeaked, hugging him.

Bri settled for a pat on his shoulder and pushed her sister out the door. "We'll wait outside."

I was painfully aware of Bell's presence—the smell of sweat and fast food behind my back. And in front of me there waited an even more destructive force of nature, rushing towards me and pulling my rigid body against him.

"*Mo ghaoil*, my darling, what have you done now? I can't let you out of my sight for a second."

He spoke loudly for the audience, his stubble scratching against my temple and the scent of chocolate and cedar wood making it almost impossible to breathe. I wanted to push him away, but he held on too tight.

"Give me ten seconds," he whispered into my ear in German. Then he pressed his lips against my mouth very hard, and my traitorous body kissed him back.

Then I was free, trembling and out of breath, like a drowning woman fished out of the North Sea. Giving me a light slap on the behind, Aidan turned to Bell, who had been watching sceptically.

"Thanks, Stew. I owe you one."

"Better keep an eye on your girl, Murray. Next time, I won't let her off that easy."

The policeman stepped behind the counter and, frowning, removed our incident report from a drawer. A shredder roared into action.

"I'll keep her on a short leash," Aidan assured him, chuckling.

Bell shrugged, as if his memory of me and my aunts was being shredded along with the paper. He seemed not to care what our canoodling meant for Vicky.

I saw a wedding band on Bell's hand, which gave me a shocking idea. Maybe the two had a gentlemen's agreement to cover for each other's adultery! Snorting derisively, I linked arms with Aidan.

"Let's go home, darling," I cooed, blinking seductively in Bell's direction. Anything to get out of here. And then—well, as long as I had a working credit card and the number of a taxi company, I depended on nobody. Aidan was not going to derail me again—even if I had to wear earphones, nose plugs and a blindfold to avoid seeing, smelling, and hearing him everywhere until I got out of this horrible country.

"Murray?"

The policeman stopped us just as I reached for the handle of the door to freedom. Aidan instinctively pulled me closer, revealing fear that surprised me. Stewart Bell's boyish eyes twinkled.

"If you're planning to take your new girlfriend and her aunts out for dinner, best avoid the Castle. They're none too pleased with the one in the hat."

"What the hell's the matter with you?" I snapped the moment the heavy doors shut behind us, pulling my sweaty hand from the crook of his arm.

He stopped on the stairs and crossed his arms. "Shouldn't I be asking you that?"

"Oh, everything's perfectly fine with me. Couldn't be better, now that I know what scum you are. You should be ashamed, cheating on your wife that way."

"My wife?" His surprise actually sounded genuine. God, this man had no conscience at all.

"And to pull your friend into it!"

Aidan touched the back of his neck. "Stewart isn't my friend. He just owes me—"

"A favour. Obviously! Did you help him cheat in maths, too?"

"Your aunt Li and I will go for a little walk," Bri said behind me.

I had totally forgotten those two. They'd made themselves comfortable on a bench and were watching us like it was guerrilla theatre. *A second-rate farce,* I thought with a bitter smile. But they would be waiting for a happy ending until the cows—or, for local flavour, the sheep—came home.

"A walk? But it's going to rain again any minute." Li took off her glasses and looked up at the sky.

And indeed, a dark-grey cloud was moving in from the mountains, its craggy edges perfectly matching my mood.

"Besides, I'd rather sit awhile. It's comfortable on this little bench, and interesting."

Li's salacious curiosity lost out to Bri's sense of tact.

"Up, Li. There's a shopping street over there. I'm sure we can find a halfway decent cup of coffee. And if you behave, I'll even give you back your phone so you can call the Frenchman." Bri winked, gesturing that I should call when I needed her.

I followed them with my eyes until Bri's red coat and Li's blue jumper combined into a purple smear in the distance. Aidan, meanwhile, had sat down on the station's steps, legs spread, elbows on his knees.

"What are you gawking at?" I snarled.

"I'm waiting until what you're saying makes sense."

He sounded so calm I got even more upset.

"Sense? Sense? I'm certain Vicky could make sense of it immediately."

"You think Vicky and I . . . ?" He laughed as if I'd just accused him of having an affair with his sister.

"I don't just think so, I know so," I hissed. "I saw the photo in the boathouse, the wedding photo of you and Vicky. And I'm appalled . . . Even if you were divorced, which you are not, I saw you making out in the pastry shop in Edinburgh—"

"You saw us making out," he repeated.

"Yes, I did. It's disgusting how you cheat on her. You're a married man, damn it!"

"So says the woman with an engagement ring on her finger."

"That's completely different."

"Is it? How?"

"It . . . it was a slip-up."

"Oh." He nodded slowly. "I understand."

"At least I was honest. You knew from the start I was engaged, but you didn't tell me you were married. I would never—"

"Josefine, stop. It's not what you're imagining."

"So enlighten me. I can't wait."

I paced on the lowest step, feeling as if I'd explode if I didn't keep moving. Above us, a blue and white Scottish flag flapped at the top of its flagpole.

"Please sit down. You're making me dizzy."

"I've no intention of getting comfortable here," I replied. I leaned against the railing, but quickly straightened up when the rusty metal made a crunching sound.

"Suit yourself, Mrs. Stone." Aidan stretched out his legs and sighed. He rubbed his finger where a wedding band should be. "Let's assume I can convince you that things are not what you think . . . I mean, let's just imagine that what we had wouldn't be affected by all this." He exhaled for so long that the air between us seemed to vibrate. "Would you reconsider whether you really want to marry that man?"

I was stunned. What was he talking about? "No, I wouldn't," I replied. My voice was trembling.

"That's what I thought."

"I don't understand what this has to do with you and Vicky." Pointing to his hand, I added, "Or the missing ring on your finger."

Lost in thought, Aidan smiled. "Who'd ever have thought we would end up here? On the plane, I thought you were sexy and smart, but irritating. Then you stumbled into my store in that hilarious jumper and I suddenly saw your tenderness, your frightened perfectionism—even though you ruined that a few minutes later. But there's something about you that I just can't shake."

"Aidan, this conversation is going way beyond weird. Could you get to the point, please, instead of flirting with me?"

He raised a hand and I saw his body sag in surrender.

"My wife is dead, Josefine. She died five years ago on a climbing trip when her group got caught in a snowstorm."

He said it flatly, like someone who has repeated the words so many times they had lost their meaning. But in his eyes was the sadness and loss that never leaves those who've lost a loved one.

"Ben Nevis was Olivia's twenty-fifth Munro, a mountain over three thousand feet—it was a jubilee, sort of . . ."

A wave of nausea forced me to sit down. I wrapped my arms around my knees.

"But the woman in the photo was—"

"Olivia. She was Vicky's sister—and, yeah, they looked so much alike." He sounded almost apologetic, as if it was his fault that I'd made such a terrible mistake.

I burned with shame. First little Maisie, now Vicky. I had jumped to conclusions about Aidan again.

"Why didn't you tell me?" I asked plaintively, though the answer was obvious.

Because there was never an opportunity, and even less a reason. Stupid cow that I was, I'd been desperate to convince myself that Aidan Murray was the last man on this planet for whom I would jeopardise my meticulously planned future.

"Honestly, I didn't think it was important," Aidan said. "I was obviously wrong. It *was* important and I'm sorry—but that doesn't change anything. You've made your decision and I'll respect it, even though I wish I'd been more than just a slip-up to you, Mrs. Stone."

I shivered, and it had nothing to do with the cold wind rattling the police station's shutters. *God, woman! Tell him how you feel. Don't let it end like this.*

"You're right. It doesn't change my decision." I closed my eyes for a moment to digest this overwhelming feeling of loss.

Mistake. You're making a huge mistake.

"Well, then . . . I know it sounds trite, but could we maybe try to be some sort of friends? Or at least declare a truce? After all, we'll still have to spend time together. It would be nice if we weren't constantly at each other's throats."

"Time together?"

I felt as if a thumb was pressed against my larynx. No! I did not want to spend one more minute with Aidan, tortured by desire and regret.

"Well, you've shown that you need someone to watch over you, and I owe that much to your fiancé, I guess. Besides, we're both looking for Charlie and Ian, and that truck *is* mine, after all. Let's just forget about last night. We'll pack up your crazy aunts and drive to Inverness right now." Aidan got up and brushed off his trousers. "Agreed, Mrs. Stone?"

"Only if you stop calling me that. My name's Josefine." My voice sounded calm and controlled even to me. But inside, I felt weak with sorrow. I forced myself to look at him. "Okay, a truce—at least until the next time you say 'Mrs. Stone.'"

"Perish the thought! I won't let myself do that ever again."

12

Deirdre Bennett was an impressive woman, and not only because she was furious right now. She slammed the pint glass she'd been drying onto the counter. With a tattered dishcloth, she treated the next glass with the same angry care.

"With my poor mother as my witness, this is the last time I'll do a favour for that ne'er-do-well, kin or not."

Another glass hit the counter and Li, who had laboriously climbed onto a bar stool, jumped.

"Barking dogs don't bite," I whispered into her ear.

My aunt looked uncertainly at the woman whose arms, from the back of her hands to her powerful shoulders, were decorated with Celtic motifs. The Hootanelly bartender not only matched her Edinburgh cousin in stature, but also shared his love of tattoos.

"Gavin's constantly talking me into giving a chance to one little drifter or another, claiming they're the next Donovan. And what happens? The snot-nosed brat stumbles in here three hours before his gig and cancels. This whole damn town is making music tonight and the Hootanelly, of all places, has no band. I can't even get a plastered bagpiper on such short notice."

"Did she just say what I think she said?" I whispered to Aidan, struggling to follow her heavily accented English.

The regret in his eyes confirmed my fears. I felt queasy—it was starting to become a habit.

"So Ian cancelled." Aidan's voice was calm, but he clutched his beer bottle so hard I thought it might shatter.

"That he did. Have to say, though, the boy didn't look good." Deirdre bent down and pulled a fresh dishrag from under the bar. "I probably should be grateful he took the trouble to let me know. Most of these types just don't show up. But I'll make that cousin of mine pay for the loss in earnings. Maybe that'll teach him not to be such a fool."

"Mrs. Bennett—"

"Call me Deirdre, dearie." She stopped in the middle of drying another glass and looked me up and down. "Can ya sing?"

"You don't want to hear it, believe me." I elbowed Aidan for support, but he was fiddling with the label on the beer bottle, seemingly oblivious to Deirdre's chatter.

"You've no idea what types of screeching I've had to put up with. It can't get much worse." Her ash-blonde spiked buzz cut now swung towards Li and Bri. "How about the two of you? I'm sure you'd make a fine duo."

Li's eyes opened wide and Bri almost spilled her coffee.

"You want *us* to sing?"

"If needs be. Or if you play a flute or a fiddle . . ."

Aidan put down his bottle, its label now striped like a zebra.

"Deirdre, when exactly was my brother here?"

"That sickly little guy's your brother?" She coughed and spat into the sink. "Well, congratulations! You're as lucky with your kin as I am. Haven't brought your guitar, have ya?"

"Sorry." Aidan's face was grim.

She shrugged and reached for another glass. "Worth a try. All Scots claim to be musicians, but when push comes to shove, they're scared shitless." Her long sigh sounded like a bad note on a bagpipe.

"Was Ian alone?" I asked, my heart pounding. "Or was there, maybe, a girl with him? Mid-twenties, wispy, dark hair?"

Deirdre thought a moment. "Nah, I saw nobody else with him."

I exhaled. Late again. What now? Had it all been for nothing?

"Maybe Charlie is no longer with this Ian person." Bri expressed what I secretly was thinking.

"Of course she's still with him." Scowling at Bri, Li put her hand on my arm.

"How do you know? Your grandniece goes through lovers like I change underwear. She could very well have ditched him by now," groused Bri.

"I just know," Li countered.

"Well, m'dears, I haven't the foggiest what you're talking about. Anyway, the lad was here half an hour ago and looked like he needed either a tubful of Glenfiddich or a doctor." Deirdre sniffed. "I sent him to Harold Finlay at the pharmacy. He's a strange one, he is, but he knows his way around herbs. His special remedy even helped my mother, and she's been wanting to join the angels for a year now." Deirdre stopped short as Aidan laid a pile of twenty-pound notes on the counter.

"Keep the change—for tonight's loss of earnings," he said briskly, putting on his leather jacket and stretching out his hand, which I reflexively took.

Bewildered, we looked at our fingers, which had quite naturally intertwined, and let go at the same time. I was immediately overcome by a strange sensation like stepping outside on a winter evening and realising you weren't wearing gloves.

"Oh my," Deirdre said. "Quite a spark there."

"Exactly," replied Bri, pushing her coffee cup away. Instead of joining Li, who was waiting at the door, she contemplated Deirdre's spiked hair. "Come up with a proper cup of coffee and a piano for my sister, and I'll sing for you next time—if you can tolerate Edith Piaf's 'La Vie en Rose.' It would be our pleasure."

"What are you talking about, Bri? Are you crazy?" Li squawked, waving her hands in embarrassment.

"Why not? You're hell-bent on adventures of late. Let's cut loose in a Scottish bar."

While Bri walked towards the door to confer with her sister, Deirdre dried her hands on the dishrag and motioned me closer.

She bent over the counter and whispered into my ear. "Hold on to this man, *mo nighean*—my girl." She patted my arm awkwardly, as if affection was a language she'd forgotten. "It's not often a chap looks at a woman like he looks at you, and I know what I'm talking about since I had a man who did exactly that until the last breath he took."

My mouth was ready for a frosty reply, but none came. I nervously looked at Aidan, who was staring out the window and bouncing on his heels. It was obvious he wanted to rush to the pharmacy, but he said not one impatient word—another trait for which any woman would adore him. Any other woman.

I swallowed and, after a polite goodbye, turned away from Deirdre. Her face had resumed its usually grumpy expression. She waved to Aidan with the pile of notes.

"*Taing, mo charaid*—thank you, my friend. I'll let Gavin know there are still some decent blokes in his neck of the woods."

That's it, I thought. *I'm too tired. I don't care where the little monster was swept by the never-ending rain. I'm quitting this game.*

Deirdre Bennett's remarks were the final straw in this tale of errors, disappointments, and one big missed chance, of which every glance at Aidan, sitting across from me in the driver's seat, was a reminder. I wanted nothing more than to give up the search for Charlie, admit I'd been beaten, and absolve myself of guilt.

The minutes ticked by on the dashboard clock as this feeling sank in. At exactly 7 p.m., the words tumbled out of my mouth.

"I can't do this anymore."

"Stop talking nonsense, Josefine," Bri said, nudging Li, who was peering at the brightly lit window of Finlay's Pharmacy. "Do you see the boy in there?"

Li rubbed the windowpane as if she could wipe away the rain. "There are so many people . . ." she whispered, excited by this stake-out. "Is there some kind of epidemic in Inverness?"

"I'm serious," I said, turning to them. "I quit."

"But, Josie, what about the ring?"

"I don't care. I'll get married without it and Grandmother will have to live with her decision if she really boycotts her own granddaughter's wedding."

"What are you talking about?" Bri demanded.

"Oh." Li waved dismissively. "Charlie stole the bride's ring."

"She did what?" Laughing, Bri poked a finger into the back of my neck. "So that's why you've been stumbling through the scenery like a shy deer, missing the stag for the trees. And here I thought you cared about your cousin!"

"Spare me your mixed metaphors, Aunt Bri!" I yelled, angry that she seemed neither surprised nor upset by the revelation. "I just want to go home!"

Aidan was straight-faced, but at least I had silenced Bri. I turned back around in my seat and covered my face with both hands.

"What if Ian's still in there?"

Li's hand found its way to my shoulder, where it rested heavily. I would have liked to shake her off, but some lingering remnant of manners held me back.

"What if he isn't?" I spat back, as if it was her fault I'd lost my nerve.

Even if Aidan's brother still was in the pharmacy, my cousin had probably sent Ian packing a long time ago. With everything that had gone wrong, the chances of actually catching Charlie felt like zero. She was gone and, with her, the bride's ring. That's just how it was.

We had been sitting outside the pharmacy with the engine running for twenty minutes, watching people come and go. None of us had made any move to climb out of the truck. Even Aidan sat like a statue next to me. Maybe Ian had become for him what Charlie seemed to be for me—an unreachable phantom. I wasn't sure whether to laugh or cry. We were in so many ways ridiculously similar, except that he wasn't going to give up.

"All right, then, I'm going in." Bri reached for the door.

"No," Li objected. "I'll go. You'd scare the poor boy off."

"Really." Bri let herself fall back into the seat. "And he'll trust your Old Mother Frost smile? Parents warn their children about witchy old ladies like you."

"I let the two of them stay in the garden house and made soup for them. He knows me."

"That might be the problem exactly, sis. It's possible they don't want to be found."

"Maybe Josefine should go," Aidan said softly.

"Me?" I looked at him in surprise. "I don't even know if I'd recognise Ian."

"You will."

"But I . . . I want to go home."

"And you will go home, Josefine—just not yet."

The words hung in the air between us, a truth we hadn't wanted to admit. I could feel my carefully constructed self-absolution begin to shake. And then Aidan showed why neither a head waiter nor a police officer could resist doing him favours.

"If I go in, Ian will bolt, either before or after I beat him up. In any case, he'll refuse to talk to me, which means I can't keep the promise I made my dad." His eyes locked with mine. "But you can, I think. You could make Ian come back with us. You're a lawyer—you're used to handling difficult conversations. Besides, you look . . . nice, trustworthy." For the first time since I'd met Aidan, he'd stopped in the middle of a sentence. "Do it for me. I beg you."

A gentle smile, three plaintive words, and I was putty in his hands. He really was a crafty bastard. What kind of person would I be if I said no? He had done so much for me these past few days. I was in his debt—and he knew it.

I unbuckled the seat belt, ignored Bri's dry "Well, that was easy," and got out of the car.

Twelve nervous steps later, I stood in front of the wooden door with inlaid stained-glass panels and an etching—"Finlay's Pharmacy. Established in 1844." An old brass bell tinkled when I pushed open the door.

I positioned myself behind a cardboard cut-out of a fat baby touting antibiotic ointment and took a moment to adjust to the overpowering scent of herbs and essential oils. Patients must have got better just by breathing the air in here. With its Victorian furnishings, the pharmacy looked like it hadn't changed since the date on the door.

The bald pharmacist behind the counter wore a white coat and pince-nez glasses. He reminded me a little of Teacher Lämpel in the old kids' book, *Max and Moritz.*

In spite of the long queue, Harold Finlay took considerable time with each customer. He had a gentleman with a walker describe his symptoms at length and then turned to the pharmacist's chest that took up the entire length of the wall. He pondered for a while and then, at great speed, filled a little paper bag with contents from various drawers. To collect the final medication, he climbed a ladder all the way up to the ceiling. I got dizzy just watching.

The customers were mostly elderly, except for one very young mother whose babbling toddler hung on to her coat with one hand

and drummed against the glass display case with the other. No Ian. I was about to turn and go when I saw a row of chairs on which more customers waited to be called.

A young man's dark-blue hoodie was pulled over his forehead, shadowing his face. But there was no question that it was Ian. His feet kept time and his hands played air guitar.

The woman next to him stood up and I took the opportunity to slide into the seat.

"Hi," I said, mustering the loveliest smile I could, terrified of saying the wrong thing.

He looked up. As soon as I saw his soulful eyes and understood why my cousin had fallen in love with Ian Murray, my phone rang.

"Justus, may I call you back?" I was shocked by my businesslike tone.

"Most certainly not, Josefine. I've been trying to reach you nonstop for two days. If this is one of those silly bridesmaid's pranks your friend Claire dreamt up . . . Well, I don't find it funny at all."

"It's not what you think," I replied, my pulse racing. "I'll explain later why—"

"So you really are in Scotland?"

"Well, yes."

Justus's dry laugh crackled through the phone.

"I sure hope you can explain. Because I couldn't make heads or tails of that note you left. What could possibly be so urgent that it couldn't wait till after the wedding?"

I glanced at Ian. His arms rested on his thighs and his hiking boots were tapping to the beat of some song only he could hear. His slender body radiated such eerie energy that I almost tapped along.

"Josefine? I want you to stop this idiocy right now and come home. Do you understand me?"

Ian fingered his invisible guitar in two-four time. I silently counted along.

"I am coming home. Just not yet."

Watching Ian's restless hands, I spoke slowly and clearly to make sure Ian could understand what I said in German. "First, I have to find Charlie, my cousin."

The tapping stopped abruptly.

"You're joking, aren't you?" Justus thundered. "You don't even like your cousin. How many times have you told me that you wished you didn't have to have her as a bridesmaid? And now you chase her all the way to Scotland? Are you out of your mind?"

"She's my cousin, Justus."

My voice sounded calm, but my insides were in knots. It was true—I really had said that the pretty bridesmaid dress was a bad investment because Charlie would first spill red wine on it and then rip it while running drunk through Grandmother's rose beds. But if I confessed to Justus about the bride's ring, he'd have me committed for sure. Belated loyalty to my cousin was less damning. To be honest, I really was beginning to be concerned about her.

Ian was now sitting up very straight, listening intently. There was icy silence on the other end of the line.

"I have to go. I need to clarify an important matter here," I said, smiling faintly at Ian. "I'll call you back."

Aidan's brother was frowning. He looked briefly at Mr. Finlay and then at the exit. If I didn't get off the phone fast, he might bolt.

"I don't understand you, Finchen," Justus said in a somewhat more conciliatory tone.

At some point I really would have to tell him how much I hated that nickname. "Well, it's the way it is," I said, and hung up.

Take a deep breath, close your eyes, find the right words . . . But it was Ian who found them first.

"So you're Jo," he said quietly.

Even his voice was musical, despite his heavy accent when speaking German. I nodded, feeling like a fisherman who watches with rapt attention as a fish circles his bait.

"She knew you'd come."

I was surprised by the relief on his face. He looked like Aidan, only younger, thinner, and more fragile. But there was something in his expressive eyes. He was afraid.

"Where's Charlie?" I asked with a trembling voice, taking hold of his hand without thinking. It was cold and clammy.

"Mr. Murray? Your fever-reducing remedy is ready," came the call from the counter.

Fever-reducing? I swallowed.

Ian jumped up and pushed his way through the crowd, mumbling apologies as he went. He took the paper bag from Mr. Finlay, listened carefully to his directions, and paid with a fistful of coins he fished out of the pockets of his torn jeans. Then he came back to me, red in the face, with an unsteady, pleading look in his eyes.

"Come on. I'll take you to her."

"First, you need to know . . ." I didn't know if I should continue. I was worried sick about Charlie, about what would happen if I said the wrong thing and Ian ran. "My great-aunts Li and Bri . . . and Aidan are waiting in a car outside."

Great, Josefine. Just blurt it out.

Ian's eyes widened. "My brother?"

My heart beat even faster. Had I ruined everything? I had to know if Charlie was okay . . .

I furtively glanced through the shop window and saw, to my chagrin, that Aidan had climbed out of the car. He was pacing up and down the pavement with the rolling gait of a cowboy, apparently ready to physically prevent his brother from escaping.

Ian followed my look. He shook his head and rubbed the back of his neck in disbelief. It seemed like forever before he sighed deeply, sounding more like a little boy than a grown man.

"Amazing," he said with a crooked grin. "Just when you think fate has bailed on you, it offers two solutions at the same time."

Together, we cautiously stepped outside, the bell tinkling in our ears. Out of the corner of my eye, I saw a raised thumb sticking out of one of the truck's windows and Li's grinning face. I fell back, letting Ian lead the way. He only hesitated for a second before squaring his shoulders and confidently approaching his brother.

"Aidan."

"Ian."

The two men looked at each other in silence.

Don't hit him, please! I watched Aidan's hands, praying they wouldn't turn into fists.

"Shit, man. Am I glad you're here," Ian said, and stretched out his hand.

I held my breath. Aidan looked directly into my eyes as if begging me to tell him what to do. I stared back, paralysed.

Grandmother once told me that anger hurts the person who feels it much more than the person against whom it is directed. She also said that when we forgive someone, we forgive ourselves.

I slightly tilted my head and Aidan instantly understood. Seeing him grab Ian's hand and pull him into an embrace made me think of Charlie. I swallowed hard. What a wise woman my grandmother was.

13

Inverness was small and, unlike touristy Edinburgh, well suited to the needs of modern Scots, who came there not to admire its sights, but to get on with their everyday lives.

Finlay's Pharmacy was a short distance from the Hootanelly, and I was shocked to learn that the hostel where Ian and Charlie rented a room was also just around the corner. Ashamed that I had almost given up looking for her, I squeezed ahead of Ian and ran up the steep hostel staircase.

But I was embarrassingly out of shape. I stopped on the second floor, completely out of breath, and stared down the threadbare corridor. The bass from a boom box hummed through the walls and made the tips of my fingers vibrate.

It seemed to take forever for Bri, Li, and Ian to catch up. Aidan brought up the rear, his eyes on his brother.

"Which room?" I asked, exchanging a nervous glance with my aunts. There was a hint of fear in Bri's eyes, adding to the queasiness in my stomach.

Ian passed me silently, pressing the paper bag from the pharmacy against his chest, and headed to the end of the corridor—number nineteen. The Scottish coat of arms under the number was missing, probably stolen as a souvenir by a previous backpacker. Ian's hand was trembling, so it took him several tries before the key slid into the lock.

I don't know what I had expected—maybe Charlie wrapped in a jumper and scarf, nestled in an armchair with one of her beloved fantasy novels in her lap and a cup of tea in her hand. Maybe the familiar sound of squeaking bedsprings as Charlie dived back under the covers so Grandmother wouldn't catch her coaxing the thermometer up a few degrees with the help of the lamp on the nightstand—that would get her out of going to church on a Sunday morning.

But there was neither a comfortable chair nor anyone faking illness. The only light came in from the hall and the room had a funky smell, as if it hadn't been aired out for days. And it was terribly quiet.

Anxiously, I stepped forward, squinting, only able to make out the vague shape of a bunk bed. Ian switched on a little lamp and something moved underneath a huge pile of clothes on the bottom bunk. It looked like someone had dumped a bunch of used clothes from a Salvation Army bag onto the bed.

"She was cold," Ian said, embarrassed.

I just nodded.

"Paaapa?"

My heart jumped painfully. Charlie had called her father "Carl" since high school, just to annoy him. Worse, the low, cracking voice didn't sound like my rambunctious cousin at all.

"It's me, sweetie," Ian answered hoarsely, with so much tenderness I got goosebumps. "And I brought someone you've been waiting for."

He gently pushed the clothes aside.

I gasped. Charlie had got even thinner. Her face was flushed and gaunt. A few sweaty curls stuck to her forehead as she looked at me with confused, feverish eyes.

"Jo?" she mumbled and closed her eyes, as if struggling to understand.

My throat closed up. I sank down on the edge of the narrow cot and took her hand, which was ice cold and terrifyingly limp. *She's gone back to her natural hair colour,* I thought, and felt strangely comforted by the insignificance, the ordinariness of the observation.

I had found Charlie. But, god knows, it was not the reunion I'd imagined.

"She needs a doctor," Ian said.

"Is it bad?" I whispered, and took the little bag out of Ian's hand, which he had been cradling like the last ounce of penicillin on a desert island. "What about the medicine from the pharmacy?" I squinted to read the handwritten label. "*Bupleu—*"

"*Bupleurum chinense*, Chinese lemon balm root—it's traditionally thought to reduce a fever. It can't hurt to make her some tea from it," Bri said, and she touched Ian's shoulder. "Get me a kettle, young man."

He sprinted from the room as if Lucifer himself were chasing him—or chasing Charlie.

My tense stomach felt like a tiny, shrivelled balloon. When was the last time I'd eaten an actual meal?

"This way, the poor guy can do something useful rather than just being in the way." Bri leaned forward and felt Charlie's forehead.

My cousin seemed completely out of it, neither awake nor asleep. She writhed around in the foul-smelling clothes and mumbled to herself incoherently.

"I don't think it's life threatening," said Bri. "But it's not just ordinary flu and, if I'm not mistaken, her fever is nothing ordinary either. I'm also worried about the rash on her arms. She does need a doctor—right away if possible."

"That might be a problem," Aidan replied. He stood in the doorway, arms crossed, like a bodyguard. I fought the urge to throw myself into his arms, sobbing. "It's Saturday night, and on top of that, there's the music festival happening. We most likely won't find a doctor willing to make a house call tonight. They'll just refer us to the clinic."

"We still have to try," I snapped, glaring at Aidan as if Charlie's condition was his fault.

"Of course we'll try." He smiled at me, apparently not offended, and pulled out his mobile phone.

I wanted to apologise, but the moment passed. Ian stumbled in with an electric kettle, which he filled with water at a little sink. He spilled some when he put it down on the nightstand and, cursing quietly, looked for a socket.

Li pushed him aside gently. She poured half of the water down the sink, then plugged the kettle into an outlet right next to the nightstand.

"The doctor will be here any moment," she said casually, and turned on the kettle.

The machine started to crackle immediately, as if it wanted to prove it was more efficient than it looked. I took my eyes off it to stare at Li, who was smiling at her smartphone.

"Antoine says it will take him about fifteen minutes to get here."

She put the phone back into her handbag with a satisfied expression and stroked Ian's head. He was shivering and looked ill himself.

"I think that the Chinese lemon balm would do you some good, too, young man. A warning, though—it's quite bitter. A spoonful of honey would be perfect, but you probably don't have any."

Watching Li take care of Ian that way took me right back to our childhood and all the times she had comforted little Charlie—the skinned knees, Band-Aids, the tantrums, the sassy grins—until what Li had said finally registered.

"Monsieur Barneau is in Inverness?"

"Of course he's here." Li blushed and looked at Bri almost defiantly. "He worked as a doctor for more than fifty years. Our Charlie will be in expert hands."

Bri frowned. "Well, let's hope your musketeer knows as much about medicine as he does about fancy food."

I'm sorry I was so brusque with you on the phone. I'm sure you had your reasons for this trip. But I need you here. The office needs you, too. So, please come back at once.

With love, Justus

P.S.: Frau Feinlaub can't find the Hohlberg file. Did you put it on the shelf?

I stared at the display and had no idea how I was supposed to feel. I was sick of feeling hurt and too exhausted to be more than slightly upset that my fiancé was unable, even now, to keep our private and professional lives separate. It wasn't really Justus's fault. He was just being himself—pragmatic, practical, goal-orientated, everything he had been these past nine years.

"Everything all right?" Aidan asked.

I switched off the phone. "How long has he been in there?" I mumbled, not really looking for a response.

I knew it had been exactly twenty-two minutes since Monsieur Barneau had come up the steps, greeted Li with a daring kiss on the cheek, and then ushered us politely out the door—all except Bri. He asked her to stay and assist him since he had heard impressive things about her medical knowledge.

I had to smile, thinking of it. Taken by surprise, Bri had no rejoinder for once, so she just followed the physician and quietly closed the door behind them. Monsieur Barneau was clearly a sly fox who knew how to win over the enemy camp.

Ian perched on an old heater at the end of the hall, looking out the window while Li made him drink the herbal infusion originally meant for Charlie. The atmosphere out here felt oppressive—all of our fear swirling around below the tasselled ceiling lamps.

Aidan sat down next to me on the staircase. It was narrow, so his knees inadvertently touched my thigh—but I didn't move away. His nearness was comforting, and right now I needed solace.

I didn't care if that made me selfish. My hand sought his and I leaned my head against his shoulder. For a moment, I luxuriated in the belief that his heart stopped for a second before it continued its calm and steady beating.

"Everything will be all right, *mo chridhe*," he whispered into my hair.

I closed my eyes, wanting to believe him.

I knew I should move, but I sat there listening to his heartbeat until I lost all sense of time.

When I opened my eyes again, they fell on a well-polished pair of dress shoes. Monsieur Barneau stood in front of us, a solemn expression on his face.

Bri had been right—this was more than a simple flu. Charlie had scarlet fever.

Monsieur Barneau and Li went to Finlay's Pharmacy for antibiotics and we decided to take Charlie back to Kincraig. I didn't want her to stay in this horrible hostel one minute longer than necessary, and taking her to the local hospital was simply not acceptable to me.

"Charlie doesn't need nurses and cold rooms—she needs pillows with little flowers," I tried to explain, earning a raised eyebrow from Aidan and a grin from Bri.

Aidan finally gave up trying to talk me into a hospital stay and went to get the car. He returned soon after with Li and Monsieur Barneau in tow. Under his arm, he carried a woollen blanket that reeked of dog.

"Genuine Scottish virgin wool, ma'am," Aidan assured me. "We can add little flowers later."

After the doctor had given Charlie an injection, we wrapped her in the dog blanket, which was no easy task. She kicked and thrashed about until, exhausted, she surrendered, and Aidan lifted her like a doll. He slowly carried her to the staircase with Ian at his side.

Ian was devastated. He had not only underestimated Charlie's illness, but it was obvious he was tormented by self-reproach for not having called a doctor. On top of it all, his physically stronger big brother had taken over.

Sensing Ian's distress, Aidan stopped halfway down the stairs. "She's gonna be all right, pal," he said. "Pull yourself together and try not to fall down the stairs. I don't want to show up at Finola's door with *two* invalids."

Ian laughed drily. "You could just tell Aunt Fi that you had to beat some sense into your stupid little brother again."

"No way," Aidan replied. "Apart from the fact that none of my smacks have helped anything before, she'd probably kill me before I could finish the sentence."

"You might be right there." Ian cleared his throat and added, more seriously, "At least about the second part."

"What about the first part? Don't tell me our last row magically taught you some common sense."

I bent over the railing to get a better look at the two brothers. Ian was staring at Charlie's sleeping face. His body suddenly relaxed and he broke into a huge smile.

"Maybe. Or maybe all it takes to see things differently is the right girl," he said. He took a deep breath as if preparing to leap into an ice-cold lake.

"I'd like to come home with you, Aidan. Would that be okay with you . . . and Dad?"

Aidan's face was inscrutable. "Let's talk about it later. Right now, open the door for me. Your little lassie weighs more than one would suspect."

While Ian ran down the steps two at a time, Aidan looked down at Charlie and mumbled something I couldn't hear. Then he continued down the stairs, his walk straighter and more relaxed than before.

Two hours later, I could almost pretend that the bleak room at the hostel had never existed. Charlie was sleeping soundly in a real bed, under a duvet that outclassed even my mother's eiderdown quilts. The little room smelled of fresh linen and flowers. A thermos with tea and a plate of scones stood on the sideboard. It was warm, it was clean, and I'd stopped counting how many times I'd mentally fallen on my knees in front of Finola since our arrival at O'Farrell's Guesthouse.

"Thank god! Her fever is breaking."

Sighing with relief, Li set aside the thermometer and stroked her grandniece's head. I had been standing at the window, not letting Charlie out of my sight. Now my knees went weak and I leaned against the sill for support.

"So it won't be long until the little monster is up and getting on our nerves again?" Bri came out of the bathroom with an armful of Charlie's dirty laundry. "Can someone tell me whatever happened to normal, white lingerie with a touch of lace?" She dumped the dark garments into a hamper as if wishing it was a dustbin.

My laugh was too loud, too forced, entirely inappropriate for this room and this moment.

"When was the last time you had something to eat, young lady?" Bri asked in the awkward silence that followed.

I waved dismissively. I was a little queasy, but food was the least of my problems. For some reason, now that everything was going to be okay, I suddenly found myself fighting back tears. I cringed with embarrassment, ashamed at losing control in front of my great-aunts, practically inviting Bri to call me a cry-baby.

My aunts exchanged meaningful glances.

"I think I'll go to the kitchen to check on the others," Li said casually. "That soup on the stove smells delicious."

Bri crossed her arms. "Besides, it would be rude to stand up Mrs. O'Farrell for dinner again, don't you think?"

Li nodded. "It's really kind of her to cook for us so late. And the room she prepared for Antoine is just lovely. I mean . . . it's . . . the view, you see—the lake."

Bri knitted her brow. "The view, Li?"

"Well, the lake, of course—"

"Mrs. O'Farrell gave your Frenchman a room in the west wing."

"Right," Li chirped, smiling innocently.

"Loch Insh is east of us, Li. Whatever you were admiring in Antoine's room, it definitely was not Loch Insh," Bri snarled.

"Listen, you two," I said. "Why don't you both go let the men know that Charlie's doing better? I'll join you in just a minute."

"You've got to eat something, child. You look green around the gills," Li objected, visibly grateful to have escaped her sister's fangs.

"Please." I looked to Bri for help, blinking frantically.

"You heard the girl." Bri motioned to the door with her chin.

A tear spilled over and ran down my cheek.

"But even Ian agreed to eat something. Josie really should come with us and—"

"We're going, Li. Now."

Only after the door closed gently and I was sure that Charlie's wheezing and my own shallow breathing were the only sounds in the room did I put my forehead against the cool windowpane and allow myself to cry.

When I finally straightened up a few minutes later, my throat felt sore, but a weight had lifted. I pulled the sleeve of my ugly jumper over my hand and wiped my face and then the window with the scratchy wool. I snuffled impolitely and cleared my throat several times. After making sure Charlie was still asleep, I tried the breathing technique Mama had picked up at some find-your-inner-centre seminar—inhaling slowly through the nose and exhaling in three short breaths out the mouth. After I did this three times, my inner centre grumbled and I had to giggle. I opened the window to cool off, and was taken aback by amazing sights that hadn't been there before. Of course, they had been there before, but I'd been so preoccupied I hadn't noticed them.

The moon was pouring a milky-white path from the middle of the lake to the jetty. A glimpse of an immaculate starry sky opened up where the pitch-black peaks of the Cairngorms poked through the clouds. A sweet, peaty scent filled my lungs and awoke memories of freshly mowed grass and bread toasting over the campfires Bri lit for us children in the back garden. Pines creaked and whispered in the wind. I saw eyes gleaming at me from the bushes before an animal silently slipped away. It was a night that made fairy tales come true, if you believed in that sort of thing.

I quietly closed the window and looked at the bed. A white foot stuck out from under the blanket. I went to the bathroom, closed the door, and reached for the light switch.

Charlie's wet laundry was everywhere. I fished a sports bra out of the sink and hung it next to matching underwear on the bathtub's tap.

I pulled the hiking backpack from the bath and shook it. Empty. I turned it inside out. Only a single sock dropped at my feet—a soiled reproach for snooping. But I pushed aside my guilty conscience. After all, it was impossible to speak to my cousin right now, and I'd gone through an awful lot to end up in this chaotic bathroom.

I spotted Charlie's purse on the floor. I was so jittery that it took forever to open the purse's zip. Then I unceremoniously emptied the contents onto the bath mat.

I exhaled, disappointed. There was lip gloss in various flavours, a pocket knife, mascara, a rumpled pouch with tobacco and matches, chewing gum wrappers, and the same peppermints favoured by car rental Deborah. There was a red polka dot scarf, broken glasses, and the missing coat of arms from room nineteen at the hostel. But no royal-blue box—no ring.

I should have been frustrated or angry, but going back into the bedroom, I looked at my cousin and felt only a strange maternal worry. She seemed so fragile—even innocent, though I knew she was nothing of the sort. I tucked her foot under the blanket and, for a moment, even considered that it might all have been a giant misunderstanding. Maybe Charlie didn't steal the ring. Maybe all she wanted was to be found and brought home. But when I remembered Uncle Carl's pinched face and his pretentious plans for his daughter's future, I seriously doubted it.

"Hey," someone said quietly behind me.

I spun around and almost upended the tray in Aidan's hands. A creamy soup sloshed about.

"Sorry, didn't mean to scare you." He calmly licked the spilled soup off his hand.

Now I was gaping at his mouth. He raised an eyebrow. I could feel myself blushing and pointed awkwardly at my chin.

"You've got . . . soup . . ."

"Really? Where?" He looked at me with an amused expression that made his eyes sparkle.

"Here."

I touched the spot under my lips again, but suddenly felt silly and reached out. He kept still while I wiped his chin, my fingers brushing against his mouth by mistake. My heart was racing.

"Your aunts are afraid you might starve any minute now." He turned away from me and carried the tray to the small table in the corner. "Their instructions were to make sure you eat this soup—to feed you myself if necessary." He pulled out the chair and looked at me encouragingly. I sat down and propped my elbows on the table.

"I'm not hungry at all," I said, my stomach growling.

"That's what Ian said." Aidan nodded seriously. "His resistance lasted exactly two spoonfuls, and then he finished off almost the entire pot. Consider yourself lucky that I managed to save a bit of Finola's Cullen skink for you." He pulled out the second chair and handed me a spoon so big it could have been a ladle. "Are you going to eat or do I have to help you?"

I took the spoon out of his hand. When I dipped it into the thick, creamy liquid, I caught a whiff of something smoked. The soup was hot—and delicious.

"What's in it?" I gasped, burning my tongue.

"Watch out. It's hot," Aidan said belatedly, and enumerated the ingredients on his fingers. "Haddock, potatoes, onions, butter, cream, and—"

"Is haddock a kind of fish?" I wrinkled my nose since I don't particularly like fish—though this Cullen skink was wonderful.

"No, sheep's balls," Aidan replied phlegmatically.

"You're joking."

"Nope. I never make jokes."

I rolled my eyes and suspiciously stirred the soup. If Scots didn't die from eating it, I probably wouldn't either. Besides, Finola would never serve her guests something so grotesque. Or so I told myself. But I made a mental note to Google "haddock."

Aidan watched while I ate. He said nothing until I pushed the empty bowl away, leaned back, and closed my eyes.

"What is it?" I asked since I could feel that he was still looking at me.

"May I ask you something?"

I half opened my lids and nodded lazily.

"Have you found what you were looking for?" Aidan, his head resting on his hands, looked to Charlie, of whom not much more was visible than a tousled head of hair and the foot that once again had inched its way out from under the blanket.

"I found my cousin."

"You were talking about a ring."

"Oh, that." My dismissive gesture was too exaggerated and I knew it. I swallowed, trying to sound convincing. "That's just a silly superstition. An old family story."

Aidan was silent for so long I felt like I'd said something deeply stupid.

"No need to do that," he finally said.

"Do what?"

"Try to make me believe you don't take the story seriously—because you do. I can see it in your eyes. Besides, your larynx twitches when you're lying." He touched my neck. "And right now, you are fibbing mightily."

He got up and moved his chair closer to mine.

"We Scots have believed for millennia in a supernatural world peopled by spirits, fairies, and other mystical beings. We tie ribbons on fairy trees and worry about being drowned by a kelpie. We're afraid fairies might steal our children, we chase kobolds away from our houses with offers of hand-sewn coats, and we dance around bonfires. We look at ghosts as being people like you and me, and we greet them as we pass." Aidan leaned forward and lowered his voice. "So I'm absolutely the right audience for your story, however mystical it might be. As a Scot, I'll believe every word."

"But it goes all the way back to the Thirty Years' War," I whispered.

"Well, I haven't got any other plans for tonight. You?"

"Well, I could . . . streamline the story a bit," I said. How do you summarise a story that has overshadowed your whole life?

"Once upon a time . . ." Aidan prodded me.

It seemed that he was neither making fun of me nor pulling my leg. He was only pushing the first domino tile that, in turn, would set the mile-long row in motion.

"Once upon a time . . . there was a young Silesian officer . . . who fell in love with a lowly seamstress."

Aidan nodded in encouragement.

"The love between Ludwig and Emilia was something special—but Emilia was not of noble birth and she was Catholic—something Ludwig's Protestant family would never tolerate—so the couple kept their relationship secret. When Emilia became pregnant and rumour began to spread, Ludwig's father had him sent to the Bohemian front at the beginning of what became the Thirty Years' War."

I fidgeted with a loose thread on my jumper for a few moments before continuing.

"But before he left, Ludwig had a ring made as a token of his eternal love and as a formal pledge of marriage to Emilia. The only thing Ludwig's parents feared more than the wrath of god and the contempt of society was losing the love of their son. So they reluctantly admitted the young Catholic and the blemished, yet-to-be-born fruit of her womb into their high and noble house."

"Tough titty for Ludwig's family," Aidan mumbled.

I slowly shook my head. My stomach turned every time I thought about the way poor Emilia was treated. "Ludwig was supposed to be working in the office at command headquarters, but a mistake was made. He was sent into battle and was blinded in the trenches. His parents told Emilia that he had died. They sent him secretly to a Swiss sanatorium, where he recovered very slowly. In the meantime, Ludwig's family spread a rumour that the child wasn't Ludwig's, and then they chased Emilia out of the house shortly before she gave birth."

Aidan sighed deeply, which made me smile. He showed so much empathy that I wanted to touch his face, but stopped myself by squeezing the edge of the table.

"She was lucky, considering. A blacksmith in her village was willing to marry her and to raise the child as his own. He was a decent, kind-hearted man who had long cared for her, and he didn't care what people might say. Emilia accepted his proposal."

"Very pragmatic, your ancestor. Reminds me of someone," Aidan said in a tone that immediately put me on the defensive.

"Do you really imagine she had a choice?"

Aidan raised both hands as if I were pointing a gun at him.

"On her wedding day, Emilia dressed in her mother's wedding gown, removed Ludwig's ring with a heavy heart, and gave it to her younger sister. 'Wear this ring when you marry the man who will make you happy for the rest of your life,' she said, and made Maria promise to hand down the ring to her daughter, and she then to her daughter. Emilia married the good blacksmith without a ring and without any hope for true happiness—she was still in love with Ludwig."

"Then what happened?" Aidan moved closer to me.

"Emilia died," I whispered. "She died in childbirth, as did the baby."

"No!" Aidan cried out.

We both jumped and then looked at the bed. Charlie didn't even stir. I couldn't suppress a nervous giggle, which made Aidan grimace.

"What happened to Ludwig?"

"He made it back home, but when he learned that Emilia and his daughter were dead—"

"Don't tell me. I can guess."

"Ludwig took his own life in 1619, six months after Emilia's marriage to the blacksmith."

Aidan turned to the window.

"My direct ancestor wasn't Emilia," I said quietly, "but her sister Maria. Ever since then, all women of my mother's bloodline marry under the blessing of the ring. And all the brides who didn't wear the ring at the wedding for one reason or other—"

"Died." Now Aidan was scrutinising me.

"Yes, either they died or there was some other calamity. What's certain is that every marriage that took place without the ring ended no later than six months after—more often than not tragically. Maybe it was just coincidence or the relationships fell apart due to incompatibility, which happens all the time."

I suddenly had a strange thought. Until that moment, I'd never actually doubted that Justus and I were well matched. We'd always just worked—like a watch you forget about because it's always on your wrist. Being with Aidan, on the other hand, was like carrying around an overactive alarm clock that constantly reminded you to stay awake. I realised I was staring at Aidan and quickly looked away.

"To this day, my grandmother is convinced that a couple's happiness depends on the bride wearing that ring at the wedding."

"Do you think she's right?"

"Maybe? I don't know anymore. I mean, I spent so many years committed to not believing in all that mumbo jumbo that I actually suppressed some very strange events."

I felt goosebumps on my arms, thinking of a distantly related aunt who had hanged herself in the basement of her Berlin apartment. Instead of a note, they found two airline tickets for an around-the-world honeymoon trip in her name and the name of her new husband. Why would someone about to fulfil her lifelong dream commit suicide?

I was surprised at how good it made me feel that Aidan didn't think I was crazy. He just sat there—chin in his hands, forehead furrowed—as if he were deciphering a code.

"What do you think?"

Aidan took my hand, turned it palm up, and gently traced the many lines with his thumb while searching for words. Then my mobile phone rang, shattering the intimate moment. Aidan's expression hardened and he let go of my hand.

"I believe you have to find this ring, and you definitely shouldn't get married without it."

This was not the answer I had expected.

"You're probably right," I said quickly, noticing how aloof I suddenly sounded. "My grandmother is incredibly important to me and it would be awful if she didn't come to the wedding. I mean, we chose the buttercream cake specifically for her." With a forced smile, I gestured to Charlie. "I just hope the little monster didn't toss the ring into one of your lochs—I'm a lousy swimmer."

Aidan ignored my lame joke. I glanced nervously at the still-squawking phone on the windowsill. Why hadn't I left it in my room?

"It's only two weeks away and I can't wait, sort of. Justus says—" But Aidan didn't give me the chance to talk more nonsense.

He got up and pushed his chair in, lining the legs up meticulously with the legs of the table.

"I'm not concerned about your grandmother, Josefine," he said when he was done. "And I don't know Justus. But I do know you and don't want you to be unhappy, whether it's because of the ring or because of a falling-out with your grandmother. That's all. Now I think it's time for me to go."

And he was gone, leaving me alone with Charlie and a gaping hole inside that had nothing to do with the fact that I was still hungry.

14

I woke up in a small bedroom with an oriental-looking rug, the sun already trying to squeeze through the heavy curtains. I was lying on top of the blankets instead of under them, still fully dressed, unable to remember how I got there. I only remembered the door in Charlie's room, white with a copper handle, and the sound it made when it slammed shut behind Aidan. At some point afterwards, I must have dragged myself here and passed out.

Groaning, I turned on my stomach and pressed my face into the pillow. I was not interested in what the morning had to offer, or the day, or those that would follow.

I held my breath, even though blood was already pounding in my ears. I would simply lie here until I died. With any luck, my problem would dissolve on its own. My *problems*. Plural.

Seconds later, I had to come up for air. All right, maybe suffocating myself wasn't a good solution to my problems. I squinted at the Laura Ashley wallpaper until I realised it was a pattern of thistle flowers. That woke me up completely.

I all but flew across the hall, flung open the white door, and stopped short. The two people on the bed jerked apart. Charlie looked at me with wide-open eyes as if I was a ghost, and Ian quickly turned away. He wasn't fast enough—I saw he was crying.

"I'm sorry," I stammered, and went to leave.

"Please don't go, Jo," Charlie croaked.

She still looked frail and exhausted, and had difficulty speaking. Her face was covered with red dots. But her eyes were radiant and the trademark mischievous sparkle was back. She sat very straight with her hands in her lap.

"I could come back later." I looked at Ian, who was now standing at the window.

He turned to me with such a sad look that I wanted to go over and hug him. But the sight of a very much alive Charlie pulled me in all directions like a bunch of kids fighting for the same doll.

It had been easy the day before. Fear for my cousin's safety had trumped everything else. But the danger was past now. Something else had reclaimed a place in my heart, advising me to suffocate the little monster with Finola's ruffled pillows.

Ian and Charlie exchanged a look.

"I've got something important to take care of." Ian walked by me stiffly, like a condemned man on the way to the gallows. He lightly touched my arm as if trying to apologise for letting me see his tears.

I watched him leave, unsure what moved me more—Ian, who openly showed his emotions, or the intense connection between him and my cousin that remained in the room even though he had left.

"His father has cancer," Charlie said quietly.

"I know." I hoped for Aidan's sake it hadn't been Finola but Aidan who'd told him.

"So, are you going to come give me a hug? The nice French doctor said I'm not contagious anymore. *Pas du tout.*" Charlie strained to clear her throat. "Is something going on between him and Aunt Li?"

I couldn't find words, couldn't move. Was I in shock?

Charlie put on a face I knew far too well. "Please don't be mad at me."

She was pushing the wrong button. She might not even have done it on purpose, but I hated it when she made puppy-dog eyes to get out of trouble. She had made this face when she drove Li's fancy car into a wall and then sobbed so uncontrollably that Li bought her a car of her own to console her. I, on the other hand, got an hour-long sermon when I brought Li's bicycle home with a flat tyre—even though it was Charlie who had insisted on riding on the luggage rack.

"What makes you think I'm mad?" The bitterness in my voice startled even me, but I couldn't stop now. "Could it be because you dragged me on a wild goose chase across half of Scotland a few weeks before my wedding? Maybe because I put my job at risk and jeopardised my marriage? Should I be mad because I was scared to death on the plane, had to spend four days with our crazy aunts, and have barely slept or eaten this whole time? This trip has been a rain-soaked nightmare where everything that can go wrong does." I took a deep breath and snarled, "While you luxuriated in your oh-so-perfect love story, I've been through hell. If it hadn't been for Aidan . . . God, Charlie! Yesterday I thought you were going to die."

I was strangely satisfied when I saw her dismay.

Quieter, but with no less hostility, I continued, "Oh no, dearest cousin, I'm not mad. I am so furious that I'd beat the living daylights out of you if you weren't still sick."

"Aidan?" A tiny smile played around Charlie's lips. "I knew it. I knew it would work."

"Excuse me?"

I felt my jaw drop. Instead of hanging her head in shame, Charlie was beaming as if she'd just won the lottery.

"All we wanted was to open your eyes." Her voice almost cracked in excitement. "Get you off the hamster wheel you've been running on for years. If I understood it right yesterday about what's going on between you and Aidan, then our plan with the ring was dead on. I'm so happy you finally realised what a complete moron Justus is!" She clapped her hands and giggled like a ten-year-old watching the scene in *Peter Pan* where Captain Hook gets eaten by the croc.

"Wait!" I raised my hand.

It wasn't the fact that my cousin, supposedly delirious with fever, had eavesdropped on my conversation with Aidan. It also wasn't much of a surprise that she'd stolen the ring to make me go on this trip, and her "moron" comment was not out of character. It was something else that rang every alarm bell in my head.

"Who is 'we'?"

A deep-seated, smouldering hunch made its way to the surface of my consciousness, where it transformed into a bubbling, neon-coloured certainty.

Charlie went pale. "Oh shit!" She burrowed deeper into the pillows and pulled up the blanket as if she wanted to hide under it.

The silence between us simmered for a while. The longer I looked at my cousin, the more certain I was. She was breathing hard, fumbling for words. But I beat her to it.

"Grandmother was behind this from the very start." My voice was devoid of emotion. It didn't even tremble.

Charlie pulled the cover up to her nose. There was no way out and she knew it.

"It was even her idea."

I was at her bed in four steps and tore away the blanket. Charlie squealed and then was wracked by a coughing fit.

"Who else is in on it? Mama? Bri and Li? Spill it, Charlie."

"Aunt Li has no idea, I swear. You know her. She'd have blabbed."

"What about Mama and Bri?"

Charlie's eyes watered—she flailed her hands and gasped for air. I picked up the bottle of water on the nightstand, but held it close when Charlie reached for it. She grimaced and I raised an eyebrow.

"Okay, we had to involve Aunt Mathilde. We couldn't have got hold of the ring without her. Aunt Bri was against it at first, but then she liked the idea of playing your bodyguard."

Charlie grabbed the bottle, drank greedily, and then let herself fall back onto the ruffled pillows with a relieved moan.

"Why are you always so mean to me?" she asked.

"You should ask yourself that question."

I rubbed the back of my neck and sighed. Of course Bri was in on it. And my mother. That's why she hadn't immediately called the police when the ring was "stolen." I had to admit, unlike my duplicitous great-aunt, I'd never have thought my mother capable of such a convincing performance. She had really seemed stunned and had even tried to talk me out of the trip to Scotland. It was a clever chess move. She knew me well enough to realise that her objections would only strengthen my resolve.

It was outrageous. My family had played me like a fiddle.

"But why?"

I could barely manage a whisper. Trembling and with my legs buckling under me, I dropped onto Charlie's bed. She moved closer to the wall, afraid I would attack her.

"Don't worry. I won't hurt you," I mumbled, thinking about the last conversation I'd had with my grandmother. Why didn't she tell me that she disapproved of the marriage? Not even Mama ever uttered a bad word about my relationship with Justus. Why would the people I loved resort to such methods?

"We meant well."

Charlie's pale hand crept across the blanket like a tiny animal and gently nudged my knee.

"Honestly, we were worried. You're so dogged, single-minded—in everything. We thought, maybe if you got away from Frankfurt and had time to think about this marriage, it—"

"It still would be my choice—mine alone."

"True. It's your choice, but—"

"There is no but, Charlie. I'm going to marry Justus. That was the plan a week ago, and that's the plan today. I'm not going to dump my partner of nine years just because"—*Some Scottish guy made plum pudding of my heart*—"some people think they know what's best for me. There is no change of plan. Period."

My heart was pounding so hard that I was sure Charlie could hear it. I was sweating, burning up with fear that my life would end up in chaos. None of them understood.

This fear often seized me at night, gripping my throat, but this was the first time I'd experienced it during the day. Even as a child, I'd had a passion for order. I always tidied up everything I could reach—cutlery trays, boxes of buttons, the tools in the shed. I loved to sort books alphabetically and clean out my knapsack. My first appointment book was a revelation. It brought order to the adult world of which I was afraid long before entering it.

I had made rough drafts for everything ever since—driver's licences, high school exit exams, university studies, jobs, friendships, and relationships. Nobody had any idea how much I depended on my future being predictable and clear. Even if I supposedly missed some of life's beauty along the way, I needed bulleted lists like I needed air. That was the sad secret of my professional success. And I needed this marriage because it would save me from chaos and failure.

I raised my chin and looked straight at Charlie for so long that she lowered her eyes.

"Grandmother says—"

"What Grandmother wants, most of all, is for me to wear the bride's ring when I walk down the aisle. She'll get her wish, even if she doesn't approve of the man at my side." The words hurt, but they sounded harsh enough to hide my panic.

Charlie looked sad. "Justus will make you unhappy, and you know it. You're just not willing to admit it to yourself." She sat up in bed and took my hand. "Life doesn't follow predetermined plans. It isn't perfect. When new doors open, it's so incredibly precious. Please don't run away from them."

"Where is the ring, Charlie?" I withdrew my hand and moved away from her.

"Are you listening to me at all, Jo?"

"Where?"

"I don't have it anymore," she whispered.

"What the hell do you mean?"

"It . . . it wasn't planned. We ran out of money and had to somehow make it to Aunt Finola in Kincraig. So I took it to a pawnshop—"

"You did *what*?" I gasped for air. "Tell me it's not true. Tell me you didn't pawn a centuries-old family heirloom for a bus ticket."

"I was going to redeem it on time with the money from Ian's gig in Inverness! But then everything went wrong."

"Where's the pawnshop?"

"In Edinburgh." Charlie swallowed with difficulty. "Mr. MacGrady promised he wouldn't put it up for sale for a few days. I thought that gave me tons of time, but then I got sick and Ian cancelled the show. So by now . . . Jo, where are you going?"

My temples pulsated with pain. My chest moved up and down, but no air reached my lungs. Breathe. I had to breathe. Outside. I headed for the door with clenched fists.

"Going to see Mr. MacGrady to pick up *my* ticket home."

I managed to tiptoe past the kitchen—the sound of clattering dishes, the smell of fresh coffee—without being noticed. Then I almost ran straight into Bri in the yard.

I pressed myself up against the wall of the house just in time and watched as my aunt took Hank for a walk, chatting to him cheerfully. She held his leash like a set of reins, fists raised and arms bent. It didn't seem to bother Hank that Bri had mistaken him for a horse. He trot-ted next to her and responded to her words with an occasional wag of his tail.

Vexed, I watched the odd couple until they disappeared from my field of vision. Bodyguard, my foot. Bri was as good at being a body-guard as a Doberman is at herding sheep.

I heard voices coming from the bench by the lake where I would have liked to stop and think things over. Li and Monsieur Barneau sat together, wrapped in blankets. With Li's cooing laughter still in my ear, I went the long way around the garden. Stumbling over roots and brambles, I ended up on the trail that had already cost me a shoe once. I briefly flirted with the idea of returning to the boathouse, but lost my nerve and turned towards the barn.

The wooden door was ajar. Relieved, I slipped into the semi-darkness that welcomed me with the sweetish scent of straw and dog. Gardening tools hung on the walls. I made my way past waist-high containers filled with fodder, bags of potting soil, and a dusty riding mower, trying not to make any noise. All of the kennels but one were empty. I looked cautiously inside and met the watchful eyes of a Border collie surrounded by five or six whimpering furry bundles.

"Hey, girl," I whispered.

She wagged her tail. Without thinking, I pushed up the bolt, went into the kennel, and sat down at a respectful distance. The mama dog paid me no mind, too focused on the blackish-brown explorer who had climbed onto her back.

Within seconds, I had two puppies in my lap, gnawing on my fingers with their tiny teeth. Exhaling deeply, I smiled.

"It never ceases to amaze me what effect animal babies have on people," an amused voice said behind me. "Especially women."

I closed my eyes—my quiet moment alone just was not to be.

"Did Aunt Bri sic you on me?" I asked, lifting my chin.

Aidan was wearing a cowboy hat and chewing on a piece of straw—a cliché come to life, even though it would have been a more fitting look in Wyoming or Montana. Still, it was a very appealing stereotype, complete with a lumberjack shirt under which I knew a fire-spewing dragon hid.

I quickly shooed away the image and focused on the puppy I had christened Little Hank. It was about to pee on my lap. I set the protesting yapper and his sibling back down in the straw.

"Why would your aunt put me on your trail?" Aidan asked.

I shrugged and tried to look casual. I got up with stiff knees and awkwardly brushed straw and dog hair from my jeans.

"Are you quite all right, Mrs. Stone?"

I shook my head and stared at the ground. I couldn't even laugh or yell about his calling me "Mrs. Stone" again. I felt no joy. On the contrary, everything in me was in messy, unbearable disorder.

"How's Ian?" I asked without answering, kneading my fingers.

"He's left to see Dad."

"And how is your dad?"

If Aidan was surprised by my sudden interest in his family, he didn't show it.

He scratched his chin. "Well, the old man has weathered worse storms. And the doctors are optimistic, even though Dad's fallen into the habit of acting as if the end is near. Sometimes, I even suspect he enjoys all the attention. I do hope, though, that he makes his peace with Ian and doesn't show him the door a second time."

"How about Finola? Has she come to terms with it? She seems very sad."

"She wants Dad to stay at her guesthouse. He'll drive her and Uncle Angus crazy, but she's determined."

"That's good." I nodded hastily. "Sounds like family."

Family. The word tasted bitter in my mouth, and I grimaced.

"So you talked to your cousin."

For a fraction of a second, I was tempted to deny it. But Aidan reached out and lifted my chin with one finger, forcing me to look directly into his eyes.

"Good," he nodded. "Where's the ring?"

"In Edinburgh," I murmured. "She pawned it."

The surprise on his face was almost immediately replaced by a grin. He turned and charged out of the kennel.

"What're you waiting for, Mrs. Stone?" he shouted over his shoulder. "Let's drive to our bonny capital."

Aidan parked on a quiet side street near Princes Street Gardens with an impressive view of Edinburgh Castle. Shivering, I turned up the collar of my trench coat and braced myself against the wind that had almost ripped the car door out of my hand.

The tiny store on Rose Street was the fifth we had visited, and looked least like a pawnshop.

We hadn't found Thompson & Halberry in the Yellow Pages, arriving there more or less by accident. The saleslady in pawnshop number four, who smirked at my yellow Border collie jumper before flirting openly with Aidan, knew old Mr. MacGrady. She'd visited his shop herself a few months before to have a necklace appraised since he was regarded as a jewellery expert.

I warily looked up at the decaying brick building. Someone had taped newspaper over the small shop window from the inside, and it took a moment for my tired brain to connect the dots. I stared at the note on the green door, the message written on it with a felt-tip pen—"Out of Business."

The ground seemed to open up under my feet. I read the sign a second time, then a third.

"That just can't be true." Aidan took a sharp breath and reached out to ring the doorbell.

"Don't."

"Why?" he replied. "Just because the shop's closed doesn't necessarily mean the inventory's been sold off."

"The ring's gone," I said, holding on to the shoulder strap of my handbag as if it was a lifeline. "Let's forget it."

"But you need that ring!"

I had to smile. His hair was tousled by the wind and his green eyes flashed defiantly through the drizzle. Had he worn a kilt and a sword, he would have given Li's romantic heroes a run for their money.

"Sometimes you just have to accept that fate has a mind of its own," I heard myself say.

"Sure—if you're talking about natural disasters or something. In this case, though, you should at least give it a try. Destiny likes to play games, so let's deal and draw cards." He gestured to the bell. "If nobody answers, maybe the ring is lost. But if—"

"Then we'll find out they've sold it," I said.

"So what? Mr. MacGrady can probably tell us who bought the ring." He raised his hands, palms up. "There's always another card in the deck, Josefine. After this, fate has the next move. Then it's our turn again. Those are the rules."

"You never give up, do you?" I grumbled, secretly admiring his unwavering belief that everything would turn out all right. "Why are you still helping me? What's in it for you?"

"You mean other than the fact that Ian has come home because of you and that I'm in your debt?" He smiled wryly. "I only can repeat myself, Mrs. Stone . . ."

His hand shot forward and rang the bell.

"I just want you to be happy."

15

"It's okay," I whispered, even though nothing was.

We had been sitting in the parked truck in front of the former pawnshop for half an hour, silently watching the wind rattling shutters and parking signs, churning puddles, and tearing young plants from window boxes.

After Aidan had pushed the doorbell several times, then held it down for what seemed like forever, a woman had opened a window on the second floor and shouted that the MacGradys had moved away a few days ago. She told us that the couple had grown tired of city life and moved to some godforsaken village further north. She said it was such a wretched place that she couldn't even remember its name. What she did remember, though, was that they'd said only a trail led to their house, and it was impassable in winter. "They're off their rocker" was her final assessment, before she shut her window loudly and indignantly.

"Off their rocker," Aidan imitated the grating voice of the neighbour, drumming against the steering wheel.

"I doubt it." I twirled a strand of hair around a finger.

We looked at each other. The corners of Aidan's mouth were twitching and my mouth stretched sideways all on its own. We burst into laughter. We laughed in the same way we had been silent—helplessly and longer than necessary—until our faces were red and tears rolled down our cheeks. Eventually, silence fell again, this time a much lighter one. I don't think I'd ever felt so close to anyone before.

I pulled out my mobile phone, remembering that I hadn't checked it the day before when its buzzing had interrupted us. I found a text message from Justus, sent at two in the morning. It consisted of just four words:

I am in Edinburgh.

For a moment, the earth stopped turning.

Aidan cleared his throat. "Well, you shouldn't leave Scotland without trying our legendary fish and chips," he said, motioning to a small food stall on the corner. "Why don't I go grab us some?" He looked at the phone in my hand. "It'll probably take a few minutes for them to make it, so you can . . ." He didn't finish, but opened the door. "Ketchup or mayo?"

I gaped. He might just as well have asked me whether I wanted to be shot or beheaded.

"Okay, both. Good choice."

I watched him saunter along the path, hands buried in his coat pockets. He jumped over some puddles and stepped aside for a woman with a rollator walker. She lifted her umbrella in gratitude, to which he responded with a friendly greeting. Then he crossed the street and disappeared into the fish and chip shop.

Justus picked up on the first ring. I didn't give him time to speak.

"What do you mean, 'I am in Edinburgh'?"

"I thought you'd be glad," he answered after a short pause that echoed in my ears.

"But . . . why?" I stuttered helplessly. "I mean, of course I'm glad. It's just . . . unexpected."

"Sorry about that. I know you don't like surprises."

Wrong. I just hated to be caught off guard.

"Like the saying goes—if Mohammed won't come to the mountain . . . I missed you, Finchen."

"Where are you?"

"I'm at the Grand Duchesse. Hard to believe this monstrosity got a five-star rating. The Wi-Fi is a joke. When can you get here to rescue me?"

"I . . ." I saw a young couple leave the fast-food shop, their arms around each other.

"Listen, sweetie. I know you're going through something difficult right now—even though I don't understand what. You needed me and I wasn't there. But I'm here now, in Scotland. Isn't this every woman's dream—the man you love chases you halfway around the globe? Well, almost."

This was followed by his usual laugh—slightly nasal, as if he had a cold. Even though everybody else made fun of it, I had always liked his laugh.

"Come on, don't leave me hanging here. We'll find a better hotel, spend one or two days shopping in the city, and then fly back to Frankfurt. Because, in case you forgot, we still have the tiny, inconsequential matter of organising a wedding to do."

"I haven't forgotten. Believe me."

My voice sounded hoarse. I was still staring at the door to the fish and chip shop, but Aidan was taking his time. Or maybe giving me time. He had this uncanny ability to sense—

Wait a minute! I was on the phone with the man I was about to marry. This was not the right time to think about Aidan Murray—not now, and even less so later on.

"I'll be there in an hour, Justus."

It wasn't that hard to sound resolute, and glad. Yes, I was happy, very happy. Justus was my home—who wouldn't like going back home?

"I love you, Finchen."

"Yes, I—"

At that moment, Aidan stepped outside with two large paper bags in his hands, and I completely forgot what I was going to say. Not only did it look like he had ordered enough to feed an entire rugby team, he had also donned a silly hat advertising the fast-food place and a matching cardboard nose. I couldn't help giggling.

"How lovely that you find my declaration of love so amusing," Justus said, sounding peeved.

A little boy stopped on the path, tugged on his mother's sleeve, and, chuckling, pointed at Aidan, who doffed his hat and waddled in my direction, Charlie Chaplin style. The boy shook with laughter until his mother pulled him away.

Pull yourself together, Josefine.

"See you soon, Justus. I just have to take care of something first."

I hung up and dropped the phone back into my bag. A foolish, totally inappropriate pain swept through my chest.

Aidan hopped into the driver's seat. The odour of fried food triggered a nausea in me that couldn't be smiled away, no matter how hard I tried. Aidan noticed this and put the food in the back seat. He inhaled deeply and steadily, the way I always did when I was trying to stay in control. Then he started the truck.

"Where are we going?" he asked calmly. His serious eyes told me that he already knew what I didn't dare to say.

That was the moment I realised how much Aidan meant to me. That was the moment my heart broke.

"The Grand Duchesse hotel," I said in a flat voice, my hands clenched in my lap, staring at the dashboard. Nothing more needed to be said.

The Grand Duchesse was, without doubt, one of the most impressive hotels in Edinburgh. It fit Justus to a tee—luxurious and over the top, a hypermodern glass palace behind a historical church façade, an old jewel in a new setting of glass and steel.

A week ago, I might have rolled my eyes at such excess, but now it really bothered me. I was annoyed that my fiancé wanted to be "rescued" from a place far beyond the reach of ordinary mortals—crummy Wi-Fi or not.

Aidan, on the other hand, was clearly unimpressed. He scrutinised the liveried bellboy, who had positioned himself at my door with an umbrella, with an expression of disgust that could also have been pity. Then he took his hands off the steering wheel and turned off the engine.

I fought the temptation to stare at the dashboard again. Every button had imprinted itself on my brain on the drive here, but I still had no idea what to say to Aidan.

"So . . ." I said, and unfastened my seat belt awkwardly.

"So," Aidan echoed. "Should I tell your aunts that—"

"Yes. Please tell them that I'll call . . . and to mail my luggage. There's nothing in my suitcase that I need right away."

"What about Charlie?"

I blinked. Charlie. I'd totally forgotten her.

"I'll give her your regards." Aidan rubbed his chin. "You two will work things out eventually. Don't worry. The lass is in good hands with us."

"I know that. Thank you," I said softly, folding my hands in my lap.

The bellboy bounced impatiently and switched the umbrella to his other hand. Aidan grinned.

"You shouldn't make the fellow wait too long, otherwise you won't be able to afford the tip."

"Yeah," I replied with a forced smile, trying to ignore the fluttering in my stomach.

"Goodbye, Mrs. Stone. Take good care of yourself," he said quietly, and bent over to me.

I held my breath, but his lips merely brushed my cheek.

"Goodbye, Mr. Murray."

There was no reason to stay any longer. The ring was lost, but I had given it my best shot. I would write a note to Li right away so she wouldn't worry. And Charlie was free to do as she pleased. What was important now was that Justus was here because of me. He was set on bringing his bride home. What could be more romantic—especially coming from someone so disinclined to romance?

So, then, why the hell did I feel that the world would end if I got out of Aidan's truck? I exhaled, slowly and deliberately. *Control.* I had to regain control of my brain, and of my emotions—heck, I had to regain control of my entire life.

I lowered my head and got out of the truck. The young bellhop, no older than twenty, had blemished skin and a gap between his front teeth large enough to accommodate an extra tooth.

The feeling that more needed to be said came unexpectedly while I stared into the boy's green eyes that were similar to Aidan's. There were a hundred things I wanted to tell Aidan, or at least one thing . . . I took a step back, out from under the umbrella and into the rain, and turned around. The truck was gone.

"How can I help you, ma'am?"

The receptionist's short blonde hair was slicked back, giving her face a strange sternness.

"I'm here to see Dr. Grüning." I pointed to her name tag—Mercedes Delafonte. "Wow, I'd kill for a name like that!"

She looked up with a surprised smile, but quickly reverted to faux friendliness, making it clear that there was no bridging the desk between us.

Embarrassed, I turned around. I was uneasy in this place, where even the cleaning lady in her blue smock was better dressed than I. To make matters worse, the entire foyer had mirrored walls to show me that I looked worse than Cinderella.

I had washed up in the lobby of a five-star hotel in rubber boots and a baggy Border collie jumper that hung to my thighs. My face was red, and the only accessory that gave any indication of the old me was my Louis Vuitton purse. It must have looked like I'd stolen it.

Sighing, I concentrated on Mercedes's chiselled face. She seemed to be waiting for something. I hoped she didn't think I was a homeless person, or a criminal.

"Sorry?" I asked.

"Is Mr. Grüning a guest in our establishment?" Mercedes repeated.

"Since he's a so-so cook and has no idea about tools or cleaning, I'd say that he indeed is a guest."

She granted me a brief smile and began to type on her computer. "Are you expected, Mrs. . . . ?"

"Josefine," I answered quietly. "Josefine Sonnenthal."

Mercedes nodded and continued typing. I brushed a strand of hair behind my ear.

"I've had a hard couple of days. Normally, I'm . . ." *Different?*

It was the truth. I usually was different, but I wasn't sure I wanted my normal self back, especially since Mercedes now looked at me with a smile that seemed genuine and even somewhat empathetic.

"There's a note saying he's expecting you. Room four-two-eight, fourth floor."

I thanked her and turned towards the lift.

"Mrs. Sonnenthal," Mercedes called after me.

I stopped, my heart pounding. She was probably going to ask me to use the staff staircase.

"Thank you. I think your name is very pretty, too."

A few minutes later, I was standing in front of Justus's door, a news anchor's professionally agitated voice blaring behind it. The sound dropped away when I knocked. As footsteps approached, I eyed the lit "Exit" sign at the end of the hall.

What would happen if I bolted? Just thinking about it was wrong and childish. But imagining the expression on Justus's face was priceless. The door opened.

"Hello, Justus," I said, forcing myself to look at him.

He looked fabulous.

"Good god, Finchen. You look horrible."

"And you sound like my mother." I grimaced to take the edge off my sharp response, but he had already pulled me into his arms.

"I'm so glad you're here."

"So am I," I said, and I really meant it. It felt good to snuggle up against his strong body, my face against his smooth cheek. He smelled crisp and clean, like the pile of fresh towels our cleaning lady put in our bathroom cabinet every Friday.

Justus hugged me so tight it almost hurt. Then he pushed me away a little and looked me up and down, lingering on my silly rubber boots. His square jaw twitched and I knew he wanted to make a derogatory remark. But he controlled himself and instead looked up and down the hallway.

"Did you leave your luggage in the lobby?"

"That's a long story," I said cautiously, checking his reaction.

Should I tell him everything, or skip the . . . inconsequential details? Aidan's haunting green eyes appeared in front of me. Since I didn't respond to his questioning look, Justus stepped aside.

"Well, come in. You look tired."

He went ahead into the room—a suite, actually, with a living room and a work space behind a glass partition. The screen saver on his laptop showed a beach on Martinique, where we had spent our winter vacation five years ago. A wildly gesticulating BBC reporter was on the flat-screen TV, reporting mutely from the London stock exchange.

I sat down on the Cubist leather sofa and was surprised at how deep I sank. Justus stood next to me while I pretended to study the financial ticker on the TV and remembered the last time I had tried my luck with lip-reading. I really should call my mother and confront her.

The silence was growing uncomfortable. I briefly considered asking about the office, but thought better of it. The great Maibach and his cigar-stained fingers would get hold of me again soon enough.

"Something to drink?"

Justus strolled to the minibar, took out a bottle of Chablis, and got two glasses from a sideboard.

"Maybe a beer—dark, if there is one."

"Since when do you like beer?"

I didn't know how to answer.

With a shrug, he took out a bottle. It was the same brand Aidan had ordered for me in Gavin's pub. Something tightened in me again. Justus sat down in the chair opposite me and watched me take a sip, visibly irritated that I didn't use a glass.

"You look like you've been through hell."

Funny. I hadn't expected a remark like that. Relieved by his surprising empathy, I finally relaxed, ready to tell him everything. But he spoke first.

"Let's get you into the shower first and wash off some of this mess. In the meantime, I'll have them bring up something pretty to wear and some shoes from the boutique downstairs. You'll feel like a new person afterwards, you'll see. Tomorrow we can go shopping on the Royal Mile and buy some more appropriate things."

I closed my mouth and looked down at myself, at the jumper that was already frayed at the sleeves. I suddenly realised I had grown fond of this scratchy, loyal companion that had braved the elements and kept me from catching a cold.

"A shower sounds wonderful, darling." I smiled weakly. "And it would be nice of you to arrange for some clothes for me. I wear—"

"Finchen." Justus shook his head, grinning. "I'm your future husband. I know your social security number and the phone number of your gynaecologist. I know you love Debussy, what lottery numbers you play, and that you're crazy for Kimoto's sushi. Of course I know your dress size."

He got up and went to the bar again to uncork the wine bottle. He poured a glass for himself, glanced at his laptop, and then looked at the TV.

I scrutinised him silently, this tall, Hugo Boss-clad man with tanned, long, pianist fingers, elegantly swirling the wine in his glass. He turned to me and I saw a gentleness and affection that somehow reminded me of my father.

"Everything all right?" he asked in his confident way that never left room for an answer other than yes.

I felt a wave of warmth in my body. This man was more than just my safe haven. Even looked at objectively, Justus Grüning was perfect— and he loved me.

"Everything's fine," I said, pushing aside everything that had turned my heart inside out these past few days. Ring or not, Grandmother or not—even if the entire family was against this wedding, it no longer mattered. It was me, after all, who was starting a family with this perfect specimen of a man—another flawless star on my to-do list, and the sooner I checked it off, the better.

"If you don't mind, I'd rather do without the shopping tour and fly back to Frankfurt as soon as possible—tonight, even," I said rather louder than necessary, as if trying to shout over my stupid heart, which kicked against my ribs like an unruly kid, shouting "Aidan" again and again.

This time, I was not going to be confused by mood swings and flights of fancy. I'd had it with this constant balancing act of external cold and internal heat. It would be best to return as soon as possible to the moderate climes of everyday life with Justus.

Justus turned back to the TV and became lost in the world of stock market winners and losers. "No problem. I'll take care of it," he mumbled. "We'll be out of here by tomorrow morning at the latest."

The kiss I blew fell unseen to the floor. All right, I still had to work on getting him to pay attention to me, but that was a minor detail.

I slipped off the rubber boots and headed to the bathroom. Taking a shower wasn't just a great idea—it was brilliant.

"Did you ever find your crazy cousin?" Justus called after me.

I felt a stabbing pain near my chest. Images appeared, staccato and in quick succession, like in the Super 8 films Papa used to shoot at Christmas. The reels showed Ian and Charlie, communicating without words, holding hands. I saw Charlie's face in close-up, exhausted and ill, but beaming with happiness—someone who had found her place in life. There was nothing of the old, angry Charlie in this woman, and it was beautiful. I was deeply sorry I wouldn't have a chance to tell her that any time soon.

I slowly turned back. "No, I didn't find her."

Justus snorted. "That's what I thought. Good. This way, she won't wreak havoc at the wedding."

Shaking his head, he turned up the TV, indicating that he had already filed away Charlotte von Meeseberg as a hopeless case, despite clear legal precedents.

16

"Well, I'll be damned," a smoky voice shouted across the salon. "Frau Sonnenthal! Is it really you?"

She was right to be surprised. I was doing something I'd always sworn I would never do—I had entered a client's shop for my own purposes. She was a previous client, to be precise, which made matters more acceptable—if only slightly.

I looked over my shoulder. Bri frowned, while Li seemed a little anxious, which I fully understood. Frau Ziegelow was intimidating, the way she rushed towards us on dizzyingly high stilettos, her bracelets jingling. In the blink of an eye, I was swept up in her soft, perfumed embrace, and knew I had been right to come here.

Frau Ziegelow then held me at arm's length away and looked at me closely, missing neither my red eyes nor the shadows below them that even a thick layer of concealer couldn't hide. Then she looked at my hair and gasped.

"Goodness gracious. I hope you are suing the person who committed this crime."

She gave me no time to answer, but grabbed my arm and guided me, like an emergency room patient, towards a hairdressing chair that had just opened up.

"I actually just came in to make an appointment. I'm sure you're very busy today," I protested weakly while glancing to the chic grey-and-pink waiting area.

Salon Tausendschön was bursting with customers on this Saturday afternoon. I could feel the disgruntled looks of the waiting clients who realised right away that I'd jumped the queue.

"Bah, nonsense! These fine ladies can wait—the Armageddon on your head can't. Besides, a little waiting helps them sufficiently appreciate what they're wasting their money on," Frau Ziegelow whispered in my ear, regally raising a hand when the receptionist, dressed in a skin-tight catsuit, approached with the appointment book in her hands. The girl spun around immediately and offered a cappuccino to a client with an already-impeccable pageboy hairdo, presumably to make up for the delay.

I dropped into the pink imitation-leather chair, which squeaked under my behind—and almost burst into tears when I saw myself in the mirror. My hair really was catastrophic—it was the icing on top of everything that had happened recently. Ever since Bri and Li had returned to Frankfurt and we'd resumed wedding preparations, I'd watched myself mutate into a bundle of nerves with each advancing hour. Li's botched flower order was only partially to blame, as was the pneumonia that befell the woman who was supposed to sing at the church. In the past, I would have easily handled these small to moderate mishaps with a cool head and lawyerly calm. Now, I more or less sat by impassively and allowed Li and Bri to make the chaos even more perfect. But when Bri's friend Mechthild had experimented with my hairstyle, I'd bawled like a baby.

And I was supposed to be happy.

I swallowed and raised my chin. Frau Ziegelow, now flanked by my aunts, was standing behind my chair, grinning with a mixture of mirth and disbelief. Li patted my shoulder and made whimpering noises until Bri gave her a little shove.

"How could we have known she'd give her an eighties perm? Anyway, it's the best Afro I've seen in ages."

"I told you that someone who cheats at cards like Mechthild does can't be trusted with anything," hissed Li. "Josie looks more like Mechthild's dreadful poodle than a future bride!"

"Bride?" Frau Ziegelow scrutinised my face in the mirror while wrapping a pink smock around my shoulders. "So you're going through with it? You're marrying your . . . 'colleague'?"

I nodded at my reflection in the mirror and widened my lips, but it was obvious even to me that this attempt at a smile didn't reach my eyes.

"Colleague. Good one." Bri winked at Frau Ziegelow and raised a thumb. "Where did you find this woman? I like her."

"Can you save my hair?" I asked.

"I can save anything, so long as it's hair," my client proclaimed, tugging at one of my tight curls.

Bri watched sceptically until she caught my angry look in the mirror and, with a shrug, followed Li to the waiting area.

Even though we had talked things through, I was still mad at Bri. She'd been far less contrite than Mama, whom I had forgiven quickly because I'm no good at dealing with tears. Bri did apologise and even offered to smooth things over between Grandmother and me, as I hadn't felt able to drive to Villa Meeseberg to face her. Worse, I wasn't sure I ever would. Yet the wedding was set for the following Sunday and the mere thought of the empty seat in the first row brought a lump to my throat.

"It would be too risky to treat the perm chemically. We might end up with your hair looking like steel wool." Frau Ziegelow tapped her manicured fingers. "I think it's best if I use a flat iron and then blow-dry the frizz over a styling brush. That way, you'll end up with nice corkscrew curls, and we can create a marvellous up-do with those. How about we just try it out today, and then we'll know what's possible for the big event?"

"You're the expert," I answered, and added softly, "Thank you. I'll never forget this."

"Nonsense. You've done much more for me—it's only fair that I contribute to your unforgettable day." The wary expression appeared on her face again, similar to the one Bri had been wearing of late. "And it will be unforgettable, won't it?"

"Definitely," I answered, wildly determined to hide my doubts.

And I did have doubts.

Not about Justus. I doubted myself.

Since my return to Germany five days ago, I had come to realise that I simply could not pretend that I hadn't changed. I recognised this when I made room for the Border collie jumper among my cashmere pullovers and fought back tears when I realised I would probably never wear it again. Since then, I'd discovered a new eerie trait every single day.

I would get up an hour earlier lately to walk to the office through Greenburg Park. I would have a caramel coffee each morning in the little café on the corner of Sebastian-Rinz Straße and had got to know the waitress, Susanne, with whom I'd never exchanged more than three words before. Buying groceries at the supermarket after work, I would put a six-pack of beer into the cart, and when I saw peppermint drops by the checkout, I almost started to cry. To top it all off, I was breaking one of the holiest rules of lawyers today by having my hair rescued by a client.

"Take a deep breath, child," Frau Ziegelow said into my ear, as if she'd heard my thoughts. "Other than death, there's nothing that cannot be reversed." She paused meaningfully and then continued smoothly.

"Trust me, an hour from now, the world will look rosy again, just as it should for a happy bride."

But her generous smile filled me with dread. *A happy bride.*

An hour later, we were headed to Sachsenhausen in my little car. I had offered to drive Bri and Li home—forgetting that this meant Villa Meeseberg. My pulse rose even before we turned onto Mörfelder Landstraße. I drove up the familiar gravel drive with sweaty palms and stopped on the carpet of white blossoms under the cherry tree. Leaving the motor running, I stared at the stone lions next to the iron gate and counted the seconds until I could get out of there.

Unfortunately, neither Li nor Bri made any move to get out of the car. Bri, her arms crossed, leaned back in the passenger seat and squinted at me while Li patted my artistically pinned-up curls for the hundredth time.

"You look like Sissi! You know, on my favourite painting of the Austrian Empress. It'll be wonderful if Frau Ziegelow can reproduce this for the wedding," she clucked, fascinated by what the master had fashioned out of my poodle frizz.

My face was framed by full and shiny corkscrew curls and Frau Ziegelow had braided genuine daisies into the chignon. Without any doubt, this bridal hairdo was a work of art, but even a perfect bridal up-do wasn't enough to make me look like a happy bride.

I glanced nervously at my watch and then out of the window to the drawing room—almost four thirty. Almost time for Grandmother's tea.

"Since you're here anyway, why don't you come in? There's cake," Bri said with forced casualness.

"Thanks, but I have to watch my weight," I replied, thin-lipped.

Bri laughed hoarsely. "You barely ate in Scotland, young lady. A piece of Li's cheesecake won't hurt you."

"Or even two," Li giggled. "Besides, you should talk to Adele. Tell her that, thanks to her awful plan, the bridal ring is now lost forever. It's not your fault, it's hers."

"The plan wasn't that bad," Bri murmured, but looked away quickly in order not to face my disapproval.

I held on to the steering wheel with both hands and pulled my shoulders up around my ears. I was freezing despite the early summer warmth. "Today was exhausting. I don't feel like talking to Grandmother right now, okay?"

"You'll never feel like having this talk with her," Bri said curtly. She grabbed my chin with her thumb and index finger, forcing me to look at her. "Let's toss a coin. Heads means we get out of this sardine tin of a car without you. Tails means you come in and eat some of the enormous calorie bomb Li baked this morning. Get a coin out of your crochet bag, sis."

"You're a real pain in the neck, Aunt Bri."

"So you'll play?"

"Do I have a choice?"

She grinned and took the coin Li offered. She tossed it into the air and skilfully caught it with one hand.

"Ready?"

"Come on, Bri. Don't keep us in suspense," Li giggled.

The fist came towards me in slow motion. Shaking my head, I stretched out my hand and felt cool metal land on my palm. I held my breath.

A silvery five-pence piece lay in my hand. Facing up wasn't the image of Her Majesty but a tiny crowned thistle, the symbol of Scotland.

While Bri and Li went to their rooms to get changed for tea, I took advantage of the brief reprieve. Instead of marching into the salon to face Grandmother with my head held high, I turned right after my usual salute to my ancestor Philipp and slipped out to the garden through a side door.

Since my great-aunts had never been very passionate gardeners, my grandmother had hired a local gardener to take care of the half-acre of greenery. The old, stooping man had technically retired, but still came by every Tuesday to slowly trim the hedges, prune the apple trees, and mow the lawn. When he got tired, he'd lean on his rake and stare at the house, which used to terrify Charlie and me. We nicknamed him "Scarecrow." By now, I knew that the poor guy had been hopelessly in love with Grandmother for half of his life, while she was equally focused on her great love—my grandfather, Gustav von Meeseberg.

He was the one who had started the kitchen garden, right behind the ivy-covered pergola where we drank Bri's homemade ice tea every summer. Since my grandfather's death, this part of the garden had become Grandmother's refuge. In summer, there was always an abundance of berries. Grandmother taught us how to grow tomatoes, sugar peas, tender baby carrots, and kohlrabi. We snacked on it all until our mouths and fingers were red, our tongues blue, and our bellies so full that there was no room for dinner. It was to this special place I was drawn now, and it was there that I ran into the very person I was trying to avoid.

She was kneeling in a freshly raked bed, weeding without gloves. She had always claimed that the point of gardening was to get in touch with the soil.

"Kohlrabi used to be your favourite," she said without interrupting her work. "Charlie always wanted to eat it right away, right when I pulled it out of the soil, but for you, I had to peel it like an apple, paper-thin rind, and make sure it stayed—"

"All in one piece." I finished quietly.

"You've always liked things to be in one piece."

She got up, groaning, supporting her back with one hand. I stood awkwardly on the narrow woodchip path.

"What you and Charlie dreamt up wasn't very nice," I said, suddenly courageous. The sooner we cleared the air, the sooner I could sleep again.

My grandmother bent down to her weeding pail and freed a little shovel from a nearby molehill. "It's never pleasant to be pushed into cold water, Josefine," she said finally. "Not for the one who does the pushing, either, unless that person is a monster."

"So you sent me all the way to Scotland because you wanted to teach me how to swim," I said sarcastically while warding off a bee that had apparently mistaken my yellow blouse for a flower.

"Well, to extend your metaphor, I just hope you went in deeper than your knees."

My sharp reply got caught in my throat when Grandmother raised her chin and looked at me from under her straw hat. For a moment, I thought she had talked to Charlie, but there was no way Charlie would have called to confess that she pawned the ring. Yes, they had plotted together, but that had surely not been part of the plan, and I wasn't the only family member who feared Adele von Meeseberg's wrath.

"I guess that means that I shouldn't expect an apology." I actually managed to display a half-hearted level of defiance, which bounced off Grandmother like a rubber ball off bulletproof glass.

"Well, I've got nothing against apologising," she said slowly. "If, that is, you tell me that you regret every minute of your journey—every single minute."

My cheeks started to burn. I took a deep breath and forced myself to sound calm and in control, even though I felt like I might swoon from the deep longing her words brought to the surface.

"What I can say is that this *journey*"—I stretched out the word on purpose—"did not change my wedding plans." I couldn't back down. I simply couldn't.

My grandmother inspected me silently. Then she shrugged, hung the pail on the crook of her arm, took the rake, and turned towards the house. Puzzled, I watched her bobbing straw hat and swaying little bucket. I ran after her as well as I could in my heels, which sank into the lawn, once again wishing for comfortable, flat shoes. Rubber boots, even.

"There's something else I have to tell you," I said.

She didn't slow down, but I had to stop to get the terrible words out.

"The ring is gone. Charlie lost it. Are you still going to—" Damn it, *now* my voice was trembling. "Will you still come to the wedding?"

"The library, Josefine. Right now. We have another twenty minutes before tea," Grandmother ordered over her shoulder, disappearing into the house without turning around once.

The library had originally been my grandfather's study. Nothing had been changed after his death—even his pipe still waited for him in the heavy crystal ashtray. While Grandmother sat down behind the imposing desk, I stepped uneasily up to the bookcase on the other side of the room. Very much aware of her eyes on me, I ran my finger over the books' spines: Böll, Hesse, Kleist, Grandfather's Karl May collection, and the collected works of Christian Morgenstern, my grandmother's favourite. Next to it stood thirty volumes of the Brockhaus encyclopaedia, which Li used to consult whenever we got stuck with our homework. Out of habit, I crouched down and looked at the lower shelves. They were still there, the treasures of my childhood—shelved at knee height so that even a four-year-old could reach them. I didn't have a chance to pull out one of the dog-eared, cocoa-stained picture books, since Grandmother cleared her throat and brought me back to the present. I straightened up, went to the desk, and sat down obediently across from her.

"Are you absolutely sure you want to marry this man?"

I nodded, uneasy, playing with the paperweight, a sphere of acrylic glass with a genuine dandelion flower inside. Grandmother seemed to sit up even straighter in her chair after my silent answer, as if a thread were attached to the top of her head, pulling her up. Her silence was difficult to bear, as were her penetrating eyes, the colour of a quiet ocean.

"But I can't wear the ring in front of the altar," I whispered and, to my dismay, felt myself tearing up. "That's why I wanted to beg you—"

"I'm not deaf," she interrupted with a gruff gesture. "I heard what you said in the garden."

My finger clutched the dandelion paperweight so tightly that my knuckles turned white. "And what is your answer?"

"My answer is"—she bent down to open a drawer—"that I won't stand in the way of my favourite granddaughter's happiness."

Confused, I looked at the wooden box that Grandmother pushed towards me.

"What's that?"

"Open it."

A strange smile appeared on her wrinkled face, cheerful and sad at the same time. My heart beat fast as I carefully unlatched the box—then skipped a beat when I looked inside.

"But that's the bridal ring," I whispered, stunned.

"Strictly speaking, it's a reproduction. One of two replicas, to be precise."

My thoughts came thick and fast. "A second copy? That's . . . That means—"

"It means that Charlotte lost a copy of the ring. Don't tell her. A little guilt will do her good." Grandmother shook her head.

"But if Charlie's was a reproduction, and this one is, too . . ." My eyes widened as I pointed to the narrow golden band with a diamond that apparently wasn't a diamond. "Where's the real ring?"

"Lost."

My grandmother slowly got up from the leather chair and went to the window. I only noticed now that she wobbled when she walked and almost imperceptibly dragged her left leg. She gazed at the cherry tree while I waited for her to collect herself. Or maybe it was the other way around, and she was giving me time to pull myself together.

"I lost it," she said softly, more to herself than to me. "It was during a boating trip on the Main, shortly before your grandfather and I got married. I was standing at the railing with my best friend, Annegret. Wanting to brag—giddy with love and silly as I was—I took it off my finger for her to admire." She smiled wistfully. "Sometimes, a gust of wind at the wrong time is all it takes for our dreams to be dashed."

I gasped as the truth sank in. "You married Grandfather without the protection of the bride's ring!"

My grandmother shrugged. "You do whatever it takes if you truly want something, and all I wanted was to marry Gustav von Meeseberg. But your great-grandmother Helene would never have allowed it. After her sister died tragically, she was obsessed with the mystical power of the ring. So I made a drawing of it and secretly commissioned a jeweller to make two identical copies. Just in case something similar happened again." She added dryly, "Didn't take long, did it?"

I couldn't sit still any longer. The dandelion paperweight rolled across the desk and dropped to the Berber carpet with a thud. I left it there and began to pace up and down.

"Just to make sure I understand correctly—the real bride's ring has been resting at the bottom of the Main these past sixty years. The ring I thought was genuine was a reproduction you had made so you could marry Grandfather. What I don't understand is . . ." I stopped and lifted both hands, more helpless than angry. "Why did you make us believe all these years that the ring meant so much to you? You sent me all the way to Scotland, for crying out loud. For what? For a copy of something that turns out to be no more than a fantasy?"

"Who says that it's a fantasy?" Grandmother asked gently.

"Please! I mean, you were happily married your entire life—no tragic disaster or any of that . . . nonsense. Doesn't that prove that it's just a silly superstition?"

How strange. Not only was I hurt and furious, but I was also disappointed like a child who had lost Santa Claus and the Easter Bunny at the same time.

"You should have told me!" I shouted, hardly able to keep it together. "It would have saved me a lot of trouble. Not to mention Li and Bri. I assume that they also didn't know that we were chasing a copy?"

"Oh, I'm sure my little sisters had a grand time in Scotland," Grandmother said. "You brought something back, too, Josefine. Your eyes are far more alive than those of the miserable young woman who stood in this room not so long ago. Moreover, when was the last time you dared talk to me like this?" A tiny smile played on her face. "A little rebellion suits you."

Rebellion? Me? This must be a bad dream. I'd wake up any minute now. But the cool hand that guided me back to my chair felt very real.

"Let me explain, Josefine," Grandmother said, and she sat down as well. She bent forward, propped her elbows on the desk, and clasped her hands as if she were praying. "In the past, the myth of the ring really had only one purpose—it helped the head of the family control who the daughters and granddaughters married. This was very important for a well-to-do family. If a future husband was considered unsuitable, they had the ability to withhold the ring. Disasters in marriages without the ring were welcomed and exaggerated because it reinforced the legend. It was a simple recipe that worked exceedingly well. Over the centuries, the family combined random accidents with the tragic history of our ancestor Emilia, shrouded the whole thing in mystery, and voilà—a perfect system for keeping the girls in line."

She cleared her throat and reached for the water decanter. In a daze, I watched her pour water into a glass in a thin stream, take a few sips, and then wipe her mouth with a handkerchief.

"There were some, of course, who defied the family and married as they wished, but if the unions were happy, they were swept under the rug." Grandmother nodded admiringly. "The mind is capable of amazing feats. It can bring a myth to life. Marriages have become very serious events in our family thanks to this ring. A bride has to consider very carefully to whom she'll say 'I do.' Ideally, the family approves and gives her the ring. But if she's denied it and marries nonetheless, then that proves hers is a true love because, after all, she believes she's risking her life."

Grandmother leaned back in her chair and closed her eyes as if she had to gather all of her strength for what she would say next. I waited with bated breath.

"I kept the myth of the ring alive because it works in both directions—for you, for Charlotte, and for all who come after. It doesn't matter if the diamond is real or a cubic zirconia. It's our belief in its magic that helps us recognise whether we truly love someone. Love is the key to happiness, my little moth. And that's what I wish for you, no more and no less."

Her ice-blue gaze seemed to penetrate my innermost core, making my stomach do cartwheels. I could guess what she'd say next, and I was afraid of my own response.

"The journey you undertook has apparently strengthened your love for Justus. I didn't expect that, but my opinion about the young man is not what matters here. In these modern times, the old should advise, not prohibit. Your heart has spoken to you and, thus, the bride's ring has fulfilled its purpose. So take it and wear it at the ceremony as a symbol of your love and your resolve. You have my blessing."

The curtains billowed in the sudden breeze that drifted through the room, as if the faint, lingering doubt in Grandmother's voice had materialised. I shivered. My grandmother looked at Grandfather's pipe in the crystal ashtray and then at the old grandfather clock, which struck five, making the parquet floor vibrate. We used to lie down flat on the floor to feel it tickle our bellies.

"Let's go to the salon, Josefine. I've felt guilty all day because I'll have to indulge in that rich cake to avoid hurting Li's feelings. Let's get it over with quickly."

I still sat there as if glued to my chair, her words reverberating in my mind—*true love . . . key to happiness . . . my little moth,* a term of endearment Grandmother had always used just for me.

She got up and smiled at me. For the first time in a long time, I didn't feel intimidated by her gaze.

"By the way, your hair looks just lovely," she said softly, and she caressed my cheek as she walked by.

With that, she left me alone with my heart, which bucked like a rodeo pony, kicking me again and again. What hurt most was that Grandmother had been wrong in one decisive respect.

I had no idea what my heart was telling me.

17

It's strange how your world tilts as soon as you look at it from a different perspective. I couldn't stop pondering Grandmother's words—not on the way home, not at dinner with Justus, and not in the shower, where I stood under the hot stream of water for so long it turned my skin lobster red, but still I couldn't wash away these unwelcome feelings. I lay awake all that night, staring at the ceiling, unable to get Aidan out of my mind while my future husband tossed and turned in bed next to me. When I finally fell asleep, the lavender-blue dawn followed me into a short, disturbing dream in which I relaxed into the embrace of a fire-breathing dragon.

"There you are, Frau Sonnenthal."

The authoritative voice catapulted me back into my fishbowl of an office. I could feel Lara give a start next to me, and the dishes on her tray tinkled. How long had she been standing there?

I slipped the bride's ring onto my finger and nodded to Lara. "Please bring another cup of coffee for Dr. Maibach."

My assistant didn't move. She stared at the boss with her mouth half-open, scared and awestruck. No wonder. The mighty Maibach showed his face on the lower floor no more than twice a year, if at all, and mostly for less than pleasant reasons.

Dr. Maibach unbuttoned his double-breasted jacket and plopped down into the visitor's chair at my desk.

"Black with two sugars," he barked, not bothering with even a hint of friendliness.

I knew Maibach well enough to anticipate what the hawk might do to an injured chick. Lara had to be removed from the line of fire.

"That's all. Go now," I said urgently, gesturing to the door with my chin.

Lara straightened her chronically drooping shoulders, set the coffee tray on the desk, and hurried away.

"By the way, you handled the Göthekind v. Henfler matter very well, Frau Busche. Keep up the excellent work!" I called after her.

Surprised, Lara stopped and turned back. I waved her away, then looked innocently at my boss, who frowned.

"Is everything all right, Frau Sonnenthal?"

"Why shouldn't it be?" I replied quickly, but my smile evaporated when I recognised the document in his hand. My yet-to-be-granted vacation request floated down onto my desk like a silent reproach, right next to my wedding to-do list. Maibach looked at the latter and picked it up without a second thought.

"I thought you might want my signature on your request for time off," he said, perusing my private list.

"The whole . . . it came up quite . . . unexpectedly."

"Did you manage to accomplish on your 'vacation' what you set out to?" Maibach lifted his head. "I assume it was a family matter that couldn't be postponed."

Blushing, I said, "A family matter, that's right."

Dr. Maibach leaned back, loosened his tie, and swivelled from side to side in his chair. He didn't take his eyes off the list that reported not only the colour of my garter, but also the number of glasses of champagne I planned to drink per hour to be pleasantly tipsy but not so drunk that I could lose control.

"Oh, don't worry about the vacation request. I'm actually here to congratulate you on your impending nuptials. You really are an outstanding team, you and Dr. Grüning."

He grinned, which made his face look more than ever like a dented egg. Even though Maibach the Great was fastidiously trim, his bald head and sturdy neck made him seem stocky.

"I've seldom come across young people who approach these matters so pragmatically."

He tapped my to-do list as if it was Exhibit A in a complicated trial. I smiled uneasily.

"It seems you leave nothing to chance. I like that. Love, romance, and all that—highly exaggerated. One marries so the accounts balance—I completely agree with your fiancé on that! Be assured that, in addition to the wedding present from the partners, a substantial, encouraging sum will also be diverted into your future husband's account—call it a little parting gift before you leave the firm."

"Why would I leave the firm?" I asked, fighting a wave of nausea and processing what he'd said about my fiancé marrying to balance his accounts.

When Maibach's eyes dropped from my chest to my belly, I had the answer I feared. Shocked, I put a hand on my stomach.

"Sir, you're mistaken. I am not pregnant and have no intention of becoming pregnant in the near future."

"Got it, Frau Sonnenthal." He winked. "Just don't let your fiancé know that I told you that he'd shared your plans with me. Take a little time if you wish. We'll hold off dissolving the family law division until you leave."

Self-satisfied as an oil baron, he rocked in the chair where Frau Ziegelow and other women had shed tears. I wanted to push him out of it.

"You're shutting down the family law division?"

"Of course." He laughed. Leaning forward, he whispered, "Don't worry. Your future husband's salary will allow you to employ a house-keeper and a nanny. Look forward to the good things in life—shopping, the gym, hair salons, all that stuff you women love—much better than wallowing in other people's divorces. Yes, you planned everything perfectly, Frau Sonnenthal. Or should I call you Frau Grüning?"

"Sonnenthal is fine," I said, pressing my shoulders against the back of my chair to keep from screaming.

Maibach examined me. He finally seemed to realise that something was wrong, very wrong. I stared at his hands with their short, square-cut nails, and tried to find an innocent explanation for what I'd just learned about Justus. I found none.

I got up, seemingly in slow motion, staggered, but caught myself on the glass table top. I felt as if I were made of glass myself, like this entire office. "Would you please excuse me, Herr Dr. Maibach? I have an important meeting with a client right now."

Unbelievable. I was showing my boss the door. And I had lied about a meeting. But as Charlie would say, "Who gives a shit?"

Lara came around the corner with Maibach's coffee, but caught my look through the glass wall and retreated. Mighty Maibach pushed himself out of the chair and nodded at me with a patronising and far-too-familiar smile.

"Yes, yes. That's how it should be—work before pleasure. It's not easy to find a woman like you, who so doggedly heads for the home stretch. Almost a pity. You could have had quite a law career."

He turned to leave and I reached to grab my phone.

"Oh, before I forget, Frau Sonnenthal, be sure to always leave the blinds up from now on—including whenever you meet with clients."

Then he headed for the elevator that would carry him to Mount Olympus, as we lowly peons called the partners' floor. Tucking the phone between my chin and shoulder, I called Lara's extension.

"Lara? Please ask Dr. Grüning to come to my office immediately. And don't let his manicured receptionist scare you off. It's important."

"I hope you have a good reason for calling me away from the budget meeting, Josefine." Justus sat down on the edge of my desk with crossed arms and glared at me. "You look just fine, so I guess your secretary was lying when she said it was a matter of life and death."

I suppressed the learned reflex of taking off my glasses for him. Instead, I went to the glass wall, caught my assistant's eyes, and mouthed a silent "Thank you." Then, in front of her flattered smile, I pulled down the blinds.

"Don't say a word about the freaking blinds," I snarled. "This is my office. At least for right now."

It gave me some satisfaction that these words made him frown as if he had a migraine, a recent quirk of his. I strutted back to my desk but made sure not to sit down. I had looked up to this man for far too long.

"So you're in a budget meeting."

"I *was* in a budget meeting," Justus replied. "God, Josefine. What's the matter with you? I barely recognise you lately."

"That makes two of us."

With a stiff smile, I turned to the window. It hit me, for the first time in all these years—all you could see from this window were the shiny façades of skyscrapers. Squinting, I followed the trail of an aeroplane until the white line dissolved in the endless blue of the sky. Grey cloud ponies would have fitted the day much better—and rain. I missed rain.

"When did you plan to let me know that Maibach, Roeding & Partners is going to shut down the family law division?"

Justus exhaled audibly. "Who told you that?"

"The boss himself," I replied. "And he told me some other interesting things, too."

"I don't know what your problem is," Justus said after a pause. "Your family cases are extremely expensive to prepare and bring in close to nothing in return. A single licence agreement brings in three times the profit—without having to spend years putting up with emotional wrecks like the Ziegeltoff woman. Besides, nobody plans to shut the department down tomorrow. The partners will vote on my suggestion at the end of the next quarter, and it'll be a while after that before all your pending proceedings are settled."

"So it was your idea."

"I will be one of the partners of this firm, Josefine. It is therefore one of my duties to make sure that Maibach, Roeding & Partners maximises its profits. Anyway, the family law division is a one-woman enterprise, and once you leave—"

"What in the world makes you think that I intend to quit?" I interrupted.

"I thought that was a given." He was genuinely surprised.

I couldn't believe it. I opened my mouth, then closed it again, realising my fiancé was truly unaware that he'd done anything wrong. He pushed off the desk and walked towards me. I raised my hand to stop him.

"But we've discussed all this, Finchen," he said, sounding like a doctor trying to convince a coma patient that she'd slept through two years of her life. "You wrote it on your list yourself—our list. Don't you remember? Our son's going to be called Valentin, or if it's a girl, Sofia. A nanny was out of the question, since you hated how your mother never had time for you. So I assumed . . ." He shrugged.

Thoughts whirled through my head like a swarm of wasps, and they didn't hesitate to sting. My list. Our list. Justus wasn't wrong, exactly. Of course I wanted kids, just not . . . like that. My pride lost the battle against crushing despair and hot tears streamed down my cheeks.

"I never said I wanted to stop working," I whispered.

His expression hardened. "You can't have your cake and eat it, too, young lady," he said. His lenience was suddenly gone, as if Cinderella's doves had eaten up all the crumbs of patience he'd begrudgingly thrown me.

"Since it's necessary for me to marry to become partner, I at least want a wife who's entirely committed to me and my children and isn't one of those stressed-out, part-time career women who do justice neither to their jobs nor their families. What the hell changed our plans? Did five foolish days in Scotland make you lose your mind?"

His words were like a slap in the face. I swallowed and clenched my fists.

"So that's the real reason you want to marry me, Justus? To make partner? I'm another one of your . . . profit-maximising schemes?"

"Don't be silly."

"Answer me."

He looked at me silently for quite a while and then shook his head as if nothing made sense to him anymore. "The two of us make a good team and Maibach values partners whose personal circumstances are up to snuff. So why shouldn't we get married if it benefits us professionally?"

"You."

"Excuse me?"

"Use the singular—benefits *you* professionally."

"So what? It's for both of us. If it makes you feel better, I'll have them draw up a prenup to make sure you'll be properly compensated if worse comes to worst." With his palms up, he asked, "What else do you want? Tell me, and you'll get it."

I was silent, letting his words sink in. Taking shallow, concentrated breaths, I wound up the next question like a toy car.

"Do you actually love me?"

"God, Finchen." He rolled his eyes. "What does that have to do with anything?"

"Everything." I looked up, and was astonished not to feel any sadness.

"You never used to be so goddamn sentimental."

He came closer and pulled me roughly towards him. I held my breath, no longer able to stand his scent of soap, of perfect cleanliness. He represented my entire life—clean, disciplined, perfect. I could no longer stand that either.

"I can't do it, Justus."

I gently extricated myself from his embrace and crossed to the window, searching for a sign, any sign, that would tell me what to do. But there was nothing out there, nothing but sky, glass, and steel. No snow-covered mountains, no green-brown heath, no calm, peaceful lake. There were no magical, fantastical clouds, either, and no eyes looking at me as if I was the only thing on earth that mattered.

Listen to your heart.

I heard it distinctly even though I knew that neither Frau Ziegelow nor Bri, neither Grandmother nor Charlie were in the room. Their insistent voices swooshed in my ears as if I held conches against them.

I looked at my hand, the engagement ring on my ring finger, and the fake bride's ring that only fit my pinkie, no matter how hard I tried. Sighing, I pulled off Justus's promise of marriage, worth twelve thousand euros—as he'd been keen to tell me.

"What are you doing, Finchen?"

I turned around slowly and placed the ring on the desk, right in the middle of my wedding to-do list with its bullet points and stars, next to the framed photo showing Justus and me on a sailing trip to the North Sea—a beaming, perfect couple with big plans for the future.

"It's not your fault. I thought I loved you, but I was wrong. This has been a mistake for years—I just didn't see it."

"You can't do this."

"I know." I nodded. "But I *am* doing it. I'm sorry you won't make partner, but I'm sure you'll find another woman to help you benefit professionally."

"What the hell are you—" He stopped. "You can't just leave."

I shook my head and picked up my handbag. "Be so kind as to let Dr. Maibach know that he'll have my written notice on his desk soon. I'm going to look for a firm that cares more for their clients and less for their assets."

"Finchen . . ."

Justus stood in the middle of the room with drooping shoulders and an expression of shock I'd never imagined he had in his repertoire. He resembled a star pupil caught cheating. I stroked his arm as I walked by, feeling he deserved some conciliatory gesture. He pulled away.

I took my coat and scarf from the rack by the door, then pulled hard on the blinds so that the slats snapped up with a loud clatter. Startled, Lara spilled coffee all over a file.

Glancing back felt like thumbing through a long-winded novel to read the final sentence. Justus still stood where I'd left him, only now he looked angry rather than sad, which reassured me. I knew from my professional experience that it wouldn't take Justus long to get over me. He was Justus, after all.

"My name is Josefine. Josefine Sonnenthal," I said with a smile.

There no longer was a Finchen.

I was free.

That intoxicating feeling lasted exactly two hours and fifteen minutes. I rushed home through Grüneburg Park, packed my belongings, then called my grandmother. She listened to my torrent of words and, when I came up for air, told me to come stay at her place. A few minutes later, I was in a taxi on the way to Sachsenhausen, wailing like a baby seal stranded on an ice floe.

With a pitying look, the taxi driver handed me a handkerchief. It was perfectly ironed and smelled of soap, which made me cry even harder. I had no man, no home, and—due to my eagerness for a clean break—no job. I had to start from scratch.

I don't know what made me pull my personal organiser out of my bag. I leafed through, finding no solace among its pages, but leaving tearstains all over the Post-it notes and to-do lists. A few business cards fell into my lap—the flower shop, the catering company, the pastry shop. I'd have to call them all. There would be no tiered buttercream cake for Grandmother and no filet mignon in Barolo sauce with duchesse potatoes—no funeral flowers either, though Li's mistaken order seemed strangely appropriate now, as if my aunt had known how everything would turn out.

I saw the stone von Meeseberg lions glide by out of the corner of my eye and, just as the taxi pulled up in front of the house, I found something tucked into the organiser that had completely slipped my mind.

I felt some resistance from the little thistle flower as I peeled it off the paper and held it up to the light. It was flattened and its pretty lilac colour had faded.

A wee little plant that knows how to defend itself, that stands for courage and deep conviction, Finola had said. And Aidan had told me I was like this thistle . . .

I snuffled and shut my eyes until I could master the lump in my throat. Wiping my eyes with the back of my hand, I looked up. My organiser slipped to the floor.

"Hallo, cousin!" Charlie shouted, drumming her turquoise nails against the window. "Are you going to bawl all over the taxi much longer or are you coming in? Bri has brought up a bottle of Dom Pérignon from the cellar to celebrate."

"Charlie! What . . . ?"

Stunned, I watched Charlie skip to the boot and help the taxi driver with my luggage. I gathered all the scraps of paper and cards and discovered that even a dry thistle has thorns. When I finally got out of the car, I stood there with the organiser pressed to my chest, trying to control my frustration. I'd told everyone that I hadn't found Charlie so they'd leave her alone with Ian. I had even made Bri and Li promise not to tell. And here she was, acting like she'd never been away.

"Is this all?" Charlie pressed a twenty-euro bill into the driver's hand and turned to me. "Two suitcases and two measly duffel bags? Who are you? What have you done with my cousin?"

"What . . . are you . . . doing here?"

The voice didn't sound like mine, but I was happy to at least have made some sound. A strange mixture of guilt and pity appeared on Charlie's still somewhat sickly face.

"I actually wanted to surprise you. After all, I promised to be your maid of honour."

"I'm afraid you made the trip for nothing," I whispered and had to fight tears again.

"Not at all. You need me now more than ever." With an anxious smile, Charlie said, "That is, I mean, if you want me to be . . . there for you. I guess I have to make amends for some stuff."

She shoved her hands into her jeans pockets, obviously wanting . . . a hug? I was moved and shocked at the same time. So it had come to this—my own cousin was afraid of consoling me.

"I'm happy you're here," I said.

"Really?"

Her look of relief was followed by the most sparkling and vulnerable smile anyone had given me in a while. I nodded and did something that even a short time ago I wouldn't have dreamt of—I pulled Charlie into my arms.

We stayed that way for some time without saying anything, even though there was a lot I wanted to tell her. I needed to apologise for all the times I'd been mean or even spiteful to her, when I was green with envy that the little monster was once again the centre of the family's attention, and for how I had always pushed her and her admiring love for me away. Apologies were especially due for the bitterness that was inside me because I couldn't be more like her—more carefree, more cheerful, more open, more thirsty for life.

There was so much to say, but words would have robbed the moment of its magic. So I was silent and just held Charlie tightly until she started to giggle and squirm.

"Honestly, Jo, you're better off without that moron."

"Justus is no moron."

"He isn't?"

"He's a stupid moron."

"Right," she said seriously.

"In a way . . . I'm actually . . . glad."

I opened my eyes wide in pretend shock and covered my mouth with my hand. Charlie grinned and then we both burst into laughter, like two silly little girls.

"We'd appreciate it very much if the young ladies came inside some-time today. The bubbly is getting warm," someone called impatiently from the staircase.

Bri was leaning against one of the entrance columns, Marlene Dietrich style, her legs elegantly crossed below her pencil skirt. I could hardly believe my eyes—my great-aunt was wearing stilettos.

"Well, move it. I'm not only dying to hear what's got into our dear Josefine, but last night, your grandmother announced she had some news she'd only share once Miss Solicitor and her luggage had arrived. So get in here already. Li's driving me nuts. She's more curious than a three-year-old in front of a monkey cage, but I bet it's just going to be another creepy ring story."

She puffed on her cigarette, blew some smoke rings into the air, and stubbed out the butt in Grandmother's precious rose bed.

"Sir, yes, sir!"

Charlie saluted, winked at me, and then dragged my two rolling bags towards the house. I picked up my duffel bags and wished I could obey Bri's command just as enthusiastically, but my legs moved as if through molasses.

These past two weeks, I had experienced more and felt more than in my entire life. I was worn out, and my chest hurt as if I'd been crying for days, not just hours. And yet, more cracks still formed in the crumbling façade of my self-awareness. Bri's offhand remark was another blow, showing me that others knew me far better than I knew myself. How else could my grandmother have already known last night that I would leave Justus so soon?

"I don't quite follow, Adele. Did you just say that the bride's ring . . . actually isn't the bride's ring?" Li lowered her teacup and stared at her sister.

Bri finally stopped circling the kitchen table, her stilettos clacking nervously. She shut the window and drew the lace curtains as if making sure the secret didn't escape.

"What's so difficult to understand, Li? Adele wanted to marry Gustav, the ring fell into the Main, and our big sister was resourceful." She nodded to Grandmother. "The replicas idea was brilliant. You should have let me in on it."

"You were eleven at the time, Brigitte," my grandmother replied.

"So what? I was a sharp cookie even as a child, not like some others."

Bri peered at Li, who was still clutching her teacup and throwing bewildered glances around the table. Nobody had touched the cake.

"But that means . . . The pawnbroker gave me two hundred pounds for the ring . . . but it's probably worth much less."

Either Charlie was embarrassed or the red blotches on her face were remnants of the scarlet fever.

"It looked valuable, didn't it? Or maybe Mr. MacGrady just felt sorry for you," I said to Charlie, smiling at Grandmother.

I was worried about her. The old lady had talked without interruption for almost forty-five minutes and her voice had grown shaky, almost faltering, towards the end.

"Who would have thought? My upright, respectable sister Adele turns out to be, in retrospect, a bigger cheat than all of us combined. A fine family we are."

"Now, Bri," protested Li. "Don't be so cheeky."

"What? It's true. We're either deceiving others or ourselves." She briefly glanced at me. "Li's the exception, of course. She can, as always, thoroughly wash her hands of the matter."

"But that's not what I want at all! And I can't believe you all left me out of the loop. Poor Josie! To think that you sent her to Scotland for nothing. And *we* could have done without that crazy trip, too—plus, we wouldn't have to cancel the lovely lilies."

"Poor Josie!" Bri imitated Li, frowning. "Do you really not understand anything, Li? *Poor Josie* could have done a lot worse than go to Scotland, even though right now she's sitting here sniffling like Tolstoy's Anna Karenina. Besides, you'd never have tripped over your French musketeer's feet if you'd just stayed in your floral armchair, waiting for some schmaltzy romance writer to explain love to you."

Li sulked silently, but could not prevent her rosy cheeks becoming rosier, which probably satisfied Bri as much as the fact that Adele had resorted to an incredible lie to be able to marry Gustav.

I took Grandmother's hand, which felt cool and dry. I needed to say something before she launched into her usual role of defusing a clash between the twins.

"It's really sweet that you're worried about me, Aunt Li, but Aunt Bri is right. The thing is, a lot has happened lately and I still have to let it all sink in. But I'm actually relieved."

And I really was, in spite of the blank page waiting for me, "Josefine's Future" scrawled across the top and with no meticulous lists beneath. Grandmother squeezed my hand as if she knew how I felt.

"Spoken like a true von Meeseberg. Bravo!" Bri made a pistol with her hand, pointed it at Li, and pretended to pull the trigger.

"But where does she go from here?"

"That's a good question, Li."

I looked around at four pairs of eyes filled with pity, curiosity, and empathy. The long silence was infused with the aroma of baked apples, flour, and yeast. The familiar scent aroused in me a feeling of peace, something I had lost among all the lists that were meant to lead me into a perfect adult life.

"Actually, I don't think I want to plan anything right now, especially since fate might have a different idea," I said slowly, thinking of the small, dried thistle. "I think I'll take a little time and see what comes up. I haven't listened to my gut for so long. I think I need to learn to trust it again."

"Whoa!" Bri laughed. "Is this really Josefine?"

"I asked the same thing," Charlie piped up with a grin.

"Yes, it's me," I answered, and knew that it was the truth.

Bri raised her glass and everyone followed suit.

"Well, then . . . To Josefine's fresh start. May her gut tell her where to find happiness. And should it be silent, I could give her a clue. She probably doesn't want to hear it, though." Bri casually cleared her throat.

"Speaking of new beginnings," Charlie said. "I have something to share."

"You're pregnant," said Bri.

"Bri!" scolded Li.

In response, her sister plopped herself down on her chair in a not very ladylike manner, her knees as far apart as her pencil skirt allowed.

Li's expression showed that, in her opinion, it allowed much more than was proper for a woman over seventy.

Charlie smiled with lowered eyes. "I'm going back to Scotland, to Ian. His brother offered me a position as an apprentice pastry chef in their Edinburgh branch. Aidan's going to teach me everything I need to know so that Ian and I can manage the original bakery in Kincraig later on. Ian isn't good with numbers, but with my basic knowledge in business administration, we'll manage somehow."

Bri raised an eyebrow. "So you'll be a baker."

"A pastry chef. I'll bake the best cakes the Scots have ever seen, let alone eaten. After all, I learned more in this kitchen than just how to lick a mixing bowl clean." Lifting her chin high and squinting, she looked ready for battle. "Don't even try to talk me out of it. I've made my decision."

Bri and Li exchanged a look and Grandmother contemplated the apple cake as if she were thinking of having a slice after all.

I was speechless as well. It wasn't because Charlie had decided to settle down—to lead a normal life, as it were. I had expected that after having observed her with Ian. It was the casual mention of a name that had thrown me off.

Aidan.

The room expanded and contracted. It was amazing what the mere sound of his name did to me—a gentle smouldering radiated from my belly to the tips of my fingers. I clung to my chair with both hands and closed my eyes.

Bri reached for the champagne bottle. "Finally! A toast to the happy couple! I can't wait to see my nephew's face when he hears the news."

"Don't remind me. Papa is going to cut me off without a penny."

"I thought he'd done that long ago."

Bri raised her glass, satisfied as a famished cat with a bowl of cream. Charlie groaned theatrically and everyone laughed, but I felt miles away.

Aidan. Aidan. Aidan. His name rang in my ears.

Bri scrutinised me before lifting her glass. "To Charlie and Josefine. To the emancipation of the von Meeseberg women. Hip hip, hooray!"

Li almost choked on her champagne. "Hip hip, hooray?"

"Why not?"

Glasses clinked and my field of vision continued to shrink until I could see hardly anything beyond the untouched apple cake in the middle of the table—a perfect circle with a light-brown crust.

Aidan, a soft, longing voice wouldn't stop singing while the rodeo pony in my chest beat time with its hooves. My pulse rate must have been a hundred and eighty.

Charlie gently touched my arm, startling me.

"I almost forgot . . ." My cousin moved closer. "I brought you something." Then she addressed everyone, her eyes sparkling. "Aidan gave me a present for Jo."

The chatter around the table stopped.

Okay. Now I was dizzy. I blinked and tried to say something, but only warm air escaped my mouth. Charlie slid from her chair, left the kitchen, and came back with a brown padded envelope that she laid on the table in front of me.

It was addressed to Mrs. Stone. I immediately recognised the flowing handwriting.

"Maybe Mr. Murray sent cookies," said Li from the end of the table, squinting through the glasses that hung from a chain around her neck, which seemed to grow several inches as she tried to look at the envelope. "But your name isn't Mrs. Stone."

"Li, you really are beyond help," Bri said.

"But why? Mr. Murray knows that Josie likes cookies, and he's famous for those lucky stars—"

"Shut up, Li," Bri and Grandmother said in unison.

Bri looked at her older sister in amazement while Li just shrugged and leaned back into her chair with a disgruntled snort.

"Open it, Jo," Charlie pestered me, raising two fingers as if taking an oath in court. "I swear I didn't sneak a peek, even though I wanted to. I hid it at the very bottom of my backpack. Out of sight, out of mind."

"Or you could take it to your room and open it in peace and quiet," Grandmother said.

Disappointed faces.

"No way! I've been praying for years for something exciting to happen in this family." Bri aimed a finger at my chest. "What are you waiting for, young lady? I highly doubt it's a bomb."

I took a deep breath. Then I picked up the envelope—only to almost drop it again. It weighed almost nothing. Definitely no cookies.

"Did he say anything?" I managed to ask, afraid of the answer.

Charlie shook her head. "He just asked me to give you the envelope. Said you would understand. That's all I could get out of him."

I wrestled with the glued seal of the envelope. I lost, and finally tore it open on one side. A small object rolled out onto the kitchen table.

Bri whistled softly. My grandmother turned pale and pressed a hand to her mouth.

"I don't believe it," Charlie said.

The chiming of the old kitchen clock seemed too loud in my ears. I noticed something wet on the back of my hand, but only realised I was crying when the bride's ring became blurry.

"Ooh!" Li's glasses slipped to the tip of her nose when she bent forward. "So is *this* the right one, then?" Confused, she gestured to the ring with the sparkling rhinestone that had duped three generations in this house into believing it was a diamond.

I reached for it in what felt like slow motion.

It felt hard and cool, but the metal soon absorbed my body's heat. The ring seemed to pulsate in my fist, like a tiny creature with magical powers that might grant me a wish if I let it go. I knew it was my own heartbeat inside my tightly closed fingers, but the idea of the magic ring living and breathing appealed to me—and I knew Aidan would have liked the thought as well.

Aidan.

I suddenly knew what my wish would be—something I wanted more than anything else in this world. I sat there as if in a trance for a minute before meeting my grandmother's knowing gaze.

"Yes, Li," I said, slowly opening my hand. "I think this is the right one, indeed."

18

Edinburgh, June 2016

I had overcome many of my fears these past few weeks. Unfortunately, my fear of flying was not one of them.

Even though the pilot had sounded very competent on the intercom, the ride had been exceedingly bumpy. One more life lesson—never trust a deep male voice cooing about the possibility of "some minor turbulence," even if a flight attendant smiles at you at the same time. I had my eyes closed for almost the entire flight, knowing I must be freaking out the young woman next to me by incessantly kneading my fingers.

Now, two hours after landing, I still felt queasy.

It seemed as if I had stood here since yesterday, on the little paved path in front of the pastry shop—actually, in front of the house next to it. I didn't want to be discovered before mustering the courage to go in. Fate apparently didn't like all this waiting and so sent me an irate downpour. Defiantly opening my umbrella, I huddled up against the house. It wasn't the best spot since people were coming and going, carrying presents and wrapped bottles. A party on a Monday afternoon—and here I was blocking the door. I had to step aside every two minutes. If I wasn't fast enough, someone would step on my feet or push me aside. When I ended up in a deep puddle, I gave up, closed the umbrella, and entered the shop.

An aroma of warm baked goods permeated the room, mixing with the smells of coffee, chocolate, and caramelised fruit. In my memory, the shop was larger, but maybe that was because of the crowd filling it now, all pushing towards the glass display cases. Hiding outside had been absurd. Nobody noticed me now that I was inside. Murray & Sons was a zoo today, and the zookeepers were busy keeping the animals fed.

I hid behind the cookie shelf with two elderly ladies in rain bonnets. If I stood on my toes, I could overlook the entire room without being seen. But this, too, was superfluous, since Vicky and Aidan had barely enough time to so much as smile at their customers. Their hands flying, they bundled butter scones and their famous lucky stars into paper bags and packed colourful cupcakes into boxes. Cake slices landed on small, round plates that Vicky rushed to the crowded tables from time to time. Aidan's little nephew stood on a stool and pushed buttons on the coffee machine with an expression like that of a ship captain. Coffee and hot water for tea emerged with equal decorum.

Despite the hectic rush behind the counter, the three radiated harmony. Aidan would fill a bag with cookies and hand it off to his sister-in-law, who tied it together with a ribbon. He'd then grab a cup from a shelf that was out of reach for his nephew's short arms. When Aidan turned to his next customer, the cake box was already waiting. I watched how Vicky smiled at him and how he winked in return.

Aidan.

I studied his face—tired but content—his kind eyes, the dimple partly hidden by his five o'clock shadow, and the flour he unconsciously wiped across his forehead. There was a new expression around his mouth that I could not interpret.

A pang of jealousy shot straight to my heart. Here I was, hardly off the plane, and I already felt out of place. Not even the Border collie jumper helped, although it had filled me with confidence in the morning.

Vicky was beautiful and she looked exactly like Aidan's late wife. Did she stir the same feelings in him that he once felt for Olivia? I breathed deeply to overcome my rising panic, without success. But nobody had noticed me. If I quietly slipped out now, it would be as if I'd never come.

Without thinking, I stepped from behind the cookie shelf and right into Vicky's line of sight. She recognised me immediately, despite the fact that my hair was still curlier than before. Her eyes widened and her slender hands stopped tying ribbons.

I had no choice. I gathered the meagre remains of my self-confidence and smiled. Her chin trembled, and she threw a heavy-lidded look in Aidan's direction. That's when I decided to run.

"Aidan, there's a customer for you," a voice rang out, silencing the chatter and laughter in the room. Vicky still possessed the vocal chords of a drill sergeant.

Vicky was pointing at me and a lady with poufy hair shook her head, probably assuming I was cutting the line. I found myself staring into Aidan's eyes through a sea of heads and hats. At first, I thought I saw slight irritation. To my immense disappointment, this was neither followed by joy, nor something bigger—something I had yearned for, the reason I was here. Seconds passed in which even the rodeo pony in my chest held its breath.

Then Aidan briefly nodded at me and continued to take care of a gentleman wearing thick glasses, who was squinting urgently at the various cakes.

I could hear myself laugh—it echoed high and clear in my ears. It was the laughter of a quiz show contestant who gave the wrong answer to the very first question and was desperately trying to save face in front of the audience. But the customers' attention had already returned to the sugary temptations in the display cases. I turned and escaped into the rain.

So this was what lovesickness felt like.

After only a few steps, a gust of wind snatched my umbrella. It cartwheeled across the street and landed in the wheel well of a parked wedding limousine, a bouquet of lilies on the hood. Apparently, Scots didn't consider white lilies to be funeral flowers. I went to rescue my umbrella, but it was next to impossible to yank it free. It resembled a twisted wire hanger with some tattered shreds of clothing still attached.

"Care to enlighten me as to what the hell you're doing out here?" a harsh voice said right behind me.

Spinning around, I almost bumped into a broad chest covered by a white apron. Blinking through my glasses, I saw annoyed green eyes flashing at me.

"My umbrella is broken."

Aidan frowned and followed my pointing finger. Then he examined my soaking wet, curlier-than-ever hair and, with tantalising slowness, the rest of me. His face did not reveal his verdict when he grabbed my wrist.

He pulled me down next to him into the red velvet back seat of the limousine. And as he had so often done before, he seemed to read my thoughts.

"My neighbour doesn't much believe in locking cars." He looked at the house next to his shop. "Besides, I doubt he's in any shape to drive on his wedding day. So don't worry. He won't mind if we take shelter from the rain."

"Okay." My teeth chattered—whether from cold or excitement, I couldn't say. Probably both.

"Take off your jumper," Aidan said.

My jaw dropped. A smile played around his beautiful mouth, which, at last, was no longer pressed into a thin line.

"Come on," he said. "Otherwise you'll catch a cold."

I pulled the wet jumper over my head. Shivering, I pressed the Border collie against my breasts, which looked much too prominent under my clinging blouse. Aidan snorted and shook his head.

"Too impatient to wait a damn minute. You'd rather run out into the rain and catch your death."

I was too rattled to come up with a reply.

"You've a new hairdo," Aidan said.

"Don't say anything about it. It's awful."

"Hmm."

"Great. That's worse than if you'd said it was hideous."

"Really?" He scratched the back of his head. "I don't think it's bad. It's actually pretty cute. In a way, it makes you look . . . younger."

"Don't make fun of me. I look like my own grandmother."

"You must have a cute grandmother."

Confused, I remained silent. Aidan pulled back and gave me a questioning look.

"Aren't you supposed to be on your way to church in a car like this?" His eyes narrowed. "Charlie did give you the ring, didn't she?"

I slowly raised my hand so he could see my finger. I hadn't taken the bride's ring off since the day I'd opened the envelope. The second replica rested in Grandmother's safe. Aidan seemed confused, but I spoke first.

"How did you find it?"

Aidan grinned. "Well, the neighbour was right. The only way to the MacGrady's house is down a damn dirt road. What she neglected to mention is that the dirt road is in the Orkneys."

"You . . ." A lump suddenly appeared in my throat. "You went to the Orkney Islands for me?"

"Obviously." He frowned as if the question was an insult.

"All of this is completely crazy—even the fact that the pawnbroker still had the ring. He must have known it was a fake. I don't get it."

"It doesn't matter if the ring is genuine gold or whatever," Aidan said. "What matters is the story that goes with it. Charlie told MacGrady about Emilia and Ludwig. The old man was apparently so moved by their fate that he gave the ring to his wife when Charlie didn't come to claim it."

"That's unbelievable."

"It was none too easy to persuade his wife to part with it. And she refused to accept money." Aidan grimaced. "Instead, I had to chop about nine square feet of wood."

"What?"

"I'd wager that the MacGradys will have a very warm house this winter."

He made a show of lifting both hands. The inside of each thumb bore barely healed blisters. My eyes filled with tears. Aidan had done everything in his power to get the bride's ring back to me, just so I could marry someone else. Either he was a zealous do-gooder or—I closed my eyes—or he felt the same things I did just from hearing his name.

"Hey," Aidan said, putting his arm around my shoulder. "I didn't mean to make you cry."

I sobbed harder still.

"What happened, Mrs. Stone?" he whispered, and I let him pull me to his chest.

His embrace was always natural and effortless—tight enough that I felt protected, yet loose enough to let me breathe and, if necessary, flee. His heartbeat was calming and, oh, how good he smelled. Breathing in the aroma of dough and sugar, of warmth and melted butter, escape was the furthest thing from my mind.

"I hate it when you call me by your teacher's name," I mumbled into his apron.

"No, you don't."

He helped me to sit up straight. Then he wiped away my tears with his thumb and adjusted my glasses, which were slightly fogged up.

"Now then, I'd like an answer."

"I forgot what the question was," I said.

"You know. The question you've been asking yourself ever since you sat next to me on the plane and turned my hand black and blue." There was a catch in his voice. "Why are you here, *mo chridhe*?"

"It just didn't feel right," I said, lowering my eyes. I took two deep breaths. Then I let it all out in a rush. "I hadn't been happy with Justus for a long time, but I couldn't admit it. When I came to Scotland, fate and similar craziness seemed to really mean something, while everything that I thought mattered burst like a soap bubble—my job, my relationship, my future . . . everything." My hands trembled as I took off my glasses. I blinked at Aidan. "I have no idea what happened. I followed your advice and took off the blinders, but what I saw on the side of the road wasn't flowers. All I saw was you. And so I thought, before I miss my chance to be happy, I should stop and ask if you'd walk a bit of the way with me."

There, I'd said it. There was no going back.

Aidan was staring at me, poker-faced, and with each passing second, my heart sank lower and lower. What if I was wrong? Was he trying to figure out the best way to let me down easily?

"It's all right if you say no," I said quietly, my heart almost breaking.

Aidan leaned over me and took my face in his hands. Placing his forehead against mine, he paused for a moment as if saying a prayer. When he opened his eyes, there was such incredible tenderness there that it took my breath away.

"I thought you'd never ask, my sweet."

Then he kissed me—a kiss filled with the same incredible tenderness, holding promises of a long, hot, thistle-filled summer and the faint taste of chocolate cookies.

Epilogue

She wasn't afraid, not the tiniest bit—well, maybe just a little. She'd never travelled such a long way all by herself. If she was honest, she couldn't remember having travelled anywhere without Bri.

For probably the tenth time, Li reassured herself with a glance at her father's old pocket watch that she'd make it to the station on time. She fumbled in her purse for the train schedule printout. Her eyesight had got worse these past few months, so she had to hold the paper close to her face to decipher it. In truth, she'd already memorised the information just in case she lost the printout, clumsy and distracted as she sometimes was. She just hoped there were no pickpockets on the train—without her ticket and her wallet, she really would be in trouble. Li pushed aside the what-if scenarios and concentrated on the timetable, which she recited quietly, like a poem.

TGV to Strasbourg. Departure 2:00 p.m., Frankfurt/Main, Main Station, Track 17.

A first-class, two-hour trip requiring no change of train. Crazy how small the world had become thanks to super-fast trains. There was even a dining car where she would have a cup of tea and a piece of cake, even if it had probably been frozen. No comparison, for sure, with the wonderful cherry cake Charlie had baked two weeks before, a goodbye present before returning to her Ian. Li already missed the girl.

Arrival in Strasbourg 4:00 p.m., no track provided.

She hoped Antoine would find her.

"Good heavens, Li, put away that slip of paper. Your constant rustling is making me nervous," Bri snapped next to her.

Li did as she was told, putting the printout back into the envelope that also contained her ticket. She looked out at the oozing city traffic, heavy even though it was well before rush hour.

"Are you sure we'll make it to the station on time?" Li asked, upset to hear herself sounding like an old fogey. But she couldn't help it. Her anxiety and excitement had become almost unbearable.

"You tell me. You're the one who's been looking at her watch every two minutes."

Sheepishly, Li nodded. She was grateful to have Bri escorting her to the station, even if her impatient sister scolded her incessantly. Li knew that Bri, elegant in her shift dress, was only covering her own nervousness. She also knew that neither of them had slept a wink for two nights.

Bri looked out the window of the taxi with a hangdog expression. After a few uncomfortable minutes of silence, Li dared to ask a question.

"Do you want me to call you when I arrive in France?"

"I'd prefer if you called every half hour so I know you haven't got lost looking for a bathroom."

Li nodded. "All right."

"I'm joking, Li."

"I see," said Li with a tiny smile.

They lapsed into the same uneasy silence as before.

"Bri?"

"What is it now?"

"I love you, you know. These two weeks with Antoine won't change that."

Her sister was silent, but Li had learned over many years to hear the words that Bri didn't say out loud. She glanced at Bri's hands, crisscrossed with tiny veins, which were tugging at the dark-blue trim of her dress. Her fingers said, *I love you, too. Mostly, though, I'm dying of fear something might happen to you.* Li smiled.

"Did you pack enough warm clothes?" Bri asked without taking her eyes off the oncoming traffic.

"Of course—three jumpers, four pairs of slacks, ten pairs of socks, and eight long chemises. I'm also taking my red wool dress and—" Li stopped when Bri lifted her hand.

Pulling out her handbag from under the seat, Bri handed Li a ribbon-wrapped box. It seemed to come from an expensive store, an Italian one. The looping script said "La Passionata."

"For me?"

Bri pursed her lips. "For your birthday."

"But our birthday was two months ago."

"So it's for the next one. Let's hope you live to see it."

Bri reached into her bag and pulled out a pocket knife, which she snapped open in front of Li's frightened eyes.

"What are you doing?"

She gave Li a surprised look that turned into a scowl. "We're long past that childish blood pact stuff, you silly goose. It's for the ribbon. They always tie these things like they contain nuclear waste."

"Oh. All right."

Li cut the ribbon, cautiously opened the lid, and peeked under the lavender tissue paper.

"Now really, Bri!" she said, slamming the lid down. She glanced at the taxi driver who, to her relief, was focused on the traffic.

"What?" Bri said. "I bet you only packed cotton panties."

"No! I . . . Yes, but . . ." Li didn't know what to say.

"You're visiting your new boyfriend, not a girl scout camp. Women have to present themselves to their advantage, and these sinful things do make a statement." Bri laughed at her sister's appalled look.

"Antoine isn't like that. He—"

Bri's expression softened. "I know that your musketeer likes you, quite apart from lace underwear. But these sexy things will make him even fonder. Come on, put them in your bag before I change my mind and exchange them for something in my size."

"Thank you," Li said, her eyes damp with tears.

The taxi pulled up to the station. Looking at her sister, Bri's sternness disappeared and was replaced by a rare softness reserved for very special moments in their lives.

"I hope it's all right if I don't come with you to the platform, sis. I have an appointment at the animal shelter and, unless I leave right away, I won't make it with all this traffic. Besides, it might be a good idea if you tried to manage without me from here on."

Li looked at her with big eyes. "You're going to the animal shelter? Why? Don't tell me you're going to—"

"What if I am?" Bri bit her lip. "Do you think you're the only one entitled to a bit of happiness? I'm sure they'll have a poor, lonely mutt who wouldn't mind being ordered around. But enough of this. Track seventeen is in the very back, to the right. Just go straight through and don't talk to any strangers."

Li swallowed again, and once more. Then she nodded and opened the door. Out of the corner of her eye, she saw the taxi driver lifting her suitcase out of the boot.

"All right, Bri."

"Promise that you'll only stick your nose into your book after you're in your reserved seat."

"Promise."

"And Li."

"Yes?"

"I wish you tons of fun with your Frenchman. He's not bad at all."
Bri's eyes opened wide. "Oh my god, did I just say that?"

Li felt a wave of relief sweep over her, washing away her fears.
Everything was all right. And whatever wasn't would be.

"So we're meeting in Scotland?"

"We're meeting in Scotland, where we'll attend the most beautiful
wedding ever," Bri said gleefully, blowing her a kiss.

Li stood at the taxi stand, waving, even when the car was long gone.

Breathe deeply in and out three times, Josie had said on the phone
when Li almost fainted with happiness at the news that Charlie and Ian
were getting married this month. It was going to be a genuine Scottish
wedding, in a castle, with bagpipes and a banquet of local delicacies
that Li was slightly afraid of. Nobody had noticed that she'd successfully
avoided the local cuisine during her Scotland trip, except for Finola's
smoked fish soup. "It's all good," as Josie said, laughing down the phone
line. "Oxygen helps everything." So Li took a deep breath. She realised
that she hadn't asked when Josie was coming back to Frankfurt. But she
had a hunch about—

"Do you need any help, young lady?"

An elderly gentleman stopped, touched his hat, and grinned. Li
responded with a reserved smile and shook her head. The man adjusted
his backpack and walked on.

She straightened her back, grabbed her suitcase with her right hand,
and pressed her handbag and umbrella close to her left side. With her
chin held high and her heart pounding, Lieselotte Markwitz walked
towards the entrance of Frankfurt's Central Station.

Just try it, pickpockets.

They wouldn't know what hit them.

Notes About the Setting

On a trip to Scotland in April 2015, I got to know the wonderful Cairngorm Mountains in the heart of the Scottish Highlands. I grew especially fond of Kincraig, a picturesque village that fired up my imagination. It is a worthwhile destination for every traveller.

I hope I will be forgiven for bending the physical truth a little for my story. Kincraig, for example, has neither a castle restaurant nor "tea" in the gift shop. You would also look in vain for a shopping street.

All characters and locations, while inspired by Scotland, are fictitious. Any similarities are purely accidental.

A Note of Thanks

There are again many people who lent support and suggestions during the writing of this novel, and helped bring its stories to life.

Most of my helpers this time were intimately familiar with Scotland, and I got to know the country and, most importantly, its people through them. I owe a debt of gratitude to John and Irene at Crubenbeg House in Newtonmore, Scotland. They not only provided me with food and shelter, but also made sure that I felt completely at home while making my first approaches to the setting and characters of this novel.

I thank John for his amusing stories about Scots and Scotland, for his interest in my writing, for valuable suggestions, and for his humour. Not only are you responsible for my greatly improved knowledge of English after just one week, you also made sure that my English language homepage developed into a perfect representation of the author Claudia Winter.

Thank you, Irene, for always being thoughtful and caring, for looking after my physical well-being, and for sharing two of your terrific secret recipes from Crubenbeg House and allowing me to use them in my book. I love your chocolate cake with beetroot.

Brian Fraser and Heike Setzepfandt, my Scottish experts from the Facebook community, allowed me to pelt them with questions and did not even lose their cool when I wanted to know how to say "crazy son of a bitch" in Gaelic; in the end, I spared the reader this expression. Above all, Heike's suggestions for various characters were invaluable. I thank both of you for being there for me.

Thanks to Andreas Schneider and Gabriele Tiedke of the Schottland-für-Alle travel agency for arranging my stay with John and Irene. It is remarkable how well you look after your customers and it was a pleasure to finally get to know you and your terrific dog in person. Anyone ever in need of a carefree Scotland package should consider these two and their small company with a big heart.

Of course, there are also special people in Germany who helped this novel along. First of all, I thank my fellow authors, Silvia Konnerth and Julia Dessalles, who agonised with me about plot and plotlines, gently praised and critiqued, and helped me out of many a dead end. Thanks for your heart, dear Silvia, and for your lovely laughter, dear Julchen—and for always believing in me, both of you.

I can't praise Nicola Knothe enough for always being amazed and enthusiastic. You were with me from the very beginning on the little raft that slowly became an actual boat. You threw yourself into the ocean of my story and provided so much encouragement that I can now cope with problems I would never have tackled before. You were, are, and remain my best friend in every way.

To those who read my story before it was published, my gratitude for their honest opinions and valuable suggestions for making the novel better—Beate Döring, with her laser-sharp eye for even tiny inconsistencies; the incomparable writer's collective, Rose Snow, for their professionalism; Christina Schulz; my colleague Eva Lirot, a mystery writer who normally doesn't like romances, but was enthralled by the lucky stars; and, of course, Anna Hingott. You are all terrific.

I would also like to thank the dedicated AmazonCrossing team and my editor, Gabriella Page-Fort, who could hardly wait for me to finish this novel. Thanks also to Lauren Edwards, my German language contact person, who took care of all my little concerns as if they were major ones. I thank my translator, Maria Poglitsch Bauer, who has given voice to my language in English. It has been a pleasure working with all of you.

I am grateful to Michaela and Klaus Gröner of erzähl:perspective, my literary agents, for your professionalism, industrious work, and a glass of champagne every now and then. There are many things I couldn't have done without you. Thank you.

And I bow to you, dear reader, because if you are reading these words, you have accompanied Josefine, Aidan, Bri and Li, Charlie, and all the others to the very end. I hope that my story brought you pleasure and possibly not only a smile . . . but a little bit of Scotland.

Recipes

Charlie's Cheesecake

Vanilla-scented and topped with a pouf of airy meringue, this cheesecake is unusual. Made with cottage cheese and sour cream, it has a bit of a tang—which is just what Charlie liked.

Serves 8–10

For the crust:

4 tablespoons/65 grams butter, at room temperature, plus more for greasing the pan

1/4 cup plus 2 tablespoons/75 grams sugar

Seeds from half a vanilla bean

1 1/2 cups/200 grams flour

1 1/2 teaspoons baking powder

1 large egg

For the filling:

1/2 cup plus 1 tablespoon/125 grams sugar, plus 3 tablespoons for the meringue

Seeds from half a vanilla bean

3 large eggs, divided

1 (16-ounce/454-gram) container sour cream

1 (16-ounce/454-gram) container low-fat cottage cheese

1 (4.6-ounce/130-gram) package cook-and-serve vanilla pudding mix

1 cup/250 ml whole milk

1/4 cup/60 ml sunflower or canola oil

Preheat the oven to 350 degrees Fahrenheit. Grease a 10-inch spring-form pan with butter, place it on a rimmed sheet pan, and set aside.

First, make the crust: in a medium bowl, blend together the sugar and the vanilla bean's seeds with your fingers until evenly mixed. Whisk in the flour and baking powder, then add the 4 tablespoons butter and egg and blend in the wet ingredients with a wooden spoon. When there are no visible wet spots left, knead the dough with your hands until evenly moist and crumbly, then dump the dough into the prepared pan. Scoot about two-thirds of the dough to the edges of the pan and, using your fingertips, pat it into the corners and up the sides of the pan, so a thin layer of crust comes about 1 inch up the sides. Pat the remaining crust into a thin layer on the bottom of the pan, and set aside.

Next, make the filling: in a large bowl, blend together the 1/2 cup plus 1 tablespoon sugar and the vanilla bean seeds until evenly mixed. Add the egg yolks and whisk to combine, then add the sour cream, cottage cheese, pudding mix, milk, and oil, and whisk until blended. Pour the mixture into the crust. Bake for 45 minutes, or until the centre is puffed and jiggles as a whole.

Meanwhile, in a standing mixer fitted with a paddle attachment, beat the reserved egg whites on high speed until foamy (about 30 seconds). With the machine running, add the remaining three tablespoons of sugar in a slow stream, then beat for another 1–2 minutes, until the whites form a shiny meringue and the whisk holds the whites in a stiff peak when you remove it. When the cake is done, pour the meringue in a pretty pattern on top, spreading it all the way to the crust (but not letting it touch the pan). Bake for an additional 15 minutes, or until the meringue is lightly browned.

Let the cake cool completely (or chill overnight, if desired), then cut into slices and serve.

Finola's Cullen Skink

(Adapted with friendly permission from Crubenbeg House, Newtonmore, Scotland.)

While some people mistakenly believe that "skink" refers to a small animal, the Cullen skink is a traditional Scottish soup from the Moray Firth area. *"Skink"* is Gaelic, meaning "shank," and in this instance means "essence"—in Scotland, it's a term commonly used for soup. You could call this Scotland's smoky version of a fish chowder.

Serves 4

1 pound/454 grams russet potatoes, peeled and cut into 1-inch pieces

1 (1-pound/454-gram) fillet cold-smoked haddock or other smoked white-fleshed fish, skin removed

3 cups/750 ml whole milk

1 medium yellow onion, cut into 1/2-inch pieces

1 dried bay leaf

1 tablespoon/15 grams butter, cut into pieces

Kosher salt and freshly ground pepper, to taste

2 tablespoons heavy cream

3 tablespoons chopped parsley, for serving

Put the potatoes in a medium saucepan, add cold water to cover, bring to the boil, and then simmer for about 10 minutes, until the potatoes are completely soft. Drain the potatoes, return them to the pan, and mash. Set the potatoes aside, covered to keep them warm.

Meanwhile, in a soup pot, combine the haddock, milk, onion, and bay leaf over a medium heat and bring to the boil. Reduce the heat to low and simmer until the haddock becomes creamy and starts to break apart and the onions are soft (about 10 minutes). Pour the mixture through a strainer into a clean pan, separating the haddock, onion, and bay leaf from the milk. When it's cool enough to handle, flake the fish apart, picking out any bones you see, and add the flakes and the cooked onion back into the milk. (Discard the bay leaf.) Stir the hot mashed potatoes into the milk mixture, then stir in the butter. Season the soup with salt and pepper to taste. Return the soup to the heat and bring back to the boil. Stir in the cream. Serve hot, sprinkled with the chopped parsley.

About the Author

Photo © 2011 Alexandra Zoth Photo-Stage

Claudia Winter has been writing since childhood. She has previously published two romantic comedies, a crime novel and several short stories in German. The author of *Apricot Kisses* and *Kissed by the Rain*, she also works as a certified specialist in social pedagogy at an elementary school. Winter currently lives with her husband and two dogs in a small town in Germany.

About the Translator

Maria Poglitsch Bauer grew up in Carinthia, Austria, and fell in love with the English language early in life. Her first translation attempt happened at age twelve, when after little more than two years of high school English, she stumbled across an abridged version of *The Great Gatsby*, judged it "great," and wanted to share it with those who did not speak the language. Fortunately, the unfinished opus languished in the drawer of a desk which was eventually stolen. The joy of hunting for the right word stayed with her.